THE WRENCH

A BRUDER HEIST NOVEL

JEREMY BROWN

WOLFPACK
PUBLISHING
— EST 2013 —

WOLFPACK
PUBLISHING
— EST 2013 —

The Wrench

Paperback Edition
Copyright © 2021 Jeremy Brown

Wolfpack Publishing
5130 S. Fort Apache Road 215-380
Las Vegas, NV 89148

wolfpackpublishing.com

Paperback ISBN 978-1-64734-571-6
eBook ISBN 978-1-64734-559-4

THE WRENCH

PART ONE

CHAPTER 1

When Bruder picked the candidate up, the guy was staring at his phone.

Not the people around him, not the traffic.

He eventually found the car handle and pulled the door open, dropped in and left the door open while he stared at his phone some more, swiping around with his thumb.

"Shut the door," Bruder said.

The guy pulled it halfway closed, swiped some more, then slammed the door shut.

"Seat belt," Bruder said.

He didn't give a damn if the guy busted his face on the dashboard, but he didn't need any overambitious cops stopping the car because this idiot didn't have a strap across his chest.

The guy kept staring at the phone and pawed around his shoulder until he found the belt.

He had to break away from the screen to thread the steel tongue into the mouth until it clicked, then he went back to the phone.

Bruder took a deep breath and pulled away from the curb.

They drove north through Brooklyn with Bruder waiting for the guy to start impressing him.

Maybe say something about the car.

It was a four-door sedan painted dull gray.

The radio didn't work and the air conditioning just moved the heavy summer air around without improving it.

It didn't have built-in GPS and if anything under the hood broke you could fix it with a wrench and other tools instead of a laptop.

It was registered with legitimate plates under a fake name, which matched the license Bruder had clipped to the visor.

Best of all, it couldn't be tracked with any software and the cops couldn't turn it off with a remote.

The guy in the passenger seat didn't notice or remark on any of it.

Bruder kept going generally north, the afternoon sun bursting through the driver's window whenever they reached a cross street. When he got close to Bed-Stuy he turned east toward Highland Park.

The guy in the passenger seat chuckled at his phone a few times.

It was the kind of laugh that was supposed to be an invitation, so other people would say, "What's so funny?"

Then the guy with the phone could show them and explain why it was so funny.

Bruder didn't say anything.

He noticed he was squeezing the steering wheel and made his hands relax.

The steering wheel hadn't done anything wrong.

He turned into the park and coasted at a low speed until he found a spot with just a few other people around. They were walking and running and paying attention to themselves or other people, not the car.

Bruder took the phone away and threw it out his window into the ditch across the road.

"Hey!" the guy said.

"No phones," Bruder said. "Kershaw already told you. Or should have."

"I wasn't on the phone. I was checking my IG."

"Your what?"

"Instagram."

Bruder got out and walked around the front of the car. The guy watched him, then squawked when Bruder yanked him out by his shirt and threw him over a low fence into a gulley. Bruder got back in the car and drove away.

Kershaw owed him an apology.

***

Bruder parked inside the warehouse and closed the door behind the car.

The warehouse was one of dozens in a commercial/industrial complex near JFK. Planes taking off sounded like they might come through the roof.

The space was three cars wide and fifty yards deep with exposed girders, pipes, and radiant heaters for a ceiling. Kalwall panels along the top of the front wall let filtered light through.

It had a square office in the back-left corner with windows overlooking the warehouse, a bathroom with a paint-stained shower stall and toilet in the middle of the back wall, and a kitchen counter and refrigerator in the back-right corner with a long table and folding chairs spread in front of it.

A stack of more tables with collapsed legs leaned against the wall near the refrigerator. They were for the computer stuff when the computer guy told them what he needed for the job.

The tables were fine, but they were going to need a new computer guy.

Two cots were lined up on the right wall with suitcases tucked underneath. Kershaw had rigged a piece of conduit between two support beams to hang their clothes.

The rest of the warehouse was open except for the one car and a small rolling tool cart, which could fit in the trunk of the car.

The space was leased by a false company and paid in advance, for six months.

Bruder was in New York but didn't live there and never would.

Too many damn people.

He walked toward the office. He could see Kershaw in there through the windows.

Bruder had dark skin and dark hair. He was almost, but not quite, the same color top to bottom, like a tree trunk.

His arms were long with hands that looked like bricks when they folded into a fist.

His knuckles were scarred.

Depending on where he had to be, he wore suits off the rack or bland workman's or outdoor clothes—whatever got him through the door.

He would seem to fit right in on an oil rig or at a logging camp or standing next to a drag line in a quarry with grit blowing into his face.

Italians think he's Italian.

Greeks think he's Greek.

Hispanics suspect he might be Hispanic, but he doesn't smile enough to convince them.

When he looked straight at people, they tended to get nervous, like he was upset with them or sizing them up for a smack.

They were usually right.

His default setting was simmering impatience, as though he could feel every wasted moment grinding through the hourglass like a shard of rust swallowed.

But he only got impatient with people—never the job.

The job took as much time as it took and required as

much work as it did.

Leading up to a job he might work eighty hours a week or more.

For a month or more.

A schlub might say that's crazy, why not get a steady career with benefits and coast through forty hours a week? Why not?

Because the idea of someone else dictating what Bruder's time on this planet was worth made him murderous.

***

He found Kershaw in the warehouse office looking at a blueprint.

Kershaw looked past Bruder's shoulder.

"Where's the guy?"

"Hell if I know."

Kershaw blinked behind his black-framed glasses.

"Is he still with us?"

Bruder knew what he was asking.

"He's still around, somewhere, but he's not with us."

Kershaw picked up the Glock 19 from one side of the blueprint, letting it roll itself into a tube, wrapping up his hopes and dreams.

"He's really good with computers."

"He was on his phone," Bruder said.

Kershaw closed his eyes. "I told him."

"Yeah, well, he was probably too busy swiping around to remember. It doesn't matter, he's out."

Bruder sat down in one of the beat-up office chairs they'd collected from trash bins. This one had chewed-up arm rests from somebody cramming it into the edge of a desk for about twenty years.

Kershaw looked at the stuff on the desk, all of it having to do with the job they were setting up.

He was a little shorter than Bruder and looked like a construction site foreman who ran triathlons on the weekend. He wore khakis and untucked short-sleeved linen or golf shirts. Some people thought he was a hipster because of his glasses and trimmed mustache, but he only kept the facial hair so he could shave it off and change his look in an emergency.

He said, "So now we have to find another computer guy."

"Do we?"

"We can't make this work without a computer guy."

"Then we can't make it work," Bruder said.

Kershaw crossed his arms. "You just don't want it to work."

"I told you from the beginning. It's too complicated."

"Maybe for you."

"Who else would I care about?"

"Look," Kershaw said, "just because you can't hold it in your hands doesn't mean it's not worth something."

Bruder shook his head. "So, we steal this data, this information, and somebody else pays us for it."

"Or the people we stole it from pay to get it back. Highest bidder wins."

"But it's not worth anything."

"It's worth whatever people are willing to pay."

"Exactly. The value is made up. It's…" Bruder looked at the ceiling and pulled the right word down. "…imaginary."

"Bruder, that's what money is."

Bruder frowned at him.

Now he wasn't making any sense at all.

Kershaw said, "What about Hamler? He was doing identity stuff, maybe he can do this too."

"He's dead," Bruder said.

Kershaw looked at him. "Since when?"

Bruder shrugged. "Since his wife shot him."

"Damn. Yarborough?"

"She knows computers?"

Kershaw leaned on the desk. "I don't know. She does that internet stuff, I figured maybe..."

"See? I told you. It's too complicated."

Kershaw was still trying to figure it out when the burner phone buzzed.

***

The phone hopped and shimmied across the desk.

Bruder pinned it and brought it up.

The minutes on the phone were pre-paid and unregistered, untraceable.

"Yeah?"

Lola said, "There's a guy who called looking for you. He said he works at the place with no neon. Does that mean anything to you?"

Bruder thought about it for a moment.

"Yeah."

"He said he has something you might want to buy."

Lola sounded irritated.

Whether it was because she felt like she was being treated like his assistant, or just because she was talking to him, Bruder couldn't tell.

He said, "Did he leave a number?"

She ran it off and Bruder had to find a pen on the desk and scribble it on the corner of one of Kershaw's papers.

"Get it?" Lola said.

"Yeah."

She hung up.

Kershaw was wary. "Lola?"

"Yeah."

"How is she?"

"The same. I gotta call this guy."

Bruder dialed the number and put the phone on speaker. It was answered on the second ring.

"Hello?"

"You called said, you might have something for me."

"Oh, hey. Yeah. This is the guy at the place with no neon. You know what I mean?"

"Yes."

"I got something you want to hear about. In person."

Bruder looked at Kershaw, who raised his eyebrows.

Bruder said, "You there tonight?"

"Wait, you're in town?"

"Close enough."

"Oh, good," he said. "Great. I'm on right now, I'll be here until close."

Bruder squinted. "What phone are you on?"

"My own, not the place's. Don't worry, it's clean."

"I'll see you."

Bruder killed the call.

He stood up and adjusted the .45 tucked into the back of his belt.

Kershaw put on his coat and dropped the Glock into the pocket and said, "Who's this guy?"

"He's a bartender. But he's worked some light stuff in the past, mostly driving or pulling lookout for some family members. Italians. It might be something. He doesn't know you."

As they walked to the car Kershaw said, "Does he know computers?"

"If he does," Bruder said, "he better keep it to himself."

CHAPTER 2

Kershaw drove.

They took the Brooklyn Bridge and dropped into the Financial District, then took Liberty to John Street and found a lot to drop the car.

The sun wasn't down yet but the tall buildings left everything at street level in near darkness, so the streetlights were already on.

They walked along John and turned onto Cliff to find the pub.

Bruder had been there the previous year to talk to the same guy. Because of this, he stood in a doorway across the street while Kershaw went inside and ordered a drink and eyeballed the situation.

People gave strange looks at anyone standing and doing nothing, so Bruder put the burner phone to his ear and faked a conversation.

"Uh-huh. Uh-huh."

Anyone close enough would figure he was married.

Five minutes later Kershaw stepped outside and turned left.

Bruder put the phone away and started across the street. If Kershaw had turned right Bruder would have taken off or pulled the .45, depending on how fast Kershaw was moving.

He stepped into the pub and smelled beer, furniture polish, and fried food. A mahogany bar with a brass rail ran along the wall on the left. The wall had a mirror behind tiered shelves of booze. A narrow path of black and white tiles separated the barstools from booths with high backs on the right wall.

There wasn't any neon anywhere.

Soft orange lights hung from black chains attached to the ceiling. The entrance and front third of the place was full of them, casting a warm welcoming glow through the windows onto the sidewalk.

But the lights got fewer and farther between toward the back, and Bruder couldn't tell how deep the pub went.

It didn't matter.

He remembered where the exits were from the last time.

Two guys were behind the bar and Bruder could see two more servers, females in black, moving around the booths.

A sign inside the door said, "Please seat yourself."

Bruder walked behind a half dozen people at the bar. Some of them watched him in the mirror, some of them stared into their drinks or phones.

The booths on the right looked about half full, and every-one in there had someone else's face to look at and talk to.

He found a stool three quarters of the way down. The nearest people were a foursome in one of the booths telling a story about a boat and the sad sacks at the far end of the bar. They hadn't bothered with him yet, and if he picked a closer spot he'd be encroaching on their territory, so he respected the border and sat down.

The bartender was a fit guy in his late twenties with dark hair and a beard that looked like it had been drawn on.

He turned around from ringing up a tab.

"Be right with you sir."

Bruder waited.

He scanned the mirror for anyone too interested in him or anyone acting too uninterested in him.

The bartender came over with his eyebrows raised.

"Beer," Bruder said.

"Sure, we have—"

"Whatever's closest and coldest."

The bartender nodded. He pulled a frosted glass out from somewhere beneath the bar and filled it with beer from a tap. He tipped the glass to let some of the head fall into the trough, then set it in front of Bruder on top of a napkin.

Bruder drank it and put a ten on the bar.

The bartender came back.

"Another?"

Bruder shook his head. He stood up and headed for the door.

He heard the bartender call to the other one, "I'm taking my fifteen."

The other bartender gave a thumbs-up.

Bruder stepped out of the pub and turned left, following Kershaw's route.

He glanced through the windows on his way past.

No one was watching or following.

***

Bruder passed two buildings and cut another left into an alley. The alley led to a wider lane running through the middle of the block.

He turned left again and walked behind the same two buildings until he was at the back door of the pub.

Kershaw was there, sitting on stack of two milk crates.

"All quiet," he said.

The battered steel door to the pub shuddered, then

popped open on the second try.

The bartender with the beard stuck his head out and saw Bruder and Kershaw.

He stepped out and toed a brick between the door and the frame to keep it from locking behind him.

"Hey man, thanks for coming."

Bruder shook his hand.

The bartender leaned toward Kershaw.

"I'm James," he said.

"Winger," Kershaw said, shaking the hand.

James hesitated, but Kershaw kept a straight face.

Bruder said, "Anybody else coming through that door?"

"Nah, not while I'm on break. We're understaffed so it's only one at a time."

They all looked at each other for a bit.

"So?" Bruder said.

"Oh, yeah," James said. He licked his lips. "So, here's the thing, I don't know if this is anything you can, you know, work with or not, but as soon as I heard it, I figured it was worth a call."

Bruder waited.

After a few seconds Kershaw said, "Thanks for thinking of us."

"Yeah, for sure."

"What did you hear?" Bruder said.

James licked his lips.

"So, we get a lot of finance people in here. Not the C-suite types, they have club memberships and shit, but the worker bees, you know? They come in and get sauced up and start quoting The Boiler Room and Wall Street, doing shots and bombs, and when that dies down there's usually just one or two guys left, and they get all mopey."

Bruder waited some more.

James said, "They start crying about how they're never going to catch a break, or how they thought catching a break would make them happy, or how so-and-so at the office is fast tracked because they know what's-his-nuts or their daddy is in Congress or some shit."

James stopped to lick his lips.

Bruder wondered if punching him in the mouth would speed things up.

Probably not.

He didn't enjoy violence, but he appreciated its efficacy in certain situations.

It was just another tool in the toolbox; there were some nuts who wouldn't turn unless they were stuck in the right wrench.

Bruder didn't think James was one of those.

So he waited.

James said, "Then yesterday, this guy comes in. He's a regular, maybe three or four times a week with a crew from work. They're all from Vanguard Investments. Every time he comes in it's a couple rum and Cokes, burger and fries. Yesterday he comes in and does the usual, but once his crew leaves, he orders a shot of tequila. Tells me straight up, 'I'm gonna get lit tonight.'"

He looked between Bruder and Kershaw to let that sink in.

"Okay," Kershaw said. He had his head resting against the building with his eyes closed.

James said, "I ask him, 'What's up bro?' He tells me he just got laid off. So, I pour him the shot on the house, try to cheer him up a little. It was the shitty tequila but he didn't notice. Just knocked it back and asked for another. He tells me getting fired isn't even the worst of it. Turns out Vanguard is in the red, overextended on some mortgages or some shit—I kind of glaze over whenever they start talking shop. So, they're letting people go and have to take a bailout to keep the doors from closing."

Kershaw opened his eyes.

"I haven't read anything about a bailout for Vanguard."

James nodded. "I know, it's all supposed to be on the low-low. They don't want investors freaking out."

"I'll pretend I didn't hear that," Kershaw said. He winked at James. "Wouldn't want to get in trouble for insider trading."

"Anyway," Bruder said.

James licked his lips. "So, they're cutting my man loose, and—get this—one of his last assignments is to process some of the bailout money into bonuses for the big bosses. The CEO, CFO, and COO."

He looked between them again, his mouth open at the audacity.

Bruder started to get interested. "Those three are getting payouts?"

"Not just payouts," James said. "Cash payouts."

"Keep talking," Bruder said.

***

James stepped next to the back door and peered through the narrow opening.

Along the alley, people went from buildings to trash bins and back.

A delivery guy unloaded boxes from the back of a truck near the end of the block.

Nobody paid any attention to the three men behind the pub.

James came back.

"After a few shots my man was getting fired up. He said the CEO was all over his ass to make sure the branch would have enough cash on hand to make a full withdrawal on the bonuses. He said the CEO kept on him, 'Call the branch, call the branch.'"

"Which branch?" Kershaw said.

At the same time Bruder said, "How much?"

James looked back and forth.

"It has to be the Vanguard on Pearl. Right by Hanover

Square."

"Why?" Bruder said.

"He kept saying, like he was talking to the CEO, 'It's right around the fucking corner, walk your old white ass over and talk to them yourself.' I looked it up, and that branch is literally right around the corner from their headquarters. Well, not literally, but close enough."

Bruder frowned.

"But he didn't say it, exactly. Pearl and Hanover Square."

"No. But it has to be."

Bruder looked at Kershaw, who shrugged.

"How much?" Bruder asked again.

James licked his lips.

"Two point five million."

***

After a moment Kershaw said, "Two point five million in cash?"

James nodded. "That's what he said."

"Why?" Bruder said.

James shrugged. "Honestly, he was four or five shots in and kinda rambling by that point. But he said something about the suits not wanting the Treasury Department to be able to track what happened to the bonuses once they got deposited. He was talking about wire transfers and paper trails...I don't know if he was stating facts or just speculating. But if they want to keep the damn bailout quiet, they for sure don't want anybody knowing about the bonuses."

"When is this happening?" Bruder said.

"A week from Friday."

"Friday's tomorrow," Bruder said, and looked at Kershaw.

"True," Kershaw said.

If they got into it, they had a week to set it up.

Bruder scowled at the wall.

"How do you know the date?" Kershaw asked.

"That's my man's last day. And he said the last thing he has to do—literally the last fucking thing—is confirm the branch has enough money for the bonuses for those assholes. Then he packs his shit and goes home."

"A week from Friday," Bruder said.

James nodded and licked his lips.

"What time?"

James spread his hands. "My man didn't say. I don't think he knows. He just keeps checking until they have the cash, I guess."

"What's his name?" Bruder said.

James blinked. "Uh, that's dicey. See, I don't know if he told anyone else about this. Maybe he doesn't even remember telling me, but if he does, and I'm the only one he told, and you go looking for him…"

"Yeah," Bruder said.

"Would he go in on it?" Kershaw said.

James looked up at the narrow strip of evening sky, like the thought hadn't crossed his mind.

"I doubt it. He's pissed off, but he's straight. If something goes down, they might go asking him questions, and I don't think he could take it."

"Can you?" Bruder said.

"Fuckin' A," James said.

"Why not take this to your family instead of us?"

"We…I mean they, mostly…don't get into this sort of thing. This requires a specialist."

Bruder nodded, then asked, "What would you do with your cut?"

"Stash it. I got a student loan, and I'd use it to make that payment. Not pay it off, just make the monthly until it's gone."

"What did you go to school for?" Kershaw asked.

"Graphic design."

Bruder said, "Then why are you tugging beer taps?"

James shrugged. "Turns out I can't sit still for eight hours a day."

Bruder and Kershaw both understood that.

Bruder said, "So your guy doesn't know anything else?"

"I think that's it, man. If he comes in again, I can try for more."

"Don't do that," Kershaw said. "If he doesn't remember telling you about it, better to leave it that way. In fact, if he starts talking about it again, shut him down or walk away. You don't want anybody else noticing the two of you being buddy-buddy."

James nodded. "What if he says the branch location changed, or the day?"

"That would be good to know," Bruder said. "But don't pump him."

"No problem, no problem. So, what are you guys gonna do?"

"It's none of your business anymore," Bruder said. "Don't call me. If something happens, I'll get you your cut. It might not be right away. Be patient."

"I'm cool," James said.

Bruder and Kershaw went in different directions away from the pub.

James licked his lips again, looking around, then nudged the brick out of the way and went through the door, back to work.

CHAPTER 3

Bruder and Kershaw got back to the warehouse and locked the door behind them.

Bruder went to the corner with the kitchen setup and sat down in one of the folding chairs. He spread his hands on the table, a beat-up slab that had come with the space. Over the years people had scored and scraped and dented it with blades, tools, sand, and pens, and there were a few gouges that Bruder was pretty sure came from teeth.

Kershaw plucked two beers out of the fridge and opened them.

He put one in front of Bruder and sat down.

"Two point five million," he said.

Bruder nodded. "With almost as many questions."

Kershaw started ticking things off on his fingers.

"We know it's the CEO of Vanguard."

"Yeah?" Bruder said. "Who the hell is that?"

"I can find out in about three minutes. We know the day it's going down."

"We think we know the day," Bruder said.

"The bank isn't going to sit on that much money for long."

Bruder turned his hands so the edges were down on the table. He started moving them in and out until he was happy with the placement, about shoulder width. Then he put one hand palm-down above the shape, maybe ten inches high. He moved it up to a foot, just to be safe.

He looked at Kershaw.

"What's that?" Kershaw said.

"That's a million dollars in hundreds. It would fit in a carry-on suitcase. Two point five doesn't take up that much room."

"You're assuming it's in hundreds."

"What, a CEO and his cronies are gonna ask for used fives and tens?"

"The volume isn't the point," Kershaw said. "It's the liability. No bank wants that much money on hand."

"So, we assume it's happening a week from Friday. We assume it's in hundreds. Who's going to pick it up?"

Kershaw took a pull from the beer. "The CEO?"

"This is grunt work."

"Yeah, but the whole point of this is to keep things quiet. Why go to all the trouble then have your assistant go pick up the cash?"

Bruder scowled at the table. "So far we're making three assumptions with zero facts."

"Three educated guesses. You want another?"

"Don't try to get me drunk. Okay, so assuming all off our wild-ass guesses are correct, the CEO himself comes down from his high tower next Friday and goes to the branch around the corner. Does he walk? Drive?"

"Drive," Kershaw said. "He'll have some heavies with him too."

Bruder nodded. "At least two, probably four. They go in, get the money, come out and get into the vehicle. Probably a Tahoe or Suburban. Armored?"

"Most likely. I mean, an IED would take it out, but the

glass would probably stop a handgun."

Bruder said, "Most likely. Probably. You see what's happening here? Now I'm even doing it. This is a goddamn
house of cards."

"All we have invested so far is a couple hours," Kershaw
said. "We don't like it, we forget it and move on."

"Yeah," Bruder said, knowing full well neither one of them
was going to let two and a half million dollars get away.

***

Bruder said, "The CEO gets back into his urban tank.
Where does he go? Home?"

"He's got a safe there, guaranteed." Kershaw said. "And
we can find out where he lives. Find a spot along the way
to hit him."

"What if he doesn't go home? What if he takes it to another bank around the block and stashes it in some Cayman
account?"

Kershaw held up his bottle. "Wait a minute. This whole
thing is for C-suite bonuses. He's gonna give it to the other
guys, the...what the hell was it...the CFO and the COO."

"So, he takes a suitcase full of cash back into Vanguard
headquarters and passes it around to his buddies? Then
they spread it out on the floor and have a wrestling match?"

"No, each person brings a case. They divvy it up in the
CEO's office and take their cuts home. Nobody knows a
thing."

Bruder was disgusted. "So now we're hitting three people?"

"Yeah, I see what you mean."

Kershaw sat down and turned his bottle between his
thumb and forefinger.

Bruder stared at the wall.

After a few minutes Kershaw said, "So now what? Back
to the computer thing?"

"Hell no," Bruder said. "Just give me a damn minute."

Five minutes later Bruder said, "Get me a map."

Kershaw got up and took a drink to hide his smile.

***

The map covered the table and curled off the edges.

They were looking at the Financial District, specifically the area around Hanover Square and Pearl.

Kershaw had a laptop sitting on the map with the address for the Vanguard Investments branch on one tab and the biography of the CEO on another.

His name was Lawrence Howell, sixty-two, MBA from Harvard and a bunch of other shit Bruder didn't care about.

He wanted a name and a photo, which he got.

Kershaw also had a Google Maps view of the branch, but Bruder wanted the paper.

The corner of Pearl and Hanover Square was shaped like an arrowhead pointing due east. Hanover Square cut northwest and Pearl went southwest, both of them one-way.

The branch was on Pearl, the third business from the corner.

Bruder put his finger on Vanguard Investment's headquarters on Water Street, southeast of the branch.

"He'll take Water to Hanover Square and turn right. Then left on Pearl and double-park in front of the branch."

"That's near the Queen Elizabeth Gardens," Kershaw said, tapping the map. "We could wait there, come running out of the bushes when he parks and be right there when he steps out with the money."

Bruder shook his head. "Too many people, too congested. One-way streets won't give us any play."

He stared at the map some more.

"If we had more time, we could make a funnel. Close down some roads so he has to go the way we want him to."

"We could set a cab on fire," Kershaw said.

"I thought about that. Fire department, cops all over. They'd probably get a hard-on and close the whole district down."

Bruder put both hands on the map and loomed over it, demanding answers.

He got nothing.

It was too flat, too sterile.

It wouldn't talk to him.

"Let's go for another drive," he said.

***

They parked in an underground lot on Pearl and emerged on foot, turning right toward Hanover Square.

It was close to ten o'clock on a Thursday and the side-walks had a steady stream of people, most of them in small groups going to or from food and drinks.

Bruder spotted more than a few workers in suits and skirts looking like they were just leaving the office, putting the whole day in for someone else's profit.

He shook his head.

They were on the south side of Pearl and walked past the Vanguard branch, across the street on the north side, without looking at it.

They got to Hanover Square and stopped to look around. Much better.

Bruder could feel the breeze coming from the East River. He sniffed the air, picking up damp decay, exhaust fumes, fried food, and coffee.

Now he could picture Howell riding through the inter-section, turning left onto Pearl and bumping over the curb to stop in front of the branch.

Bruder looked that way.

The Vanguard Investments branch was discreet. No back-lit sign against the dark brick or hanging over the sidewalk.

It had a gold placard framed in black next to a set of mirrored glass doors. Bruder couldn't read it from the corner, but it probably said something like, "Vanguard Investments. By appointment only. Otherwise piss off."

Howell's vehicle would stop in front of the doors and his security goons would get out.

They'd look around, trying to turn their little heads on their thick necks, then Howell would slide out, buttoning his suit coat and looking straight ahead.

Through the doors and into the branch.

Bruder and Kershaw crossed Pearl and turned right on that corner, not bothering to look back at the Vanguard branch again and crossed Hanover Square against the pedestrian light. They wandered into the Queen Elizabeth Gardens, a bunch of trees and shrubbery that ran the length of the block. Bruder found a semi-circular concrete bench and sat down. He was looking south across Pearl with the branch off to his right.

Kershaw kept walking for a bit, getting a feel for the place and checking angles. He came back and sat down next to Bruder.

After a few minutes they got up and walked down Pearl, on the same side as the branch this time. They turned their faces away from the doors and the placard to stay off any video.

They walked past the lot where they'd left the car and kept going.

They passed Coentis Alley and Coentis Slip, pedestrian-only malls that ran north and south off Pearl.

The street widened after the alleys with a single lane of one-way traffic and parking lanes on both sides. Bruder checked a sign—the parking lanes were metered and for commercial use only from seven a.m. until five p.m.

They walked all the way to Broad Street. It was the first place Howell, and his vehicle would be able to turn off Pearl.

Bruder spent a while looking around the intersection of

Pearl and Broad, then they crossed over again and walked back along Pearl toward the branch.

Along the way they stepped into a stretch of sidewalk enclosed by scaffolding covered in chipped green paint. Signs warned them about men working above, New York's way of saying if you get hit in the head with a brick, hey, we tried to tell you.

The scaffolding had orange plastic fencing zip-tied to the frame along the street side to keep people from wandering into traffic, but it had been broken through and left that way in enough places to render its sharp forked edges more of a hazard than a help.

Halfway through the scaffold tunnel Bruder stopped and looked around.

To the right, the Vanguard Investments branch was about a hundred yards away.

To the left, Broad Street was the same, maybe a bit more.

Howell would have to come this way along Pearl, one lane of traffic with a restricted parking lane, right in front of the scaffold.

If his vehicle got to Broad Street he could go straight, right, or left.

Two point five million, gone.

Bruder reached out and wrapped a hand around the scaffolding.

The steel was cold.

He leaned into it.

It didn't budge.

"Here," he said. "We have to do it here."

Kershaw looked around and nodded. "Who's 'we'?"

Bruder sucked a tooth. "Yeah…"

CHAPTER 4

They took FDR Drive along the river toward the Upper East
Side and Harlem to break up the pattern.

Kershaw drove and they talked through how to do it.

After a few false starts and unrealistic scenarios, they
landed on something that felt right.

Bruder stared out the window for a while, then nodded.

"That's how it's going to go."

***

For the rest of the drive Bruder worked the pre-paid burner
phone.

It was creeping up on midnight in New York, but the restaurant he called in Philadelphia was open until two. They had
one of the private dining rooms available for that Saturday,
and he reserved it for five people at four o'clock in the afternoon.

The rest of the places he called never closed.

He dialed from memory, starting with a number in Louisville.

"Diner," the woman on the other end said. She sounded

like she was two days into a twelve-hour shift.

Bruder said, "Is Pablo there?"

"Huh?"

"Is Pablo there," Bruder repeated, more of a statement the second time.

"Oh, uh, not right now. But he can call you back."

"This number is good for another day or so."

"Okay," she said.

"You got the number?" Bruder wasn't sure if they had the technology in Kentucky.

"Yeah, I got it."

"Great."

"Whatever."

As she hung up Bruder could hear her yelling at someone about something.

He shuddered and hoped that person was armed.

***

Bruder called Detroit next.

A man answered. "Who's this?"

"Is Ramone there?"

"Fuck no. Wrong number."

The call ended.

***

He called a Virginia number next.

He would have rather called Arizona, but time was tight, and he didn't want anyone to have to jump on a plane.

A man with a slight southern twang answered.

"Hello?"

Bruder said, "Is Elmore there?"

"Elmore? Wait...Bruder?"

Bruder closed his eyes. "Is this connection good?"

"Yeah man, we're secure. I check it every day. Hey, it's good to hear from you."

"Yeah. Listen, if you're not busy let's grab some dinner. Maybe tomorrow or Saturday, there's a place in Philly with some great soup."

The guy said, "Philadelphia?"

"That's right."

"Umm…Yeah, I can swing up there. Am I gonna need any tools?"

"Bring 'em just in case," Bruder said. "Eight o'clock."

He gave him the name of the restaurant and hung up, then glanced at Kershaw.

"What are you grinning about?"

"Let me guess," Kershaw said. "That was Gator."

"Damn jackass."

Kershaw laughed.

The most irritating thing about Gator was how shaky and unreliable he seemed, making everyone worry, then coming through flawlessly when the job started.

Like now—did he remember the meetup was always the second suggested day and four hours earlier than the time, or would he be at the restaurant on Friday at eight, sitting there all alone looking around like an idiot?

And coming right in with names…

They were driving off Randalls Island onto the Robert F. Kennedy Bridge and Bruder considered tossing the cellphone out the window.

But he'd already left two callbacks to the number and didn't want to miss them and waste time.

He also didn't want to talk to that woman at the diner again.

So, he kept the phone and cursed Gator a few more times until he felt better.

***

The first callback came as Kershaw was pulling into the warehouse.

Bruder was already inside, having opened the overhead door.

He walked into the empty concrete lot that ran in front of the units and answered the call.

"Yeah?"

"This is Rowe."

"Rowe, Bruder."

"What's up, man?"

Bruder could hear the grin on the big man's face.

Bruder didn't smile but he was relaxed. Rowe wouldn't use names unless he was on a good line.

"Let's grab some dinner and catch up. How about..."

Bruder checked his watch.

It was past midnight.

"Tonight or tomorrow, I know a place in Philly."

Rowe was silent for a moment.

"That's pretty short notice."

"Not ideal, I know. But I'm only in town until then."

"I got you," Rowe said. "Yeah, I can make that work. What time?"

"Eight o'clock."

Bruder told him the name of the place and hung up.

***

Bruder found Kershaw looking at the map on the table again.

He had a notepad with a list started.

Bruder looked at the list but couldn't decipher Kershaw's shorthand.

"Just some ideas," Kershaw said. "I'm still percolating on it."

Bruder nodded and went into the bathroom. He put the cell phone on the sink and hung his suit pants and coat on the wall and took a hot shower, letting the steam work into the suit.

He took the rest of his clothes into the shower with him.

They were ExOfficio, and he lathered them up and wrung them out and rolled them inside a towel, stomped it, then put the clothes on hangers to dry.

When he was done, he checked the phone, just in case— no missed calls.

Still waiting on Louisville.

If he didn't get a return call soon, he'd have to try someone else.

Kershaw was still frowning at the map and scribbling notes. His laptop was open, showing a bunch of components Bruder assumed were made by aliens.

Bruder hung his clothes on the piece of conduit and got onto his cot.

He asked Kershaw, "You need anything else from me?"

"Nah."

Bruder put the cell phone on the floor next to his cot and fell asleep.

***

FRIDAY

Bruder woke up to the phone bouncing around and chirping.

He snagged it before it disappeared beneath his cot.

"Yeah."

"This is Avery."

Louisville, checking back.

The Kalwall panels above the overhead door were orange and pink.

Bruder sat up and checked his watch: 6:04.

"This is Bruder."

"Yeah, I figured. What's up?"

"Who the hell do you have answering the phone down there?"

Avery laughed. "That must have been Sheri. She's a peach, huh? I'll tell you what, she runs a tight ship at the diner."

Bruder told Avery about the dinner and timing.

"Seems urgent," Avery said. "You in a jam?"

"No."

Avery waited for more, then said, "Okay then. I guess I'll see you soon."

Bruder hung up.

He touched the .45 resting on top of his suitcase under the cot. It was still there and hadn't been fired during the night, which was good.

Bruder wasn't a gun guy.

Over the years he'd held, pointed, and fired just about every handgun out there, and he found that when you pointed a gun at someone, they rarely noticed the caliber or manufacturer.

They saw a black hole ready to swallow them up, then they looked away.

He checked Kershaw's cot and found it empty, then saw him standing at the kitchen table with a cup of coffee under his chin.

Bruder went that way.

"You sleep?" he said.

"A little. The wheels are spinning."

Bruder grunted. The sudden change of tempo surrounding the work had thrown him off a bit. From grumbling about computer nonsense to putting together a two point five million dollar smash and grab...he hadn't yet shifted into where he would normally be a week out from a job like this.

Kershaw was ahead of him, which irritated him even more.

He put on a fresh suit and headed toward the bathroom.

Kershaw said, "That was Avery?"

"He's on his way."

"So, two drivers. Me and Avery."

"If he's in."

"He's in," Kershaw said with a grin. "He loves this kind

of job."

He bent over his notes and crossed some things out before adding more tangents and hieroglyphics.

Bruder brushed his teeth and splashed cold water on his face.

He emerged somewhat better prepared for Kershaw's enthusiasm, and was pouring a cup of coffee when Kershaw turned from his laptop with a dangerous gleam in his eye.

"I need to know what kind of vehicle Howell will be in."

Bruder poured the coffee back into the pot and grabbed the keys off the table.

"Let's talk about it over food."

***

They found a diner fifteen minutes away in Lawrence and ordered coffee and food.

Two tables away from theirs, a road construction crew in fluorescent vests talked loudly about a fight coming up that weekend.

They weren't paying any attention to Bruder and Kershaw, and no one else in the place was close enough to listen in.

Kershaw flattened a paper straw wrapper on the tabletop.

"This is Pearl Street."

He pulled three sugar packets from the little white coffin and put one near the end of the wrapper.

"This is Howell. We need him to have one vehicle. Unless it's an armored car, then we're screwed. We're also possibly screwed if he has two cars."

He added another sugar packet and tapped the first one.

"If he has two, we need him to be in the lead vehicle."

Kershaw wedged the third packet between the first two.

"In that scenario, we can cut behind him and block the chase car."

He reset the sugar and tapped the second packet.

"If he's in the second car, the lead team could cut us off

before we get to Broad Street."

He wedged the third packet in again, then slid the first packet down the road a bit before spinning it ninety degrees, blocking the end of the wrapper.

"We'd be trapped on Pearl. No good."

"What if he has three vehicles?" Bruder said.

"Then we enjoy a lovely Friday in New York City and try to forget all about it."

Bruder grimaced. "Let's say he has one. Tell me what you've been chuckling about all goddamn morning."

Kershaw told him while Bruder finished his breakfast.

When he was done, Kershaw sat back and drank some coffee in triumph.

Bruder let him have a moment, then said, "You have time for all the prep work?"

"Sure. Especially if Avery is around. We only need it to work once, so it doesn't have to be a masterpiece."

Bruder looked out the diner window at the gray car.

"Do we need a different vehicle?"

Kershaw shook his head.

"And we can drive away in it after?"

Kershaw chewed his bottom lip. "Yeah. I'll make sure of it."

"Okay. What do you need?"

Kershaw slid the list over.

Bruder glanced at it, saw actuators and solenoids and PSI specifications.

He said, "Use what we pooled for the computer thing."

"I figured. So, we're a no-go on that one?"

"For now, yeah. If this works out, we'll have a much bigger pool. We'll just hire somebody in India to do the computer thing."

"Really?" Kershaw said.

"No. Does the stuff on your list take you anywhere near Pearl Street?"

Kershaw frowned. "No. They don't have any of this gear around there. It's too greasy."

"Fine. I'll take a cab."

"What are you going to do?"

"See what a Friday looks like around there. Stroll over to the headquarters. Who knows, maybe I'll spot Howell and take him hostage."

"Please tell me you're joking," Kershaw said.

"Probably."

Bruder put money on the table and walked out.

CHAPTER 5

Bruder took a cab to the corner of Broad and Pearl and paid in cash.

He walked up Pearl on the south side, retracing the steps he and Kershaw had taken the night before. In his gray suit, white shirt, no tie and sunglasses he looked like four out of five men walking along Pearl. The fifth guy was a hipster, and nobody paid attention to him either.

The street looked and sounded different on a Friday morning.

The air was thick and damp and already hot and full of exhaust.

A few rays of sunshine found their way through the city and bounced off the upper windows of the buildings on the north side.

Pearl had a steady stream of cars moving toward Broad. Bruder made note of the vehicles parked in the commercial-only parking lanes. A few were city trucks, some were delivery, construction, or service vehicles.

Vans and trucks.

That was good.

But the majority of spots were filled with regular cars. They had meter receipts on the dashboards, so maybe the city didn't care who parked there as long as they paid.

That was good too, as long as Bruder and his crew could get the spots they wanted in a week.

He walked past Coentis Slip and Coentis Alley. People sat on benches and at cafe tables drinking coffee and talking on phones.

Bruder kept going. He walked under the scaffolding, which was like a tunnel now with vehicles parked along the street and the buildings on the other side. It was crammed with people, some of them turning sideways to slide through. Others kept square and left it up to everyone else to move or get bumped.

Bruder turned his shoulders, hugging the side with the buildings, and kept a hand on his money clip. The .45 was back at the warehouse. He didn't plan on needing it, and if he did, it meant things had gone horribly wrong and it would be time to get the hell out of the city anyway.

He came to a set of double doors behind the green scaffolding. They had plywood over the glass, and he couldn't tell where they led.

Without slowing he gave the handles a tug.

Locked.

He passed two more doors, a single and another double set.

The other double set was also locked.

He couldn't try the single door because it was tucked into the face of the building, too far in to reach, leaving a space a little larger than a phone booth between the scaffold and the door.

Stepping through the scaffold and trying the handle would raise some eyebrows.

He kept moving and glanced through the crowd and across Pearl, at the Vanguard branch, to check the distance.

No vehicles were parked in front of the branch and no one was coming or going through the mirrored doors.

He noted traffic cameras on poles and fish-eye security cameras mounted above some of the entrances across the street.

And of course, the Vanguard branch had cameras, but they were too subtle to pick out from where he was.

But there was nothing he could do about those.

And the distance from the branch to the single door would work.

***

Bruder followed the sidewalk on Pearl until he crossed Hanover Square.

He grabbed a coffee to go from a shop on the corner and sat in the Queen Elizabeth Gardens again, drinking the coffee and watching the activity in front of the Vanguard Investments branch from behind his sunglasses.

He knew how things would go between now and next Friday.

The bailout money would be wired to the Vanguard Investment account.

The accountant, or whatever he was—the guy who got sauced up and ran his mouth at the pub—would confirm with the branch that a full withdrawal on the bonus portion would be made on Friday.

Somebody at the branch would make a request to have the withdrawal amount included in the next currency delivery.

The currency transport company would pull the amount from the Federal Reserve and transport it to the Vanguard Investments branch in an armored car.

On Friday, the armored car would stop in front of the double doors and the hopper would get out of the passenger seat.

He'd look around and see nothing unusual.

He'd get the lockbox of cash from the back and move it on a rolling cart from the truck into the branch.

They might have a third guard to keep watch while the hopper was moving.

They could have twenty guards, it didn't matter.

Bruder and Kershaw had briefly discussed hitting the armored car instead of Howell. There would be more cash if they could get into the truck, but that came with exponentially more risk.

The armored car team would be armed and trained, dialed in and ready for trouble.

They would have emergency protocols and direct lines to backup and first responders.

Bottom line, they'd be a huge pain in the ass.

Bruder didn't know about Howell's security team. Not yet anyway. He assumed they would be expensive and well trained, but not as twitchy as the armored car crew.

Bruder watched the branch until his coffee was gone.

Nothing interesting happened, which was good.

He wanted everyone bored.

Bored people are easier targets.

He got up and walked south on Hanover Square toward the Vanguard Investments headquarters.

***

The Vanguard Investments headquarters was located on the corner of Wall Street and Front Street overlooking a tiny park.

He didn't know what the place had looked like when it started, but it sure as hell didn't look like a park now — a few trees and bushes and benches running between the high-rises and Wall Street.

Across Front Street the headquarters was a tall building with dozens of businesses listed on the directory outside the front doors.

Bruder stood on the corner and looked southeast through the narrow park toward the water. If Vanguard was high enough in the building, they'd be able to see Brooklyn across the East River.

Good for them.

The building had underground parking with access on Front Street.

Bruder figured, come next Friday, Howell would load up in the subterranean garage, turn right on one-way Front Street, and right again on one-way Old Slip.

Then a left on Water and an immediate right onto Hanover Square to Pearl.

But even if Howell came out the front door of the headquarters and met the vehicle on the street, it'd be the same thing.

Bruder had walked that route in reverse from the Gardens to the headquarters and couldn't see a reason for Howell not to take it.

There wasn't any construction or congestion beyond the other possible routes he'd checked along the way.

Bruder watched people come and go through the Vanguard building's doors. He wondered if any of the males were the guy who'd talked to James the bartender.

It was getting close to noon. The sun blasted down on the intersection unobstructed, and the windows above Bruder reflected more of it down onto the concrete, giving it to him from all directions.

He was sweating through his shirt.

He looked around one more time and walked into the Vanguard headquarters building to cool down.

***

Bruder pushed through a revolving door into a cavernous lobby.

The floors and walls were marble, except the wall he'd come through, which was all glass to let in the morning light.

Even with the sun beating through the windows, the lobby was at least twenty degrees cooler. Bruder took his sunglasses off and ignored the long counter on the right with three security guards behind it.

He walked past a small fountain in the middle of the floor, then past another counter on the left that looked like a check-in desk at a hotel. Two women and a man were behind that one, dressed well and talking softly to people who were lost or trying to see someone on an upper floor who didn't want to see them.

Bruder kept going.

He didn't want to stop and risk someone asking him if he needed help.

He didn't want anyone paying attention to him.

When he got past the second counter, he saw the security checkpoint.

It was three walk-through metal detectors in a row, each one with a badge scanner.

He kept walking and saw a young woman ahead of him put her briefcase on a short conveyor belt, which sucked it into an X-ray machine watched by another security guard.

The woman touched a badge on a lanyard around her neck to a reader on the frame of the scanner.

A light turned green and she stepped through the booth and reclaimed her briefcase.

Bruder heard her say, "Thanks, Paul."

She veered left toward a bank of elevators set into the marble wall.

Bruder was almost to the checkpoint.

He reached into his pocket like he was going to pull everything out and drop it into one of the dog bowls for the X-ray machine.

Then he stopped and just pulled out the burner phone.

He frowned at the screen, which was dark, but only he could see that.

He put the phone to his ear and softened his voice a bit. "Are you here?"

He waited, not looking at Paul the security guard.

"No, the other corner. You're right outside."

In his periphery he watched Paul go back to doing whatever he did between cattle.

Bruder turned and walked back toward the front of the building.

"Yeah, that's the park. Turn around and look at the tall building…No, the other one. Hold on, I'm coming out."

He said this as he passed the first security desk.

No one gave him a second look as he pushed out into the heat and walked toward the park.

***

Bruder crossed Front and walked along Wall Street with the park on his left.

Traffic was backed up to the river and he walked among exhaust fumes and blazing brake lights and turned right on South. Vehicles rumbled along on the raised FDR, and beneath that Bruder caught a glimpse of a ferry crossing the East River toward Brooklyn.

He still had his phone out and called Kershaw.

"Finding what you need?"

"So far so good," Kershaw said. "You?"

"The security company at headquarters is Ardent Security."

"Ardent? Lame."

"It might be the same company the CEO uses to drive him around. You tell me where their office is, I can take a look. See if they have a motor pool."

"They should have something parked on-site."

"Yeah. The garage is underground. I'll get in there if I have to, but I already had to turn around in the lobby. I don't want the same people seeing me on a camera wandering around in the garage without car keys."

"You need the car?"

"Not yet."

"Okay, hold on."

Bruder walked past a bank of red garage doors. Two of them were open, showing the gleaming chrome and giant windshields of FDNY trucks.

Kershaw said, "They're in Astoria, near the train yard."

He gave the address, then the address of a parking structure within walking distance, and Bruder picked up on some concern in his voice.

"What is it?"

"I don't think our CEO would use this crew for his personal security. The website says they do executive protection, but…"

"But what?"

"It's all pretty cheesy. They're trying too hard. And think about it—he's the CEO of a multi-billion-dollar investment group. Would he use the same security company as the guys watching the garage?"

"I don't know. I haven't met him yet. I'll call you."

Bruder put the phone away and turned right on Old Slip and headed northwest, back toward the Vanguard branch.

It was possible Howell would take this route, but it would take more time coming down Wall Street and dealing with the mess at South Street.

Bruder walked it anyway, just to get a feel, until he ended up back in the Queen Elizabeth Gardens. He was starting to like the spot, with its shade and green smells.

He stayed there for a while, watching things happen, then flagged a cab and gave the address for the parking garage in Astoria.

***

The ride took close to forty minutes with Friday traffic.

Bruder paid in cash and went into the parking structure on 32nd, walked through the first level, and came out the exit on the other side.

He walked a block toward the train yards until he spotted the address Kershaw had given him for Ardent Security.

"Damn," he said.

Kershaw was right—Howell wouldn't use these guys for his personal security.

Bruder checked the other sidewalks. Foot traffic was light, light enough that a man in a suit standing on a corner and swearing at a building might get noticed.

He kept walking toward Ardent.

The building was a one-level red brick structure with a sign attached right to the brick. The company colors were black, red and gold.

The place was narrow but deep, running all the way back to the middle of the block. Windows that looked like they wouldn't open were covered by mini blinds, some of them crooked, some of them missing ends like teeth broken out of a comb.

Ardent had its own parking lot, which looked rare for the area, surrounded by a ten-foot fence with cyclone wire bundled on top.

Bruder walked along the fence and checked the lot through his sunglasses.

Weeds sprouted from gaps in the concrete and formed a miniature hedge where the lot met the base of the brick building. Creeper vines were using some stretches of the fence as a ladder.

Ardent Security vehicles were parked in the lot, some four-door coupes covered in Ardent colors, and some black SUVs with no markings.

That would be the executive protection fleet. Sitting in the sun, getting hot.

The lot also had employee vehicles. The people who drove here in their uniforms and loaded up in the Ardent fleet to swarm across the city to places like the Vanguard headquarters building.

The personal vehicles were all at least five years old, most of them much older. They were dusty and faded with random stickers in the windows and car seats stuffed in the back.

Blue collar all the way, hard-working stiffs like Paul at the security checkpoint.

Not good enough for somebody like Howell.

Bruder kept walking past the front of the building and called Kershaw.

"Where are you?"

"The warehouse," Kershaw said. "You check the place?"

"Yeah."

"And?"

Bruder could tell he was grinning.

"You were right. Let's go back over the bridge, I want you to see it."

"I'll be there in...twenty or thirty. I gotta take some stuff out of the car."

"You get everything?"

"Not yet," Kershaw said. "One of the places had to order a part."

"But it'll be here in time," Bruder said.

"Their truck comes Monday. No problem."

"See you," Bruder said.

***

They walked around the Financial District for the rest of the afternoon.

Bruder showed Kershaw the Vanguard headquarters building but they didn't go inside.

Traffic started to ramp up at quarter to five, so they split up.

Bruder found a spot to sit near the intersection of Front Street and Gouverneur Lane, one block down from the Vanguard headquarters. Looking up Front Street, he could see the exit of the underground parking garage.

Kershaw was across the street in the park, where he could watch the front doors and look northwest up Wall Street.

Neither one of them expected to spot Howell, but it was worth a shot.

At six o'clock Bruder saw Kershaw coming toward him. He had some sort of green drink in a clear plastic cup with a straw.

"Matcha latte," he said when Bruder frowned at it. "It's good. Earthy."

They crossed Front and walked up Gouverneur Lane.

"I saw at least a dozen vehicles that could have been him," Bruder said. "Tinted windows. Run-flat tires. Sitting low on the springs."

Kershaw grunted around the straw. They'd figured Howell would be in something armored.

He said, "I saw some people come out the front and get into cabs and hired cars, but nobody who looked like our guy."

Bruder didn't say anything.

They stayed on Gouverneur Lane across Water Street to Pearl and turned left, walking past the Gardens and the Vanguard branch. It was closed.

They waited fifteen minutes for a table at a Thai place on Pearl, right across from the spot in the scaffolding Bruder had picked the night before.

He sat so he could see the spot through the restaurant's window.

He watched it without staring and played through what would happen in one week.

They ordered food, and when the server left Bruder said, "So we have to find where he lives."

Kershaw nodded. "I'm on it."

They sweated and coughed and blinked through the Thai meal, Bruder cursing quietly between gulps of water. The server was amused but did a good job hiding it.

"Why couldn't this be a steakhouse?" Bruder said.

Kershaw swiped his forehead and grinned. "It's good for you. Like being in a sauna."

"Yeah. But I can get out of the sauna."

They survived the meal and emerged into the evening air, slightly cooler now but heavy with coming rain.

Bruder tested his lungs to make sure they weren't seared.

He glanced around one more time, Pearl Street starting to look and sound and smell like it had when they walked around the night before.

"All right," he said. "Let's see what you got today."

***

Kershaw had moved two of the folding tables to the left wall, opposite the cots, and spread the parts and tools he'd purchased that day across the surfaces.

Bruder took his suit coat off and draped it over the open car window.

He stepped over to the tables and started with the one on the left, covered with pneumatic components.

There were four actuators—air cylinders with piston rods that could extend and retract based on the solenoid valve feeding them. The cylinders were two inches in diameter. Bruder picked one up and pulled the rod out, seeing it had an eighteen-inch stroke.

He put that down and checked out the valves, hoses, clamps, mounting hardware and solenoid valves.

He turned a solenoid over in his hands.

Bruder had always appreciated them.

They looked like a chunk of aluminum from the outside, but inside was an intricate array of springs and magnets and seals and washers. It could sit forever and do nothing, but as soon as you told it to go, one click, and it could release enough force to flip a bulldozer.

He put the valve down and looked at the tools and hardware on the second table.

Kershaw had found a used wire welder, mask and gloves.

A stack of dirty angle iron in four-foot lengths sat edges-down next to the welder, looking like a long, tiny A-frame building. Three cans of flat gray primer spray paint were next to those.

A twenty-gallon air compressor with wheels and five-gallon portable air tank were under the table.

There were fat drill bits and thick lag bolts and a cordless impact drill.

Bruder glanced at Kershaw's rolling toolbox, which doubled as a stool. There was already a cordless drill in there somewhere.

"'What's wrong with that one?" he said.

"The chuck isn't big enough for the new bits."

Bruder grunted. "How many stops?"

"Six. I could have done it in three but didn't want anybody remembering the guy who came in and dropped a bunch of cash."

Bruder looked at everything, including the slab of treated lumber leaning against the warehouse wall. It was eight feet long, two inches thick and ten inches wide.

"How'd you get that back here?"

"Strapped to the roof with rags underneath. There were guys in the parking lot with trucks, nudging each other about it."

"Everything else you need comes on Monday?"

"Yep."

"We'll be in Philly tomorrow. You might find it there."

Kershaw shrugged. "If there's a convenient place to stop. If it doesn't come Monday, I'll go find it somewhere else."

"We don't have a lot of time to jack around."

"I know. This won't take long. Especially once Avery is here."

Bruder nodded. "If we can find where Howell lives, maybe we drive past it before heading to Philly. See what we can see."

"I'll poke around," Kershaw said.

Bruder headed for the bathroom. "I'm gonna take a shower. I stink. Goddamn Thai food."

***

Bruder spent five minutes under scalding water then switched to straight cold for three, breathing through the urge to bellow.

He came out of the bathroom in lightweight hiking pants and a t-shirt feeling like he'd slept for ten hours.

Kershaw was in the office with his laptop. When Bruder walked in Kershaw shook his head.

"Howell is unlisted, no shock there, but I can't find anything in the tax assessments or county deeds. I checked everything around the city, but maybe I'm not looking in the right spot."

"Or it's all listed under his wife's name," Bruder said. "We already know he's into some shady shit when it comes to finances."

"Yeah." Kershaw pulled on his bottom lip.

It was always tricky trying to find information on an individual before a job. You didn't want to ask around or leave a bunch of footprints, because once the job went down and word got around—maybe even made the news—the people you asked would put it together.

They might come around asking for a cut.

Or put you on the chopping block if they ever got

squeezed by the cops: "You know that thing that happened three months ago? I know somebody who was asking about it before it happened..."

So, Kershaw was being careful.

Bruder left him to it and messed with the radio near the refrigerator, jabbing buttons until he found a baseball game. He turned it up and started working on the car, prepping the interior of the trunk.

He didn't do anything that could be seen from the exterior and he didn't touch any wires. They didn't need any faulty taillights before the drive to Philly.

After an hour and a half he checked with Kershaw again.

"Anything?"

"I found his wife. I think I'm onto something."

"I'm going to sleep."

"Dream of Thai food."

Bruder swore and went to bed.

CHAPTER 6

SATURDAY

Bruder's watch woke him up at six.

Kershaw was still sleeping, curled in his sleeping bag and facing the wall.

Bruder grabbed a clean suit and slipped into the bathroom and took another shower—he could still smell the Thai spices on his skin.

When he came out Kershaw was standing up and putting his glasses on.

Bruder started making coffee on the short kitchen counter and asked Kershaw, "Any luck?"

"Good morning to you too."

Bruder paused with a scoop of grounds hovering over the filter.

"Yeah. Any luck?"

Kershaw yawned and shuffled toward the bathroom.

When he got to the door he said, "I found him."

Then he went in and turned on the shower.

Bruder blinked at the closed door.

He dumped the grounds in and started the machine and went to beat on the poor car some more while he waited for the coffee and Kershaw, with his damn suspense.

***

"It was the wife," Kershaw finally said.

They were in the warehouse office, both of them wearing suits with no ties, gathering what they needed for the day.

"Her name's Sally. Some art magazine interviewed her because of a collection of dollhouses she has, and in the interview, she talks about how she keeps all of them at the Chappaqua house because the one on Sanibel could get washed away in a hurricane."

Kershaw closed his laptop and slipped it into a pouch inside a steel briefcase, then closed and locked the case. He had the Glock 19 on his right hip in a belt holster and a folding knife clipped to his left pants pocket.

Bruder had the .45 stuck in a holster in the middle of his back, with a folding knife clipped to the right side of his belt.

Kershaw said, "I found her maiden name and tracked down the tax assessment records for a property in, sure enough, Chappaqua. From there it was just a matter of time."

Bruder said, "What the hell do we need a computer guy for, if you can do all of that?"

"That's nothing," Kershaw said. "I didn't even need to hack anything, it's all public record. My grandmother could do it."

"She want a job?"

Kershaw shook his head. "You two wouldn't get along. And if we're gonna do the computer thing, we need a computer guy. Or girl."

"We're not doing the computer thing. We're gonna do Howell and get the hell out of town and not come back for at least a year."

"You'll miss the Thai food."

"Never again," Bruder declared. "How far is the Chappaqua house from here?"

"At least an hour. Almost due north."

Bruder grimaced. An hour north just to turn around and make the drive to Philly, which was two hours already. And they had to get there early.

"I don't want to rush it," he said. "We'll check it out tomorrow."

***

Kershaw popped the trunk and surveyed Bruder's work.

"Tap the brakes for me, will you?"

"They're fine," Bruder said.

"I just want to see something."

"Yeah, bullshit."

Bruder sat in the driver's seat. He tapped the brakes, turned the hazards on and off, then the lights and blinkers.

"Happy?"

"Practically giddy."

They switched places and Kershaw backed the car out of the warehouse. Bruder locked the place up and got in.

They had breakfast at a diner in Flatbush then worked their way to 278 and eventually I-95.

The sun was out, and they kept the windows down and their suit coats on.

They wanted to take their time on the two-hour drive across Staten Island and through New Jersey to Philadelphia, and they needed to be there a few hours early.

***

They made decent time on a Saturday morning, even with the tolls, and stayed on 95 into the middle of the city. They took Callowhill to Christopher Columbus and went north to drive past the restaurant.

It was a steakhouse on North Delaware, wedged between

the road and the Delaware River. The reserved dining rooms offered a view of the Benjamin Franklin Bridge and New Jersey, for no reason other than geography, but Bruder had booked one for the privacy, not the scenery.

It was just before noon and the restaurant wasn't open yet.

Kershaw drove through the parking lot and rolled over speed bumps into the adjoining lots of other business along the riverfront.

Then he got back onto North Delaware and matched the flow of traffic. He started in a tight loop and spiraled out, winding around whole blocks while Bruder scanned parking lots and alleys and garages.

He didn't see anything that looked like a bunch of cops staging for a raid on the meetup.

Avery, Rowe and Gator were all standup guys, but Bruder and Kershaw knew what could happen when law enforcement got hold of someone.

They twisted and pried and made nice and dangled and misled, and eventually, sometimes, even the guys you thought you could count on cracked and gave something, or someone, up.

If that had happened to one of the men coming to the meet, the cops would come too.

There were ways for them to tip Bruder off if something was going down, but so far none of those methods had been employed.

So, either everything was fine, or everything was fucked and Bruder and Kershaw just didn't know it yet.

They didn't have any warrants out on them.

Their prints weren't even in the system.

But they were connected to enough things, and enough people, that the cops would love to spend a few hours or days trying to learn something new.

They didn't have a few hours or days to waste, and they

sure as hell didn't want to get dropped into the system at this point in their lives.

So, they drove and watched.

***

Kershaw wanted to see where the Liberty Bell was, so they wandered that way, stood outside the building for a while, then had a light lunch at an outdoor cafe.

At two o'clock in the afternoon Kershaw dropped Bruder off a few blocks from the steakhouse and pulled away to check the surrounding area again.

Bruder took his time.

He found his way to the Delaware River Trail and walked it for a bit, watching, then turned around and walked around Waterfront Square.

He didn't see anything of interest besides the history of America.

At three forty-five he called Kershaw.

"Looking good," Kershaw said.

He was parked somewhere close, watching.

"I saw Rowe scoping the place. He gave me the finger. No sign of the other two yet."

"Gator won't bother," Bruder said. "Avery...you might not see him."

"Does that mean he's that good, or I'm slipping?"

"Nobody gets to slip."

Bruder hung up and walked into the steakhouse and gave the hostess the name on the reservation.

The hostess had blonde hair and a black dress.

"Your dining room isn't quite ready yet," she said. "But it won't be long. Would you like to wait at the bar, and I'll come get you?"

"Fine," Bruder said.

He went to the bar and ordered a beer. The place was only a third full and the staff was still setting tables and chatting with each other at cash-out stations.

Nobody looked like a cop about to slap on a vest and kick through a door, but that was the whole point.

"We're ready for you," the hostess said. "Right this way."

He followed with the rest of the beer, and she turned and smiled at him over her shoulder.

"Special occasion?"

"Just a business meeting," Bruder said.

"Oh? What business?"

"Tool and die. It's about as interesting as watching grass grow, only louder."

She laughed because she was supposed to.

He didn't want to say anything too interesting, but it couldn't be too corporate either.

He had no idea how the other guys were going to look when they arrived. If the hostess thought they were meeting about corporate mergers and Gator showed up in a tank top and denim cutoffs, she'd raise an eyebrow.

She took him to one of the private rooms and swept a hand so he could take in the view of the river.

"Perfect," Bruder said.

"I'll make sure your tool and die friends know where to find you."

Bruder smiled and nodded.

She left the door open a crack.

Bruder eased it all the way open so he could see and hear what was happening outside the room, then sat down.

The .45 pressed into his back.

He sat and waited for everyone to show up or for Kershaw to call and tell him to get the hell out of there.

***

Rowe arrived first.

The hostess brought him to the door, smiled at Bruder, and walked away.

Rowe filled the doorway and laughed when he saw Bruder.

"Look at you," he said.

Bruder shook his hand. Rowe had on dark jeans with a collared shirt and linen suit coat.

"Dinner's on me," Bruder said. "We'll wait until everybody gets here."

"Sure," Rowe said.

A male server came in and pointed at Bruder's beer.

"Another for you sir?"

"San Pellegrino with ice," Bruder said.

"Of course." He turned to Rowe. "And for you sir?"

Rowe pulled the wine list off the table. "I'll need a minute."

The server nodded and left.

Bruder said, "They have wine in Detroit?"

"Fuck you," Rowe said. "By the way, I spotted Kershaw out there. I gave him the bird."

"He mentioned that."

"Good. So, this thing—it's in Philly?"

Bruder shook his head. "Be patient."

The server came back with Bruder's sparkling water and a basket of bread. He poured the San Pellegrino over ice in a glass and left the bottle.

Rowe ordered a bottle of something Bruder had never heard of. It sounded expensive.

The server asked Rowe, "You'll be having steak?"

"Indeed."

"An excellent pairing. I'll check back when more of your party arrives."

Rowe looked at the empty chairs. "Who else we got?"

"You'll see."

"You're a somnolent motherfucker, you know that?"

"Somnolent?"

"Drowsy."

Bruder shrugged.

"Exactly," Rowe said.

***

A man with shaggy hair pinned back by wraparound sunglasses and a horseshoe mustache stuck his head in the door.

"What's up, assholes?"

Rowe said, "Oh, no."

The hostess was behind Gator, blinking like someone had just hit her with a camera flash. She looked at Bruder and he nodded. She started backing away.

Gator turned. "It's a date, right? After dinner here we go get ice cream."

"Okay," she said, laughing.

"And I'm lactose intolerant, so I'm willing to die for you. Or, you know. Get bloated or whatever."

"Okay, bye."

She walked back toward the front of the steakhouse. Bruder assumed they wouldn't see her again for the rest of the night, which was good. He needed Gator to focus.

Gator hugged Rowe, slapping him on the back, and shook Bruder's hand. He wore lightweight gray 5.11 pants and a black golf shirt.

He sat down and plucked a piece of bread out of the basket.

"Nice choice, man. I don't remember the last time I had a good steak. What are you drinking? Soda?" He looked at Rowe. "Where's your drink?"

Bruder could feel the table shaking from Gator's bouncing knees.

"It's coming," Rowe said. "But you should have some of Bruder's water. It has minerals."

"Minerals?" He looked at Bruder's glass with suspicion. "Nah, I'm fine, guys. Look."

He held his hand out, palm down to the table. It wobbled

like a wet moth.

Then it froze and Gator laughed.

"I'm just fucking with you."

The server came in with Rowe's bottle and a glass bigger than Bruder's fist.

He talked to Gator while he poured a small sample into the glass for Rowe.

"Good evening, sir. Can I get you something to drink?"

"Do you have tequila?"

Bruder and Rowe looked at each other.

The server said, "Of course. We have—"

"Nah, I'm kidding," Gator said. "I'll take a Coke."

"We have Pepsi products."

"Yeah, that's what I meant."

"Very good."

He presented the sample to Rowe, who stuck his nose in the glass and inhaled, then closed his eyes and turned his face toward the windows.

Gator watched him like he was waiting for the punchline.

Rowe opened his eyes and swirled the wine around, tilted the glass and watched it run down the inside of the bowl.

"Hm," he said.

He took a sip and worked it around like mouthwash.

Bruder checked his watch.

Rowe finally swallowed and nodded to the server.

The server added more wine to the glass. "Glasses for anyone else?"

"No," Bruder said.

The server left.

The table shook.

"Knock that off," Bruder said.

Gator frowned. "What?"

"The knees. You're gonna shake the building apart."

Gator looked under the table at his legs.

"Oh, man, sorry. I don't even notice."

He stopped for about four seconds, forgot about it, and started shaking the table again.

Bruder said, "Dammit, go run around the block or something."

Gator frowned again. "Huh?"

Then Avery came in and it was time to get down to business.

***

Avery stood in the doorway in a lean tailored suit with his palms pressed together, his fingertips touching his nose.

He spread his arms to take everything in.

"My friends," he said.

He shook hands with everyone and sat down next to Rowe. He examined the bottle of wine and whistled.

"Excellent choice. You're getting steak then?"

Rowe said, "You know it. Want a glass?"

Avery glanced at Bruder. "Are you buying?"

"For now," Bruder said.

Avery grinned. "Then I'm getting my own bottle."

The table shook and Gator jabbered while Rowe and Avery snorted wine and Bruder gnawed a chunk of bread, compelling Kershaw to hurry the hell up.

***

Ten minutes later Kershaw walked in carrying his briefcase. He said his hellos and closed the door behind him.

Everyone picked up where they left off with the small talk while Kershaw opened his case and took out a small black device with red LEDs on its face and a collapsed antenna.

He pulled the antenna out and switched the device on.

The LEDs cycled once, then went dark.

Bruder watched him sweep the room and everyone in it.

He even swept the bread and wine and spent a little extra time checking Gator's mustache.

The black box told them no one else was listening in. Kershaw said, "Nobody's creeping around outside either, unless the table is shaking because they're tunneling up from the sewers."

Gator said, "Naw, that's just me."

The table kept shaking and Bruder grabbed a heel of bread to keep from gnashing his teeth.

Kershaw put the scanner away and set his briefcase against the wall.

The server came back with a refill on Gator's Pepsi and took Kershaw's request for an Oberon, then listed the specials.

Everyone ordered steak anyway.

When the server closed the door Bruder said, "This Tuesday through Saturday. New York City. Can you be there?"

Nobody pulled out a phone to check a calendar because they all knew not to bring phones into a meet.

"I can," Gator said.

Rowe nodded. "I'll make it work."

Avery said, "I'm available...and if I stay at this table any longer, I'm committed?"

Bruder nodded.

Avery looked at him, waiting for more.

When Bruder didn't say anything, Avery raised his wine glass. "Cheers, gentlemen."

"Okay," Bruder said. "The take is two point five million."

Everyone sat up a little straighter and listened.

***

Bruder told them about the bartender and the accountant, about Howell and the bailout and the cash withdrawal happening on Friday.

He told them what was going to happen with the scaffolding and the two vehicles they would use.

Kershaw jumped in a few times to elaborate on the vehicles.

Then Bruder told them about the getaway and the primary, secondary, and tertiary hideouts.

He told each one of them what, they would need to bring.

The door opened as he finished, and the steaks rolled in.

Rowe, Gator and Avery leaned back from the table and let the plates slide in front of them.

Rowe gently swirled wine in his glass.

Gator stroked the ends of his horseshoe mustache and stared at something in the middle of the table. The table wasn't shaking anymore.

Avery lifted the edge of his steak and inspected the juices underneath.

Kershaw watched them with a small, amused grin.

Bruder watched the door.

***

When the servers left Rowe said, "This doesn't sound right."

"Go ahead," Bruder said.

"I mean, I don't know anything about what CEOs do. I've never been one, and I've never had one. Like, as a boss."

He looked around the table.

"But I don't think it's common for them to run cash courier errands. Grunt work. Am I wrong?"

"We thought the same thing," Kershaw said. "But this is different. He wants that cash out of the system as soon as possible, and he doesn't want anyone in the system to know what happens to it."

"Why not?" Gator said.

Kershaw shrugged. "Bad press. Angry investors. Main Street vs. Wall Street triggers."

Bruder said, "It doesn't matter. What matters is he's up to something, and when we take the money from him, he won't go to the cops about it."

Avery relished a bite of steak. "Methinks he's in some sort

of bind. Do we know if he likes the horses?"

"If he owes this money to someone else, that's his problem," Bruder said.

"But if he owes the money," Gator said, "and we take it… whoever he owes will come after us."

"How?" Kershaw said. "Think about the takedown. What's he going to tell them? Or anyone?"

Avery raised a hand. "Purely hypothetical, but why are we leaving any witnesses in the first place?"

Rowe put his silverware down and leaned back from the table.

"I said hypothetical," Avery said.

"We don't want the police involved," Bruder said. "We leave a slaughterhouse in the Financial District, a lot of people will care."

"But we have contingencies."

The word hung over the table like unexploded ordnance.

"Yes," Bruder said. "Everyone will be armed. Don't worry about bringing your own, I'll take care of the equipment."

"It won't come to that," Rowe said. "I'll make sure. What's the split?"

Bruder said, "Thirty percent each to me and Kershaw. We're bankrolling it and doing the legwork. You guys all get twelve. Four percent goes to the bartender."

Rowe shook his head and smiled. "Man gets a hundred grand for being in the right place and keeping his ears open."

Bruder watched for any surliness about the percentages.

He and Kershaw would get seven hundred and fifty thousand dollars each while the others would get three hundred thousand apiece—tax free—for a few days of prep and less than thirty minutes of work if everything went right.

It wasn't a retirement score, but it could give a person a few years of a good lifestyle if they spent it right.

Rowe lifted his silverware again. "So, Tuesday?"

***

They finished the steaks while Gator and Kershaw talked about baseball and Rowe and Avery talked about the wine.

Bruder paid the bill with cash.

"I'll call and tell you where to meet on Tuesday."

"When?" Gator said.

"Tuesday."

"But..."

"Just drive toward the city. I'll let you know where to go."

Avery smiled. "Mr. Paranoia."

Gator said, "What are we supposed to do until Tuesday?"

"Your truck still has that camper on the back," Kershaw said. "Go camping."

Gator thought about it, then shrugged. "Okay. Anybody else wanna come?"

"Fuck no," Rowe said. "I'm going back to Detroit."

"Camping's better than Detroit," Gator said.

"Not camping with you."

Kershaw raised the last of his beer. "Here's to not camping with Gator."

They toasted.

Bruder stood up and walked out.

***

On the drive back to Brooklyn Kershaw said, "What do you think about Gator?"

"He'll be fine," Bruder said.

"He was jittery. You see his hands when he wasn't paying attention to them?"

"We should have handed him a gun. That's the only time he holds still."

"Yeah," Kershaw said. "Too late now, I guess. He knows the plan."

They crossed over the Delaware River and the highway

switched from the Pennsylvania Turnpike into the New Jersey Turnpike. The brown water looked a lot better in the setting sun.

Bruder said, "It's not too late. He's going camping. Campers go missing all the time, don't they?"

Kershaw looked at him. "You think that's necessary?"

"No. I think he'll be fine. But you seem to think otherwise."

"It's just...this is going to require patience. Stillness. For hours, maybe. I don't know if he's up for it."

"Avery will keep him in check," Bruder said.

Kershaw grinned. "Yeah. They can talk about wine."

"If that happens, one of them isn't coming out of the van."

After a while Kershaw found a game on the radio.

Bruder closed his eyes and ran through what would happen on Friday, again and again, trying to find the weak points.

He tweaked and adjusted, added new gear and removed anything extraneous, until he couldn't see any more gaps.

Something would go wrong—something always did—but they would control everything within their power and make sure that whatever did go wrong was so minor it wouldn't have an impact on the job.

Then he slept the rest of the way back to the warehouse.

PART TWO

CHAPTER 7

SUNDAY

On Sunday Bruder went shopping.

He went to three different secondhand stores and collected six pieces of decent-looking luggage, none of it matching, some quick-dry shorts and shirts for him and Rowe, running shoes for himself, and a set of hooded painter's coveralls that fit him loosely.

Then he had to try two army surplus stores—one of them all the way up in Astoria, north of the Ardent Security offices—before he found some coveralls that would fit Rowe.

Bruder's were gray and Rowe's were dark blue, but that didn't matter.

Along the way he dropped pieces of the burner phone into random trash bins.

***

He went to a big box home improvement store and risked getting everything he needed in one purchase. The place was packed, and people were buying an endless assortment of tools and materials.

The chances of anyone remembering him were zero.

He got two respirator masks and two sets of safety goggles, the kind that strapped on like a diving mask.

He got a bucket with a lid and a fire extinguisher and a package of extra-large mechanic's gloves with reinforced knuckles. Even though Rowe was taller and heavier, their hands were about the same size, so the gloves would fit both of them.

He also grabbed a box of latex gloves from the paint aisle for the rest of the guys and a three-pack of heavy canvas drop cloths.

Bruder checked the list from Kershaw and found a few of the hardware items—bolts and washers and lock nuts—but struck out on the rest. They were too specialized.

The self-checkout lanes had video cameras right in your face so Bruder waited in line for an actual person.

The woman was short and happy with a butterfly tattoo on the back of her neck beneath a pony-tail. She started scanning Bruder's items and dropping them into bags.

"Big project?"

"Finally getting that man cave," Bruder said. "Just have to make a big mess first."

"Good for you," she said. "Demo days can be so therapeutic, don't you think?"

"Absolutely. If I'm not careful I might keep going and tear the whole house down. They call it home ownership, but the home really owns you, you know?"

She laughed and didn't pay any undue attention to what he had in the cart.

He paid in cash.

As he pushed the cart away, he heard her ask the people behind him, "Big project?"

***

Bruder took everything back to the warehouse and unloaded the trunk onto two more of the folding tables.

As soon as the trunk was empty Kershaw got to work with the wire welder.

The fire extinguisher was next to his feet.

Bruder carried the coveralls and drop cloths outside and walked around the corner of the warehouse toward the fenced-in Dumpsters.

Nobody was around on a Sunday afternoon, and Bruder felt unobserved.

He walked past the garbage bins and off the asphalt lot, into the weeds and scrub grass. Trash was everywhere— plastic tops, receipts, broken glass, condoms.

Bruder ignored all of it and walked around until he found a spot with more dirt than grass.

He dropped the coveralls in the dirt and dragged and kicked them around, then did the same with the drop cloths.

After about fifteen minutes of that—fifteen surprisingly relaxing minutes—he grabbed a sleeve on each of the coveralls and a corner of each drop cloth and dragged all of it back toward the warehouse.

By the time he went back inside they were covered in dust, dirt, grass stains, grease, oil, and something he couldn't identify but hoped wasn't from a person.

He stuffed everything in plastic trash bags and dropped them by the tables, then walked into the small office.

Kershaw was dropping the two-way radios into their chargers and testing the press-to-talk mics with D-ring earbuds. The radios were construction grade, designed for teams working on job sites.

Which, technically, is what Bruder and his crew would be doing on Friday.

He asked Kershaw, "Does the car still work?"

"No, I welded the engine shut."

"Let's drive past the other two spots."

He and Kershaw had scouted the secondary and tertiary hideouts during the week, but Bruder wanted to see how they looked on the weekend. If they had to hole up for a day or more, he wanted to make sure nobody was renting them out for Bible studies or anything.

Kershaw put the last radio in its base and made sure the charging light went on.

"You want to go van shopping after that?"

Bruder shrugged. "If we see something we like..."

***

They drove through the Financial District and noticed the muted, sleepy feel of it compared to Friday and Saturday.

People were still hustling with their phones stuck in front of their faces, but they didn't seem as frantic, like they were following directions to the Brooklyn Bridge so they could jump off.

Kershaw had the police scanner next to his leg, out of sight with the volume low but loud enough so they could hear the chatter.

They drove past the closed Vanguard branch, then the spot along Pearl where the job would go down. Nobody was walking around on the scaffold or—Bruder's biggest concern—taking it apart.

He hit the stopwatch even though it was irrelevant, Sunday traffic vs. Friday.

Kershaw turned right on Broad Street, easing along the getaway route.

He drove one block and took a right on South Williams.

This was the part Bruder didn't like.

The best way to the warehouse required a short back-track, parallel to Pearl and one block north.

They got to the next intersection, made up of five streets branching out in a mess of one-ways going north and east.

South Williams had a stop sign and Bruder looked out

his window.

He knew Hanover Square and the Queen Elizabeth Gardens were right down there but couldn't see them.

The chances of anyone who witnessed the job sprinting up the block, around the corner, and up to this intersection and spotting them were nearly zero, but something had to go wrong and Bruder figured this is where it be.

Kershaw rolled into the intersection and cut right from South Williams onto Beaver, took that to Hanover Street, then a right from Hanover to Wall Street.

They crossed Pearl going southeast but Bruder wasn't worried about it by that point. They were a good five-minute walk away from where they'd leave Howell and his security team.

All off the intersections had stop signs rather than lights, and the only left turn was Beaver onto Hanover, which were both one-ways. This would let Kershaw and Avery make fast turns and, if they had to, cut people off without crossing any lanes of traffic.

Once they got to Wall Street the Holiday Inn Express, designated as the secondary hideout, was a block away.

They had three rooms reserved there for Friday through Sunday, all under fake names and credit cards linked to those names. The cards were used periodically and always paid in full on time.

If things went sideways right after the grab—or before they got off Manhattan, for that matter—they would dump the vehicles, strip coveralls if they had them on, and wander separately to the hotel.

There wouldn't be enough time to split the cash before then, so Bruder would carry it along with the risk. If it came down to making a choice between keeping the money and getting shot or arrested, he'd find a place to stash it or just drop it and run.

But anything less than those outcomes and he'd get as

ugly as he had to.

If any of the other guys got snatched up, they had cover stories that couldn't be easily confirmed or proven false; as long as they stuck to those they'd be okay.

On the bright side, the hotel had a decent-looking continental breakfast and they could stay there as long as necessary, if they made it that far.

Kershaw found a place to park and they walked around the area for a while, scouting discreet paths to the hotel and whether they could get to it through adjacent buildings.

Too many doors were locked that would probably be open on Friday, but they couldn't count on that, so they noted the routes that would absolutely be available and went back to the car.

They continued along the route toward the tertiary hideout.

**

They got on the Williamsburg Bridge and drove over the East River, dropping onto Roebling, the first exit they could take once they were over the bridge. If the scanner blew up, they didn't want to be stuck on the Brooklyn Queens Expressway between exits.

Bruder knew that come Friday, if they made it this far, they would likely be clear to head for the warehouse, the primary hideout. But to be safe, they had rooms reserved at another hotel just inside Brooklyn.

They took Roebling to Lee, then down Williamsburg Street West to Wythe.

Once they crossed Flushing, the hotel was right there.

Again, any trouble in that area and they'd just dump the vehicles and hoof it to the hotel.

Kershaw found a spot to park—much easier here than around Wall Street and they scoped the streets and corners and lots and alleys around the hotel.

If things went to complete shit on Friday, five guys spreading out into the streets and making their way back to the hotel ought to be okay.

Walking back to the car they saw a faded blue van parked in an alley along a bike shop. It was far enough from the street you'd have to be right at the end of the alley to see it or someone working on the door.

Assuming the doors were locked.

Bruder and Kershaw both looked at it for a moment.

Then Bruder said, "Too close."

If they stole the van on Sunday then had to dump it nearby on Friday, it was close enough to the hotel that any police activity surrounding the van would cause problems.

They got back to the car and Kershaw pointed at Bruder's watch.

"Are you still timing this?"

"No. I didn't see the point anymore. I'll do it again during the week. All three spots."

"With that traffic?" Kershaw shook his head. "The things we do for money."

The sun was starting to dip, throwing the street into shadow and brushing the top floors with orange.

Bruder said, "Let's find some dinner. Then back to the warehouse. I need sleep."

"Chappaqua in the morning?" Kershaw said.

Bruder nodded. "Before dawn. In case Howell's an early riser."

CHAPTER 8

MONDAY

Even though there was barely any traffic at three in the morning it still took Bruder an hour to go north from the warehouse near JFK through Queens and the Bronx and White Plains to the hamlet of Chappaqua, in New Castle.

Once he was there, he followed the turn-by-turn list from Kershaw to find Howell's street. It was wide and smooth and lined with mature trees. It meandered back and forth intentionally, not as a result of the landscape.

Most of the driveways were gated and had plantings and mulch and decorative house numbers on the pillars or carved into a big rock.

Bruder could see the security spotlights tucked off to the sides, ready to bathe the entire street in millions of lumens if anyone got too close.

He didn't like any of it.

The whole damn neighborhood was designed to make somebody like him stand out like a mushroom on a doily. Any strange or cheap car cruising the streets or parked for too long would attract suspicion.

These residents were the kind of people who assumed their taxes and donations to the right politicians meant the police would actually care if they got upset.

And they were right.

Bruder got more unhappy the further he wove along the street. When he finally passed Howell's driveway on the right, he was ready to knock the gate down, grab the CEO by the scruff, and shake the money out of him.

But Howell didn't have the money yet, so that would be counterproductive.

Bruder rolled down the empty street. It curved gently to the right until he found the next intersection, a slightly narrower street going off to the left.

He killed the lights and risked a tight U-turn, then hugged the curb on the outer edge of the bend until he could just see the end of Howell's driveway.

He stopped there, under a tree hanging over the street like a canopy.

Across the road was the sidewalk, then a six-foot fence with vertical black bars and a dense hedge.

Through the hedge he caught glimpses of low-watt landscaping lights, which he thought followed the path of Howell's driveway.

More dim lights floated above those, possibly Howell's house but he couldn't tell for sure.

Bruder glanced at the map in the dash lights, then the satellite view Kershaw had printed.

It had to be Howell's place.

The guy had thirty acres, so the lights were either his mansion or his barn or his garage or his carriage house…

Bruder shut the engine off and turned the police scanner on and waited for sirens.

***

When Bruder was watching a place, he could usually slip into the waiting, the stillness, and just blink and breathe and watch.

But not here.

He cursed under his breath and glanced at the mirrors and couldn't get comfortable in the driver's seat.

It was a bad spot, and he was going to blow the whole thing.

He had a manila folder in the passenger seat ready to go for civilians who got too nosey, but if a cop—real or rented—showed up, he only had a flimsy cover story with no paperwork to support it: He and his girlfriend had a fight and she kicked him out and he didn't have enough money for a hotel and didn't want to drive all the way back to the city, but she was probably cooled down enough now for him to go back, thank you very much Officer, have a nice day.

But if the cop asked who his girlfriend was and where she lived, Bruder was cooked.

He had a fake name and phone number and a real address from Kershaw, but whoever lived there may or may not be a female, and if she was, she sure as hell hadn't kicked Bruder out of her bed.

Well...the chances were very slim.

The .45 was in the center console, but that was the last resort of last resorts.

He checked his watch.

It was 4:13.

He rubbed his face and looked at the mirrors and listened to the scanner.

So far it was just Dispatch checking in with two patrol cars, and those two seemed to be at the same location chatting with each other.

Then Dispatch interrupted one of the patrol cars talking and Bruder held his breath.

"Unit 1-7, we have report of a coyote running through a

backyard on Commodore. Request to check it out."

"1-7 en route."

Bruder checked his map.

Commodore was on the other side of New Castle, and it didn't sound like they were using any sort of code.

He started to relax, just a bit.

If they were worried about coyotes running around, maybe no one would notice the wolf just sitting and watching.

***

Lights started coming on in Howell's house at 4:35.

From Bruder's spot it looked like they were all on upper floors, then more windows lit up closer to the ground.

Maybe Howell was one of those maniacs who woke up early to attack the treadmill while he watched CNBC. If he had live-in help, they'd be making coffee and fresh juice, or a smoothie, or whatever CEOs had for breakfast.

The rest of the street started to move around 5:00.

A Land Cruiser went past him first, coming out of the side street behind him and rumbling past on black, knobby tires that might see gravel or a puddle if the driver got lost on the way to the golf course.

Then came a Tesla, and Bruder didn't see or hear that one until it was right next to him.

It floated by without pausing and through the tinted window Bruder could see the illuminated screen of a phone in front of the driver's face.

Over the next twenty minutes he saw three more vehicles, all of them going back the way he'd come in, leaving the neighborhood and probably heading into the city.

During that time Bruder realized he could make out more details in the landscape and parts of houses he could see.

The sun was showing up.

Bruder found a toothpick in the glove box and proceeded to destroy it.

His new burner phone vibrated at quarter after five.

"Yeah."

Kershaw said, "Anything exciting?"

"I'm basically a vagrant here. They need to pick up the pace."

Kershaw chuckled. "I'm headed downtown. See you there."

Bruder dropped the phone.

Kershaw was taking a cab to watch the Vanguard branch and see what time the armored car made the currency delivery and how the routine went.

Bruder went back to being irritated and impatient.

At 5:22 he saw headlights coming toward him from around the curve.

He leaned toward the passenger seat and opened the manila folder like he was checking something. Only his left eye and ear were above the edge of the dashboard, and if the headlights kept coming, he'd dip all the way down so his face wouldn't glow like a dinner plate in the beams.

The vehicle behind the headlights seemed to take forever to swing into view, and when the beams dipped Bruder realized the driver was slowing down.

Then the headlights swept right to left on the asphalt and the vehicle turned into Howell's driveway.

Bruder sat back up.

He couldn't see the vehicle but knew it would be sitting at the gate.

He watched the hedge and the landscape lighting, sparkling through gaps in the shrubbery, and after a few moments the lawn and driveway lit up as the headlights pulled up to the house.

The satellite view showed a circular drive that ringed a small fountain and passed right below the front entrance. The headlights moved through an arc and ended up pointing almost right at Bruder, but from a few hundred yards away and through a bush.

He could picture what was happening.

Howell's driver and one or two more personal protection specialists—fancy security guards— were in the vehicle.

The one in the passenger seat gets out, looks around for ninjas hiding in the fountain and snipers along rooftop, then opens the rear door on the vehicle and goes to the house entrance.

Howell comes out, or the help lets him know his ride is there, and the guard escorts him to the back seat and closes the door and the vehicle takes off.

Bruder was running all of this in his head, in real-time.

He was getting ready to turn the ignition key when he saw the woman coming around the curve straight toward him.

***

She wore white shorts with a long-sleeved red golf shirt and had white hair sprouting from the top of a red golf visor.

She was on his side of the street, walking a small dog the same color as her hair and shorts.

She was also talking into her phone, which she held at chin level in front of her face.

Bruder could hear the other person talking too, on speaker. He pulled the manila folder in the passenger seat a little closer.

The woman looked like she was going to walk right past without even noticing the car, then she looked up and gave a start, like it had suddenly erupted from the asphalt.

She frowned at the car, then at Bruder behind the wheel.

She looked away and said something to the phone, then looked back at Bruder and grew a deeper frown.

"I'll call you back, dear."

She stopped to punch some buttons, then strode to Bruder's open window.

She bent down and peered into the car, seeming to disapprove of all of it.

Bruder ignored her.

"Hello," she said.

"Yeah."

"Do you need some help?"

"No."

She started to get flustered and pursed her lips, which were painted the same red as her shirt and visor.

"Well, can I ask what you're doing here?"

"No."

"Let me rephrase that, sir. Do you have a good reason for being here?"

"Yes," Bruder said, losing his patience.

"Well? What is it?"

"None of your business."

She blinked and put her hands on her hips. The movement tugged the little white dog, who had to hop to keep up.

Bruder thought about sticking his knife out the window and slashing the leash to give the poor thing a chance.

Then he looked past the woman without being obvious about it and saw the headlights coming down the driveway.

The woman interrupted him.

"I'm afraid it is my business," she said. "I live on this street and we pay a lot of money to keep it safe and quiet."

"It is safe and quiet." He glanced at her. "Well, safe anyway."

The woman huffed and fumbled with her phone.

Bruder watched the headlights disappear as they approached the gate, then he saw the beams splash onto the asphalt.

The woman was still at his door with her phone.

"Let's just see if you take this attitude with the police."

Bruder picked up the manila folder and waved it at her.

"I'm serving subpoenas, lady."

She froze and stared at the folder. She was still upset,

but Bruder could see the curiosity catching up.

"Oh? Is it for—" She caught and composed herself, "Well, ah...for whom?"

"For you if you don't get the hell out of here."

Her mouth fell open, showing gaps of pale flesh where wrinkles had blocked the red lipstick.

She stormed away, dragging the little dog behind her.

The vehicle pulled out of Howell's driveway and turned left, away from Bruder. He watched the headlights sweep the far side of the road and disappear.

He looked at the side mirror.

The woman was chugging away.

She glanced back once, but not long enough to be checking his plate, and when she faced front again Bruder started the car and took off after Howell.

***

When Bruder rounded the curve, he saw Howell's taillights a few hundred yards ahead.

He couldn't tell how many people were inside and didn't try to get closer to find out.

He called Kershaw on speaker.

"Yeah."

Bruder said, "Can you talk?"

"I wouldn't answer otherwise. I'm having a lovely espresso across from the Queen's bushes. And you?"

"I'm looking at the ass end of an Escalade," Bruder said.

Kershaw grunted. "A Caddy. My man is living his best life."

"It's black."

"Of course it is. Can you tell the year?"

"Not from here. Maybe when it's lighter out."

"I don't think it varies that much year-to-year, but I'll check. Is it riding low?"

Bruder watched the Escalade slip through the orange

pool of a street light and come to a stop sign. They weren't going out the same way he had come in.

He took his foot off the gas and let the car coast.

The Escalade sat at the stop sign. It could go left or right, but no blinker was on.

Bruder got ready to hit the gas again if the doors opened.

He told Kershaw, "Hold on."

The car was closing in on the Escalade's back bumper.

Bruder swore and put his hand on the turn signal lever.

They were waiting to see which way he was going to turn before they chose.

If he just sat behind them and waited, then followed, he'd be burned.

"Ahhh, shit." Bruder said.

"What is it?"

"They—"

Then the Escalade turned right without using a signal and pulled away at the same speed as before, no evasive maneuvers or screaming acceleration to see what Bruder's car did in response.

"Well, wait a minute," Bruder said.

He used his signal and got to the stop sign, performed a complete stop, and turned right.

The street was narrower and had more bumps and fewer driveways.

"What's going on?" Kershaw said.

"We're out of the snooty neighborhood. On a feeder road that…"

Bruder looked for the rising sun through the trees and checked his own sense of direction.

"Yeah. We're heading north. Toward downtown New Castle."

"Manhattan is the other way."

"Yeah."

"Hmm," Kershaw said.

They both knew a guy who'd been tailing another guy, a guy with a security team, and they'd caught onto the tail. The security team called ahead to the police department and wandered that way and pulled the guy right into a blockade of police cars.

Uncomfortable questions had ensued.

Bruder turned the scanner up.

So far, no talk of ambushing a car that looked like his.

They went north and west.

A car pulled out between Bruder and the Escalade, which was a relief. It even sped up and rode the big vehicle's rear end. The Escalade didn't respond.

They turned on South Greeley and drove north into a small downtown that should have been inside a snow globe. The canopied two-lane road opened up on a library and baseball fields and a school that looked like a castle.

Bruder listened to the scanner.

Still nothing.

The street got crowded with cars and trucks heading into work.

Howell's Escalade kept going north into the heart of downtown, past banks and restaurants not yet open.

They were coming up on an intersection, slowing down, and Bruder was waiting for the whole turn signal thing again when the Escalade jerked across the oncoming lane and bumped up onto the curb near the corner.

The back door on the driver's side popped open and a thick-necked guy in a suit stepped out and walked with a purpose into the cafe on the corner.

"You gotta be kidding me," Bruder said.

Kershaw was still on the phone. "What? What happened?"

Bruder went past the Escalade without looking at it and turned left at the intersection down a one-way. He found an angled parking spot across the street from the cafe. He pulled in and killed the engine and looked back. He could just see the nose of the Escalade peeking around the corner.

The big truck was blocking the crosswalk and forcing anyone going south to swing out into the oncoming lane.

Bruder said, "He sent one of his protection guys in to get him a coffee."

Kershaw snorted. "What an asshole. Real men get their own java. Like me."

"It's a late model Escalade, by the way."

He recited the plate number from memory.

"Got it," Kershaw said.

Bruder could smell the coffee coming from the corner cafe. He considered going in and getting a cup to go but didn't want to be stuck inside when the Escalade left; there was a steady stream of people dressed for work and moms in yoga pants going into the place.

He wouldn't have made it to the door anyway.

Either the baristas bumped Howell's guy to the front of the line, or the protection detail had called ahead, because the Escalade lurched away from the curb pulled a U-turn in the intersection and went back the way they'd come.

"Dammit," Bruder said.

Kershaw said, "Again?"

Bruder backed out and continued in reverse the wrong way down the street, then swung into an empty slot to get his hood pointed toward the intersection.

A Mercedes coming the right way down the road and aiming for the same slot blasted him with the horn.

Bruder ignored it and nosed into the intersection and caught sight of the Escalade a block away taking a road that curved to the right.

Too far away to notice the horn or him coming the wrong way out of the intersection, he figured.

The Mercedes honked again, and the driver's window started to come down.

The old man behind the wheel said, "Hey buddy, get that

piece of shit out of here!"

Bruder ignored him again and pulled onto Greeley, then followed the road that curved to the right, which turned out to be Quaker.

The Escalade was moving now. He caught glimpses of it four vehicles ahead, one of them a furniture delivery truck, which was good as long as it didn't create a total blind spot for Bruder.

Bruder risked speeding to close the gap a bit. Quaker rose above the town in a short overpass, then dropped back down and took him through more canopy trees.

Kershaw said, "Where are you?"

"Following signs for the Saw Mill River Parkway, whatever the hell that is."

After a moment Kershaw said, "You're good. That'll take you to 87, all the way into the city."

The Escalade was in the left lane, pulling away like the driver was trying to make up the time spent on the coffee run.

"They're moving now," Bruder said. "I'll see you."

He followed the Escalade and a bunch of other traffic through a wide loop that took them from Saw Mill to Sprain Brook Parkway, which spread into three lanes both ways with a grassy median in between.

The exit sign for Sprain had also said New York City, and Bruder relaxed into his seat.

He kept the police scanner on and stayed about eight vehicles behind Howell all the way into Manhattan.

***

Things got harder as soon as they hit the FDR Drive.

Traffic into the city was snarled and Bruder had to make some aggressive moves to keep Howell in sight, but everyone else was doing the same for different reasons, so he didn't stand out.

They took Exit 2 to Pearl, crept along that to Water and ground out the rest of the way to Wall Street.

Bruder was two cars behind the Escalade when it turned left.

He followed it to the intersection with Front Street, the Vanguard headquarters right there on the corner.

Howell and his security turned right onto Front and Bruder followed, one car behind now. There was enough going on around them he felt safe getting close enough for a better look, but the tinted windows kept him from seeing anything inside the vehicle, even silhouettes of passengers.

When the Escalade cut right and dropped into the underground parking lot Bruder checked the time.

It was 6:50.

He kept going straight, just him and the traffic now.

CHAPTER 9

Bruder called Kershaw and picked him up at the corner of Pearl and Broad.

Kershaw had two large coffees and handed one to Bruder. "They already delivered the cash. So come Friday, it might all go down right around now."

Bruder nodded. He fought through traffic and one-way streets to make a loop and ended up driving past the Vanguard branch.

When they got to the spot in the scaffolding Kershaw noted the time on his watch.

"Mark," he said.

Bruder immediately turned more aggressive at the wheel. He didn't bump anybody or roll up on the curb to get around slower cars, but he did cut people off and earn the honks they gave him. He hovered right at the edge of what was acceptable in the city and what would make somebody take a photo or video of the car.

Kershaw held onto the handle over the door and tried to keep the coffees from sloshing too much. He watched the mirrors and kept an ear on the police scanner.

Bruder only had one thing to do: Get to the warehouse.

***

The car was still rolling toward the front of the warehouse when Kershaw hopped out and opened the overhead door.

Bruder goosed the car inside and Kershaw closed and locked the overhead behind him.

He checked the time again.

"Twenty-six minutes. Not bad. It's gonna feel like six hours on Friday."

Bruder got out and stretched his back. He'd been sitting in the car since three in the morning, and he wasn't built to sit anywhere for that long.

He said, "Let's run it again tomorrow morning. With the secondary and tertiary. You drive, like it'll be for the job. And again, on Wednesday and Thursday with Avery."

"Sounds fun," Kershaw said. "We'll need the van by then."

He got the coffees out of the car and put them on one of the tables next to his laptop.

He started tapping keys and swiping around while he talked.

"The armored car stopped in front of the Vanguard branch at 6:35. I was going to shoot some video, but somebody was sitting too close to me. The hopper got out of the passenger side carrying a currency transport bag about the size of a small cooler. He went straight into the branch and came out two minutes and forty-three seconds later. He got into the passenger side and the truck drove away."

Bruder was quiet for a moment. Then, "What do you think?"

Kershaw shook his head. "Still a bad idea to go for the armored car. The hopper was in the open for about two seconds, crossing the sidewalk, and if they smell anything dicey they'll just drive away."

"Okay."

Bruder drank some of his coffee.

Kershaw nudged the laptop screen toward him.

"The Escalade is registered to Platinum Protection. Look here—the website is very discreet, just a single page with no contact information, along with a statement that they typically work by referral only. No photos of guys in sunglasses with earpieces standing around while somebody gets off a private jet. My guess is they hire ex-military and ex-Feds. Definitely not the crew you saw inside the headquarters building."

Bruder shrugged.

"Whoever they are, they're sleepy. No counter-surveillance at all. When we were on the phone, I thought they were pulling something with the turn signals to see what I'd do, but they were just waiting for Howell to decide if he wanted coffee or not."

"And he sent one of them inside to get it," Kershaw said. "Some former Ranger or Recon stud, schlepping lattes for a dirtbag."

"They left the Escalade right on the curb, probably unlocked."

They both thought about the new scenario for a moment—taking over the vehicle right there at the cafe then driving it into the city and forcing Howell to get the cash for them.

Then Kershaw said, "But that's today. Just like with the armored car."

Bruder nodded. "Things will be different on Friday. And for now, they're sleepy."

Kershaw worked the laptop some more and brought up a spec sheet with the dimensions of the latest Cadillac Escalade.

Bruder looked at that, then the car in the warehouse.

"It'll work," he said.

Kershaw raised his coffee in agreement and celebration.

***

Bruder took a quick shower to wash the road off and dressed in work clothes.

The warehouse didn't have air conditioning and they couldn't risk leaving the door open, but Kershaw did crack it at the bottom to get some air flow while they worked on the car with drills and wrenches and the welder.

They kept all the modifications inside the trunk and didn't modify anything on the outside.

Those changes would have to wait until the others showed up on Tuesday with more vehicles to use.

Once they modified the exterior of the car, it wouldn't leave the warehouse until the job.

***

They went out around noon and stocked up on groceries and got lunch from the deli inside the store.

Then they made the rounds to the surplus stores and picked up three used cots and assorted blankets, sleeping bags, and pillows.

Kershaw went inside the stores Bruder had been to on Sunday in case any of the same employees were working.

At one of those stores, Bruder drove to the far corner of the parking lot, away from everybody else, and made a phone call to a store in New Jersey.

An older man's voice said, "Harold's."

Bruder said, "I need five pizzas to go."

"This is Harold's Carpets, moron."

The call ended.

Two minutes later Bruder's phone rang with a number he didn't recognize.

"Yeah."

Harold said, "I know who this is! It's been too long, my boy. How can I help you?"

Bruder looked around the lot. "I need three shorts, one long with spread—cut down is fine—and one long with full capabilities."

"Of course, of course. When will you be needing these?"

"Tomorrow."

"Oh dear," Harold said. "You're not on a vendetta, are you?"

"No."

"Not on the warpath?"

"I said no."

"Okay, okay. I'm just making sure."

"What do you care, anyway?"

Harold gave an offended gasp. "I don't sell to just anyone, my friend. Professionals only. If you're doing something amateurish, go to an amateur."

Harold was getting picky in his old age.

Good for him.

Bruder said, "Tomorrow, then?"

"You won't be disappointed."

Harold hung up and Bruder circled back toward the store to wait for Kershaw.

***

When they were unpacking everything in the warehouse Kershaw stopped with a can of coffee grounds in his hand.

"Oh, shit."

"What?" Bruder was carrying a cot and froze, the awkward frame held in front of him like a shield.

"I don't think Avery will drink this coffee."

Bruder waited a moment, then said, "Are you serious?"

"You saw him and Rowe with the wine. I've holed up with Rowe before, he'll drink sock water if he has to. But Avery...he probably roasts his own beans and grinds each one by hand."

Bruder walked the cot the rest of the way and dropped it

against the wall near his own.

"He doesn't have to drink it."

Kershaw said, "I just don't want to deal with his snark all week."

"Then tell him to shut his damn trap."

He walked back to the car and noticed Kershaw was still standing in the tiny kitchen, staring at the can of coffee grounds.

Bruder cursed under his breath. He knew what Kershaw was really worrying about, and he was right. The days leading up to a job were tense, even more so when everyone was in close confines. They'd seen guys come to blows over which way the toilet paper roll should unspool.

Bruder said, "I'll tell him to bring his own when I call him tomorrow."

That might cause a whole different kind of trouble, with Avery unwilling to share his small-batch artisan beans or whatever the hell they were—with anyone else.

But Bruder was already irritated about it and decided if anyone caused trouble he'd go with the original plan and just tell them to shut up.

***

At three in the afternoon Kershaw said, "You see any point in taking Howell home today?"

Bruder shook his head. "Too risky to sit outside the garage waiting for the right Escalade to come out. But let's run the primary route again during rush hour. I want to know the absolute longest time it will take."

"Masochist," Kershaw said.

"And I want to see if anything is changing around there now that the week has started. New road work, a damn parade. Anything like that."

Kershaw said, "If they take that scaffolding down..."

"Don't even think it."

***

Nothing had changed that they could see from walking and driving around.

The scaffolding was still there and seemed uninhabited.

The Vanguard branch was still a set of mirrored doors and a gold placard. There weren't any sudden barricades erected or blast-proof doors slapped over the entrance.

Bruder and Kershaw walked together and split up and met again.

They spent time in the Queen's garden and Coentis Slip, watching and making mental notes and sweating through their suits.

The only other people Bruder interacted with were the cashier at a cafe, where he got an iced tea, and a busker with a guitar who he gave five dollars to go away. The busker treated it as commonplace.

Bruder was walking under the scaffolding from Coentis Slip toward Hanover Square, the branch on his left across the street, when his eyes lingered on a face coming toward him.

The face was different from the rest.

It wasn't looking down at a phone or at the sidewalk or straight ahead.

It was looking around.

It floated in the masses like a radar dish, turning back and forth, and Bruder pegged the guy as a tourist until he got a good look at him.

"Dammit," Bruder said.

He was wearing sunglasses and tucked his head down and looked away, but he was going to walk within two feet of the guy and was almost certain he'd already been spotted.

Bruder clenched his jaw and kept moving with the stream of people.

He willed the guy to look the other way and miss him

as they passed.

When they were next to each other the guy turned and fell in with him, step for step.

They walked ten steps before Bruder muttered, "What the hell are you doing here?"

James, the bartender, said, "Things have changed."

***

"I think it's happening Thursday now," James said. He was sweating.

Bruder took a casual look around.

They were standing near a concrete planter at the east end of the Queen Elizabeth Gardens. Bruder didn't know where Kershaw was, but knew he'd stay away.

Two guys talking is two guys talking.

Three guys talking looks like a plan being hatched.

James said, "I tried to call you, but nothing happened."

"I don't have that number anymore."

"And I tried the other one, the woman who knows how to get in touch with you."

"She doesn't have the new number yet."

"Yeah, that's what she said."

Bruder waited.

James said, "Okay…well, I came over here from work on the chance I'd run into you. I've been walking around for about three hours now."

Bruder just looked at him.

James seemed to be waiting for an apology, or a thank you.

The way Bruder saw it, the guy stood to come out of this with a hundred grand. He could walk around for a few hours.

Finally, Bruder said, "You said you 'think' it's happening Thursday."

James blinked at the slight change of subject. "Right, yeah. My guy came in for lunch today. He was all upset, even more than the last time. His last day was supposed to be this Friday but they bumped it up to Wednesday."

Bruder worked to keep from grabbing James' shirt.

"So it could be Wednesday?"

James, shook his head. "He was ranting about that. He tried to tell the guy, the CEO, about how there was no way he could get everything done by Wednesday. Then he goes, 'And you know what that bastard told me?'"

James' tone changed to mimic the finance guy, and a few people walking past looked over to see what the problem was.

They didn't stop, just looked, but Bruder still told James, "Lower your voice."

"Oh, yeah. Sorry. It's just my guy was amped up. He said the CEO told him, look pal, I don't give a shit. You stay here as late as you have too on Wednesday. Get it done. My guy said he'd be there on his last day until midnight, easy."

Bruder thought it through.

"So, he's setting up the branch delivery for Thursday morning."

"That's what I think," James said.

"And there's no chance it could happen Wednesday."

James shrugged, helpless. "I don't know, man. I'm sorry. I don't know how it works. And I didn't want to pump him, you know? Because of what you guys said."

"Yeah. You did right."

Bruder chewed his cheek for a bit, then pulled out the new burner and called James' number. He killed the call once it rang through.

"Don't save it," Bruder said. "Don't call unless you have too. And don't come back down here."

James nodded. "I know. I'm sorry man, I just didn't want you guys left hanging."

"Us and your cut," Bruder said.

"Well...yeah."

Bruder couldn't fault him for that.

He waited for James to leave. Once he was around the corner of Hanover Street Bruder turned and walked the other way.

He called Kershaw.

"Yeah."

"We got a problem," Bruder said.

***

Bruder and Kershaw were sitting in the little kitchen area at the warehouse. The table held two beer bottles and the remains of a pizza picked up on the way out of Manhattan.

Nobody had spoken for a while.

Then Bruder said, "I'm half ready to walk away."

"You were half ready when this whole thing started."

"We've been guessing from the start. Which day. Which route. How many security guys. All in a compressed time frame. It's no good."

Kershaw pointed his beer bottle at the tables next to the parked car.

"We have less than ten grand invested, all told. Plus time. We get staged for Thursday morning. If it doesn't happen on Thursday, we'll consider it a practice run and do it again on Friday. If things don't look right, we call it off."

"And pay the other guys out of our pockets," Bruder said.

Kershaw shrugged. "Yeah. Maybe five each for the inconvenience. Rowe won't want to take it, but I'll make him."

"So, then we're twenty-five grand in the hole with nothing to show for it except a perfectly good car we tore apart."

Kershaw looked at the car. "I can undo most of what we've done."

"Great. More time and money wasted. And you're just talking about the financial cost. We'll be sitting on that street for two days in a row. Some cop or meter maid comes up and taps on the glass, or Howell's team doesn't like the look of us, we're cooked."

Bruder drank the rest of his beer, stewing.

After a few minutes Kershaw said, "But is all of that worth the risk for two point five million? Seven hundred and fifty thousand for you and me. Each."

"That's not all of the risk," Bruder said.

"What am I missing?"

Bruder said, "If we're going to do it, I want to be there on Wednesday morning too."

Kershaw's eyebrows went up. "Wednesday. The day after tomorrow."

"Things changed once already. They can change again. Can we get it done?"

"If the guys get here early tomorrow...and we can find a van..."

"We'll find a van."

"Yeah," Kershaw said. "We can be ready for Wednesday."

"I'll call the guys," Bruder said.

CHAPTER 10

TUESDAY

When Rowe pulled into the parking lot in Highland Park at ten after eight in the morning Bruder was already there, sitting on a bench. The sun was just peeking over the trees.

The parking lot was near where Bruder had tossed the computer guy out of the car the week before. He'd glanced at the ditch on the way in, and the guy wasn't still in it.

Rowe's car was the only one in the lot. Kershaw had dropped Bruder off and backtracked to watch the guys come in from a distance.

Rowe unfolded himself from the driver's seat and stretched. He looked around and saw Bruder walking toward him.

"Ten hours straight," he said. "I only stopped for shitty food and stank-ass rest stops."

"We have a shower at the place," Bruder said.

"First dibs. I'm counting on you to make sure."

Bruder nodded.

He pulled out the small device Kershaw had used at the

restaurant and swept it around Rowe, then checked the car. It was a cobalt blue Dodge Charger, a few years old with some road and salt wear. He made it seem like he was checking the vehicle out like a potential buyer would. He even kicked one of the tires.

The car was clean of anything giving off a signal.

"This yours?"

"Nah," Rowe said. "The plates are good for another week or so."

He didn't elaborate.

"The others should be here over the next thirty minutes."

Rowe frowned. "What, everybody's meeting here?"

"We don't have time to drive all over the place."

Rowe's frown stayed in place. "I had a bad feeling when you called last night and said get here soon as possible. Now you're saying we don't have time to mess around. What's changed?"

"I'll explain when everyone is here. When we're at the place."

Rowe shook his head. "I don't like time crunches, man. People start to rush, and hurry, mistakes get made."

"I understand. Hear it out, then speak up if you don't like it."

"I already don't like it."

Bruder waited.

If Rowe got back in his car and drove away, he wouldn't try to stop him.

Rowe said, "I'm gonna take that shower first. Then I'll listen."

"Deal," Bruder said.

***

Avery pulled in at 8:20.

He drove one of the new Impalas. It was deep maroon. His hands were sheathed in calfskin driving gloves and he used just his fingertips to guide the wheel.

He parked next to Rowe's car and slid out.

Bruder swept him, then the car.

They were both clear.

Bruder didn't ask Avery about the car. Avery considered every vehicle to be his, for as long as he needed it. He didn't actually own any of them.

Avery reached inside the open window and popped the trunk.

Bruder and Rowe walked over and looked inside.

A messenger bike was nestled in the large space with the front wheel removed and resting on top of the frame.

Avery joined them at the trunk. "Sufficient?"

"Can you ride it?" Bruder asked.

"I'm goddam Lance Armstrong on it."

Rowe snorted. "He's got one more ball than you do."

Avery gave a thin smile and glanced around the parking lot.

"First the call last night, which I would categorize as borderline distressing. Now we're all meeting at the same place like a family reunion."

He looked at Bruder.

"Consider me officially distressed."

"I'll explain it."

"I hope you realize, if the plan changes and I don't like it, I'm walking away. Regardless of what I already know."

Bruder said, "If you guys walk the job is over. So, it doesn't matter what you know."

"Fair enough."

Rowe said, "Dibs on first shower."

Avery sniffed the air. "I should hope so."

***

They heard Gator's truck before it made the turn into the parking lot.

He had an aftermarket exhaust package on the black crew cab Tacoma and a camper in the bed. Music heavy on guitar solos drifted from the open windows.

Gator saluted at them and parked a few spots away from Avery's car.

Bruder went through the routine, taking extra care around the camper because of the height.

The device was silent.

All four men in the lot had officially gone dark.

Gator said, "I gotta take a leak."

He jogged to a cement bunker that housed the public restrooms.

Bruder stepped away from Rowe and Avery and called Kershaw.

"All good," Kershaw said. "Nothing moving on the road in. I'll wait here and follow you back."

Bruder hung up and watched Gator jogging back, wiping his hands on his tactical pants.

When Gator got to the lot, he looked at Bruder and Rowe and Avery standing there.

He nodded and said, "So, things have changed, huh?"

***

Bruder rode with Rowe.

He knew Avery would want to complain in his "I'm not complaining, but…" way, and he didn't want to deal with the noise of Gator's truck.

The caravan left the parking lot. Bruder told Rowe where to turn and Avery and Gator followed on what seemed like a random route back to the warehouse.

It wasn't random.

The turns allowed Bruder and Kershaw, who was trailing from a few blocks behind, to spot anybody following them.

So far, nobody was.

With all the precautions and planning, Bruder still felt like they were a rolling parade with flags that said, "Arrest us."

He didn't take his hand off the grip of the .45 until all four vehicles were inside the warehouse with the door closed.

***

True to his word, Rowe headed straight for the shower with his black leather duffel bag hanging from his shoulder.

Kershaw got the coffee pot going and opened the box of bagels, rolls, and donuts they'd picked up before the meet at the park.

"Help yourself," Bruder said.

Gator stroked his horseshoe mustache while he perused the box, then chose a donut and waited with his stainless travel mug near the coffee maker.

Avery ignored the baked goods and picked up one of the tubs of cream cheese that accompanied the bagels. He found a white plastic fork and used it to scoop the cream cheese into his mouth.

Bruder frowned at him.

"I'm keto," Avery said.

"You're what?"

"Ketogenic. I only eat fats and proteins. No carbs."

"Since when?"

Avery shrugged. "Eight months or so. It's great. You should try it. I'll give you a book."

Bruder thought about the groceries they'd picked up.

"Why didn't you tell us this on Friday?"

"I didn't think it mattered. Don't worry, I brought my own food."

Bruder looked at Kershaw, who said, "You had wine at dinner on Friday. Wine has carbs."

"Well, that was a special occasion."

Bruder lost interest.

The tables with the tools and pneumatic parts were pressed against the left wall with the gray car parked right next to them to make room for the additional vehicles and cots.

Bruder walked toward the tables and said over his shoulder, "Come over here."

Everyone followed.

He let Kershaw explain the components to Gator and Avery. Everything was pretty much assembled, it just needed to be dropped into the trunk with the final adjustments made on the exterior of the car.

Rowe didn't need to know any of it—just that it would work when the time came.

***

When Kershaw was done Avery said, "Inelegant, but effective."

He turned and looked at the car with the open trunk. He had the plastic knife stuck in the corner of his mouth like a popsicle stick.

"You've reinforced the frame?"

"Enough," Kershaw said. "It only has to handle it once."

Avery took the knife out and pointed it at the car. "Someone might need to dive into that back seat. I just want to make sure it's not going to be a mangled mess of upholstery and padding and bad welds."

"So, check it out yourself," Bruder said.

Avery did, and Gator followed him.

Kershaw lingered to answer any questions and eavesdrop on the commentary.

Bruder drank coffee and ate a bagel without cream cheese.

He didn't think about carbs once.

***

When Rowe emerged from the bathroom in baggy shorts and a Mahorn Pistons jersey he claimed to be a new man.

Bruder gathered everyone in the kitchen area. The maps were spread out on the table.

"You're right," he said. "Things have changed."

He ran through the new information, sparing the part about how James had found him walking around the job site.

"We're running this on Wednesday," Gator said. "As in, tomorrow."

His knee bounced like a jackhammer.

Bruder nodded. "It's unlikely anything will happen. But it will give us a good test run, and we'll be there just in case."

"It will give us a good opportunity to get burned," Avery said.

Bruder said, "If everyone does their job, we'll be fine."

"'If you see something, say something,'" Avery recited. "It's plastered all over the city. If somebody sees us, it's going to look like something."

Bruder shook his head. "No it won't. You only think so because you know why we're there. To anybody else we're unremarkable."

"Until the time comes," Rowe said.

Kershaw set his coffee mug down. "And then we're gone within a few seconds."

"How long are we supposed to sit there tomorrow morning?" Avery said.

"The currency got delivered at 6:35 Monday morning and 6:38 this morning," Kershaw said. "We were there before we met you at the park. Both times the hopper came out of the truck with a locked currency bag. If he does the same thing tomorrow, it's a safe bet Howell isn't coming. Two and a half million in cash is going to require a rolling cart. The hopper won't want to make two trips."

Rowe said, "So we're in place before the armored car gets there. If the guy just has a bag, we're done for the day."

"We'll wait a little while, just in case," Kershaw said. He looked at Avery. "But we won't be camped out on the street all day."

Avery was sitting bolt upright in one of the chairs with his arms crossed. "I'm still not happy. We go back on Thursday and do the same thing, and what happens if the hopper just has a bag again?"

"We do the same thing," Bruder said. "And again, on Friday if we have to."

He was getting impatient with the picking but also because Avery was right—the job was turning flimsy.

He said, "The risk of us sitting there for a couple hours over two or three days is worth the potential take."

"The risk," Avery said. He scoffed at the last word. "You're not the one sitting there in a stolen van. Oh, and by the way, where's the stolen van?"

"You and Kershaw are getting that today," Bruder said.

"Oh? Where?"

"Wherever you find it."

Gator raised his hand. "What happens if Howell gets off the X? Say he squirts through because somebody steps into the street at the wrong time, or they're running a five-truck convoy or something."

Bruder said, "We can't see them going high-profile like that. But if we can't spring it on him here," he touched the spot on Pearl street, "we'll use the radios to coordinate another spot. Get in front of him and wait for a stop sign, or a red light."

Avery was stupefied. "A rolling snatch? Are you joking? Why don't we knock over a few convenience stores along the way?"

"Gator asked a hypothetical question. That scenario won't happen, but if it does, that's what we'll do. And we know where Howell lives, so if a helicopter drops out of the sky and whisks him away with the money, we'll go to his house. But those aren't going to happen. The job is going to happen the way we make it happen."

"This isn't like you," Avery said. He looked at Kershaw. "Either one of you. There is too much uncertainty here."

"You want certainty, get a real job," Bruder said. "Waste your life chipping into a retirement plan. Then you'll see how real criminals operate."

He put a hand flat on the map.

"This is the new plan. If anybody doesn't like it, you can leave. But come Thursday, around seven in the morning, you're going to get the feeling like you just let two and a half million dollars slip away."

Bruder looked each one of them in the eye.

"Or you can wait on the side of a street for a couple hours, hot and sweaty and nerved-up, do the job, and drive away from here in a few days with enough money to take it easy for a while."

Avery squinted at him. "When did you get into pep talks?"

"Just now. That'll be the first and last."

The warehouse was silent for a while.

Then Rowe said, "Fuck it. I'm still in."

"I mean, yeah," Gator said. "Why not?"

"All spoken by men who will not be driving a stolen van," Avery said. He stared at the floor with his lips pursed.

Bruder waited.

"Okay," Avery said. "But if we hear one whisper on the scanner, or if one parking cop gives me a look, I'm rolling out."

Bruder considered pushing it but knew he might send Avery in the wrong direction.

He nodded.

"Let's get to work."

CHAPTER 11

Bruder took Rowe and Gator in the gray car and drove them along the routes.

He started at the Vanguard headquarters and showed them the exit from the underground garage.

From there he took the turns Howell was likely to make on his way to the branch.

He showed them the branch and the scaffolding and the spot where it would happen, the X on the map.

He found a spot to park and let them walk around for a while to get a feel for the place.

Bruder stayed in the car with the windows rolled down. He smelled the city and listened to the traffic and waited to see if anyone would ask him what the hell he was doing or tell him to move.

Nobody seemed to notice him at all.

After a while Gator strolled back and got into the passenger seat.

"Looks good to me," he said.

Bruder nodded. He wondered what it would take for Gator to say things didn't look good.

Incoming artillery, probably.

Nobody stopped to see why two men were sitting in a parked car doing nothing.

Bruder took this as confirmation things would work out fine.

***

When Rowe dropped into the back seat the car rocked that way, then settled back and continued to tremble via Gator's bobbing knees.

"It'll work," he said. "I walked past the spot in the scaffolding. The little doorway?"

Bruder looked at him in the rear-view mirror and waited.

Rowe was smiling. "It has to be the two biggest guys, huh?"

"I hope you packed deodorant," Bruder said.

"Don't worry about me. I'll smell great. You just worry about yourself."

Bruder started the car and pulled into traffic to show them the secondary and tertiary hideouts.

Rowe mumbled to himself in the back seat.

"Place is gonna smell like coffee breath…Maybe bring some gum…Some Mentos…"

***

Bruder took them around the Holiday Inn, the secondary hideout, then across the river to the tertiary spot.

He told them the names to use if they had to check in at either place. They were the same names on the credit cards used to make the reservations, for which Bruder and Kershaw had photo IDs.

He circled the blocks, pointing out alternate routes to take once they were on foot.

He wished they had more time to go through it, but the men seemed comfortable.

Gator said, "Where to next? Back to the warehouse?"

"I'll drop you two off," Bruder said. "Then I'm going to New Jersey."

Rowe frowned. "Jersey? Why?"

"Contingencies."

***

It was close to one in the afternoon when they got back to the warehouse.

The space was crammed full with cots, tables, Gator's truck, Avery's Impala, Rowe's Charger, and now a beat-up white van with an extension ladder and PVC pipes strapped to the rack on top.

Gator hopped out of the gray car and offered guidance, waving his hands around like he was on a flight deck while Bruder backed in, squeezing the car into the remaining space along the left wall.

Bruder got out and looked at the back end. There was enough room to get the final work done on the car, but just barely.

He walked over to the van. A name had been painted on the sides in blue at some point in time, but it was just patches and chips now.

Kershaw met him there.

"Clean?" Bruder said.

"No LoJack or anything. It had cobwebs in the wheel wells, so it might not be missed until we're long gone. It didn't even have a plate. I found one on the front of a carpet cleaning van."

"Nice," Bruder said. "Where'd you find it?"

"Some idle demolition site along Rust in Maspeth. I was showing Avery the other hides and we cruised around."

Bruder tried to picture Rust Street on the map. And Maspeth.

"It was about a twenty-minute drive from the tertiary

hide," Kershaw said.

Not close enough to cause trouble.

Bruder nodded.

He opened the back.

"Holy hell."

The van was full of construction junk. Pipes, buckets, pieces of trim with bent nails sprouting from the wood. It smelled like damp newspapers.

"Yeah," Kershaw said. "We'll put all of that in the trash after dark. And leave the doors open overnight."

Bruder shut the doors.

Avery and Gator were already attacking the gray car with tools.

Kershaw went that way to help.

Rowe stood over the maps in the little kitchen, using his finger to trace routes and commit them to memory. Every few seconds he'd close his eyes and visualize it. His body swayed with the left and right turns.

Bruder said, "Rowe, I need your car."

"Keys are in it."

***

It took Bruder about an hour and a half to get out of Brooklyn, across Staten Island and onto the Garden State Parkway for the drive south into New Jersey.

The carpet shop was in Toms River, part of a strip mall with half of the stores empty. The other half were a used bookstore, a check cashing place, and a vacuum repair shop.

The windows for Harold's were covered on the inside by long strips of paper that had possibly been red at some point but were now brownish pink.

The outside of the glass had names and prices painted on it.

Bruder didn't know what any of it meant.

He parked and went inside, tripping a doorbell chime.

The sunlight and humidity got replaced by fluorescents and air dry enough to crack a sponge.

Harold's place was wide and shallow and stuffed wall-to-wall with carpets and rugs.

Rugs were stacked up on large, low pedestal tables with just a corner of each carpet showing until you got to the one on top. The tables had solid sides instead of legs to carry the weight.

Carpets were rolled up and stuck in bins and barrels.

Rugs and carpets and tapestries—Bruder thought that's what they were—hung from the walls and special racks that let people sift through them like pages of a newspaper.

Harold came through a door along the back wall. He was more bent-over than the last time Bruder had seen him, but it looked like he was wearing the same vest and had the same glasses perched on top of his head.

"Bruder my boy, so good to see you!"

He pumped his arms to show he was trying to hurry through the maze of tables and bins.

"Harold." Bruder scanned the width of the shop again. "Did you expand?"

"I did, I did, maybe…four or five years ago? The place next door was a tanning salon and the owner got cancer. It was a shame. The place closed down even though she had throat cancer, nothing to do with the tanning. But still, I took over her lease and applied my price per square foot—she was taking a beating, let me tell you—and we knocked the wall down. What I didn't plan on is how many walls a tanning salon has. The mess! But they were all just the steel studs and drywall, no insulation or anything, so that was a blessing."

Harold finally arrived at the front of the store, out of breath and grinning.

"I could have come to the back," Bruder said.

"Nonsense! You want some coffee? Tea? Sparkling water?"

Harold was a foot shorter than Bruder, even more with his stoop, and he turned his head to stare up into Bruder's eyes with the intense need to get him something.

"Sure, I'll take a water."

Harold clapped his hands once and turned around. "Splendid! Let it be so! Follow me!"

They started the odyssey toward the back of the store, where Harold kept the guns.

***

The back room had more rugs.

Some were stacked inside the battered overhead door, still rolled up and wrapped in plastic or burlap like they'd just been pulled off a truck.

There were two more of the big, low pedestal tables painted black. The one on the left had a single carpet swirled with blue and maroon and gold laid out on it. The carpet had a charred hole near the center.

One of Howard's grown sons—Irving, Bruder pulled from somewhere—was crouched over the hole picking at charred lumps of fabric under a harsh work light. He had large spools of blue, maroon, and gold thread staged nearby.

"You have the front?" Howard said to him.

Irving slid off the table and grimaced as he straightened his back. He nodded at Bruder and went into the front of the store.

A refrigerator was hiding along the back wall among the bins and boxes. Howard pulled a bottle of sparkling water out and handed it to Bruder, then turned to the table on the right.

There were probably two dozen rugs and carpets spread out on it.

Howard started folding them in half, pulling the corner

closest to the front of the store toward the back wall.

Bruder moved across the table from him and helped.

Halfway through the pile he said, "What's the difference between a rug and a carpet, anyway?"

Howard shrugged with one shoulder. "A few thousand dollars."

When they got to the bottom Bruder noticed a fine layer of grit spread across the surface of the table, particles shaken loose from the merchandise. Howard used a small whisk broom to swipe his side of the table clean, exposing the painted wood. It was scuffed and scored by hundreds of runs by a utility knife.

Howard pulled a bulky keychain from his pocket.

While he searched for the right one Bruder walked around the table and stood next to him.

"Ah," Howard said.

He slid the key into a lock on the side that was perfectly concealed by the black paint and texture of the wooden table and turned it.

A three-foot wide section of the table, top and side, popped up.

Howard lifted the hatch the rest of the way and reached inside to hit a switch. A string of lights showed the narrow wooden stairway and a concrete floor below.

Howard held out a hand. "After you, my boy."

***

The basement was more like a tunnel, six feet wide and fifteen feet long.

It had cinderblock sidewalls and a poured concrete floor and a low ceiling made of treated lumber, held in place by posts anchored to the floor. The wall at the far end of the basement was compact earth held in place by layers of chicken wire.

Bruder didn't have to duck his head but he felt like he

needed to.

The place had been dug out and reinforced twenty-odd years ago by Howard and his two brothers and the eight kids between them. It hadn't caved in yet, and every time Bruder had gone down the steps he wondered if today was the day.

The wall on the left had a locked steel mesh gun cage next to a narrow wooden table.

Bruder saw the dull gleam of black metal from inside the cage.

Howard pulled the hatch down behind him and secured it, then came down the narrow steps and stopped in front of the table, which held five guns.

"You said you needed three handguns, a shotgun, and a semi-automatic rifle with full auto capabilities. Here we are."

Bruder looked them over but didn't touch anything yet.

The handguns were two Glock 17s and a Sig Sauer P365. The slides were all pulled back in the locked position and the empty magazines were next to them.

The Sig was the only one with a manual safety, which could be good or bad depending on who was using it. If things went kinetic, someone unfamiliar with the weapon or suffering from fine motor skill decline might just start pulling the trigger and get nothing.

Rowe would have the shotgun and Gator the rifle, so that left the pistols for Avery, Kershaw, and himself. Kershaw was a Glock guy, so Bruder would use the Sig.

Everyone back at the warehouse had their own guns, but it was better to use clean gear for a job. If they didn't get used or dumped, Howard would buy them back for fifty cents on the dollar.

It was a better deal than Bruder would get on a rug.

The shotgun was a Mossberg 590A1 Compact Cruiser with the slide and pump pulled back to show an empty chamber. It was about twenty inches long and looked to be a few years old. The pistol grip and folding foregrip were both a little worn out and the Parkerized steel finish was scuffed.

Bruder pointed at it. "Anybody looking for this one?"

"It's never been fired in anger," Howard said. "But it made the rounds at the gun shows before I acquired it, that's why it's a little shabby. It still booms just fine."

Bruder grunted. "Would be nice to still have all those fingerprints on it."

"Those cost extra."

Bruder turned to the rifle. It was a Colt M4 Carbine Magpul with a foregrip and the standard A2 front and Magpul rear sights. The bolt was locked back and an empty thirty-round magazine was next to it on the table.

"Of course," Howard said, "I have higher capacity magazines and better optics if you need them."

"I don't," Bruder said. "But I need a sling for the Mossberg."

"I'm sure I can scrape one up."

"Okay. Let's see how they do."

***

Howard opened one of the gun cage doors and brought out two pairs of shooting glasses and electronic ear protectors, a box of disposable gloves, and a paper plate.

He handed the plate to Bruder, who put the gloves on first then walked to the end of the basement and hung the plate on the chicken wire at about chest height with a clothespin already there.

Bruder walked back and watched Howard load the weapons. He had strong, stubby fingers that handled the weapons with surprising delicacy, like a surgeon prepping his tools.

He put three 9mm rounds into each of the handgun magazines and six 5.56 rounds into the M4's magazine.

He lifted the shotgun and asked Bruder, "Will you be using slugs or shot?"

"Shot."

Howard slid two buckshot shells into the Mossberg's tube and set it back down, then stepped away and clasped his hands behind his back.

"At your leisure, good sir."

Bruder put on the shooting glasses and the ear protection and went through the handguns first.

They worked fine. The safety on the Sig Sauer was smooth and had enough travel that he could tell where it was with a touch.

He put all nine rounds through the paper plate and moved on to the M4.

He checked the magazine. The first round was on the left side of the double column mag. He seated the magazine and hit the bolt release with his palm, then ejected the magazine and checked it again. The top round was on the right now, so the M4 officially had one in the chamber and the loading mechanism worked.

Bruder slid the magazine back in, brought the weapon up and fired the first three shots with breath control, then switched to full auto and cycled through the remaining three in a burst.

No complaints.

Howard hit a switch next to the gun cage that turned on a small fan, piped through the wall and into the vacant lot behind the strip mall. The smoke hanging in the air drifted into the spinning blades.

The shotgun was about as simple as shooting got. He tucked his right elbow against his side, worked the pump with his left hand and turned the paper plate into confetti. The second blast of buckshot sent a small shower of dirt onto the floor.

He set the shotgun down with the pump and slide pulled back and checked the other guns.

They all had ejected mags and open chambers, as they'd

been when Bruder arrived.

He turned to Howard. "How much?"

Howard feigned surprise at question, like he didn't already have a figure in mind.

"All in...let's say six thousand."

"Do I get free wall-to-wall carpets with that? Five."

"Five and a half, and if you bring them back, I'll take them off your hands for sixty percent."

Bruder chewed the inside of his cheek. It was a lousy deal but he didn't have time to haggle or drive to another seller.

Howard, on the other hand, seemed to be relishing the back-and-forth and could have done it all day.

Bruder found a small victory in watching the grin drop from Howard's face when he pulled out the cash and told him to wrap the guns up.

***

Discipline and rush hour traffic kept Bruder at or below the speed limit all the way back to the warehouse.

The guns were in the trunk, rolled up inside a rug that, if need be, could be tossed into the woods or off a bridge to get rid of them all at once.

He stopped to pick up some pizzas in Brooklyn and thought about Avery.

He asked the guy behind the counter, "Do you have anything ketogenic?"

"For pizza?"

Bruder shrugged. "I guess."

"Nah. But we have gluten free, and dairy free. You know, if you wanted to do something keto, we could throw some cheese and pepperoni in a pan and—"

"Never mind," Bruder said.

CHAPTER 12

When Bruder knocked on the locked warehouse door Gator's voice came back at him.

"Password."

"Open the goddamn door."

"Correct."

Gator raised the overhead and dropped it after Bruder pulled Rowe's car inside.

Bruder handed him the pizzas and carried the rolled-up rug over to the tables near the gray car, which were empty except for some leftover bolts and brackets.

The car's rear bumper was on the floor along the wall.

Kershaw had his head and arms in the trunk, fiddling with something, and Avery was in the driver's seat reading a book.

Bruder unrolled the rug and used a rag to spread the guns out on it.

Kershaw stood up.

"How's Howard doing?"

"The same. How's the car?"

"You wanna see?"

Bruder peered into the trunk. The actuators and hoses and solenoid valves were all hooked up and connected to the portable air tank, which was strapped down between the actuators. It all looked like a combination of a nitro boost kit and an overzealous attempt to make the rear end bounce.

"Stand back," Kershaw said.

Bruder moved to the side and nodded at Avery, who hit the switch mounted on the center console.

It was fast and loud, and when it was done Bruder grinned.

"Knock knock."

***

They gathered in the kitchen area and sat down for pizza and beer.

Avery ate salami and yogurt out of the packages, and when he reached for a beer Kershaw gave him a look.

"This is also a special occasion," Avery said.

He opened the beer and raised it.

"To the night before."

The men raised their bottles.

Bruder sat back in his chair. There was a good chance Wednesday would be a test run, but he couldn't go into it thinking that way.

He had to be ready to do the whole thing, all in.

Every one of them did.

He looked around the table.

Guys were talking and laughing and busting chops and nobody was going through the beer like they needed it.

It was just a matter of time before someone started talking about retirement—someone always did the day before a job and Bruder and Kershaw had a wager going.

Bruder figured it would be Rowe, ready to move from Detroit to a place in the south where the winters didn't last six months.

Kershaw was certain it would be Gator. He'd been talking

about starting his own hunting and fishing guide service in Minnesota, or Montana, or somewhere.

Of course, they would both be full of shit.

Because they could be retired and napping on a golf cart in Palm Springs or bobbing around in a fishing boat on Lake Minnetonka and if the right job came along—easy money with just enough risk to get that rush—they'd be right back in it.

But when Avery said, "Well boys, I think this might be my last hurrah," Bruder and Kershaw looked at each other, both of them surprised.

***

"Bullshit," Rowe said. "You're not done."

Avery shrugged. "I think I might be. The jobs are getting harder to come by, cash is dying, and security and the cops are sucking all the air out of the world. I feel like a fish in a pond that's slowly been shrinking, evaporating, until it's just a puddle. I'm in the middle, waiting for it to dry all the way up so I can flop around for a while before I die."

Bruder checked the bottles in front of Avery again; one empty and one halfway there.

So, he wasn't getting all weepy because of the beer.

"There's plenty of work," Kershaw said. "You just have a be agile about what you're willing to do."

Avery frowned at him. "Are we about to get into how much my conscience is worth?"

"No, no, the cash thing. Money is everywhere, just not in cash. You might have to learn a new skill."

"Like what?" Avery said.

Kershaw glanced at Bruder, then said, "Computers. Programming."

"Hacking? Oh, sure, I'll just move back into my mom's basement and grow a neck beard. You guys, a couple months ago I had to start a side hustle as a damn driver to get some walking around money."

Gator looked around the table, confused. Because Avery had always been a driver...like he was on this job.

He said, "What was the job?"

Avery turned to him. "Driving."

"Yeah, for what?"

"People. Like Uber, Lyft, that sort of thing."

Gator winced and sank in his chair a little, like he felt bad for making Avery say it, now that he knew what it was.

"It's not all bad," Avery said. "It's a good way to pay a little bit of taxes to keep the IRS away. And I meet some interesting people."

"Chicks," Rowe said.

Avery smiled. "I do alright. I even had a guy from the Lab one time."

The table was quiet, then Rowe said, "The Lab?"

"Labyrinth," Avery said.

"Yeah, I know what it is, jackass. Ain't nobody from the Lab taking a ride share."

Avery just shrugged.

Kershaw said, "He told you he was with the Lab?"

"No, he was on his phone the whole time."

Kershaw waited, then said, "So..."

"So that's how I knew. The things he said."

"Like what?"

"Plans. Connections. Doing a thing with a guy."

"So, he was mob," Bruder said.

"Or politics," Rowe said.

"Or a cop," Gator added.

"He was Labyrinth," Avery said, jabbing his fingertip straight down onto the table, like it pinned his statement there and made it fact.

"Did you introduce yourself?" Rowe asked. "Give him your resume?"

"Like I said, he was on his phone the whole time."

The table collectively dismissed Avery as full of shit.

They'd all bumped up against the Labyrinth one time or another and nobody came away from it happy. Even the grunts clinging to the lowest rung of the Lab were puffed with a blatant arrogance, right on the edge of disrespect, along with the certainty that they were untouchable so what the hell was anybody gonna do about it?

Nothing.

Just eat shit and walk away.

Bruder had left a few ripe jobs dangling, due to the property belonging to the Lab or somebody hinting they had an interest in the same take.

It still chafed him to think about it.

Rowe was grinning at Avery, ready to keep digging at him, then he got serious. "Wait a minute. You need a legit car for ride sharing. So, the customers know which one to look for."

Avery was silent.

"But you don't own a car..." Rowe said.

Everyone looked at Avery.

"I do now," he said. "It's a Prius."

Rowe said to Bruder, "That's it. The man's retiring."

"Can you blame me?" Avery said, the Lab forgotten. "I mean, look at us. We're scrambling around to put this job together on a half-assed whim that the money might be there."

"It'll be there," Bruder said.

Avery held up a hand. "No offense, I know you guys have been busting your asses, and that's my point. All that work, you might as well have a real job."

Kershaw said, "Real jobs don't pay two point five million in one day."

"They do if you're the CEO of Vanguard Investments," Avery shot back.

Nobody could argue with that.

Then Bruder said, "That's for years in the grind. Decades.

You should see the guy's house. This isn't his first multi-million dollar bonus. He's probably given up his whole life just to grow a portfolio."

"Then guys like us come along and snatch the bonus right out of his hands," Avery said. "So, what's the point of any of it?"

Bruder nodded. "That is my point. Anybody can take it away. The Feds. The corporation. The stock market, whatever that is. Somebody puts a decimal in the wrong place, the price of soy beans drops and the whole world spirals out."

Bruder pointed at the warehouse, the van and gray car.

"With this, at least it's up to us. Nobody can take this away unless we're stupid or greedy. Unprofessional. And that's not going to happen."

They all took a drink and sat in silence, thinking about the life they'd chosen and how they fit into the world, which wouldn't hold still and just let them work without hassles.

Then Rowe said, "A Prius, huh?"

Avery closed his eyes. "Ah, shit…"

***

They played cards and talked and laughed some more and Bruder tried to ignore the rhythm of Gator's bouncing knees.

Around nine o'clock he stuck his head outside and said it was dark enough.

They gathered the pizza boxes and empty bottles and stuffed them into the van, then Bruder backed it out and met Kershaw and Gator at the corral of trash bins in the corner of the warehouse lot. They pulled everything out—armloads of junk and a couple things that needed two guys to carry safely—and tossed it all in the bins.

Bruder kept the side and rear doors open on the short drive back to the warehouse to clear some of the dust and lingering mildew odor.

He backed it into the warehouse next to the gray car and

left the keys in it.

Rowe was next to his cot with the coveralls, respirator, and safety goggles on. He had the hood up and the front of the coveralls open. His arms were loose at his sides, then in a smooth motion he reached into the coveralls with his left hand and brought the Mossberg shotgun out by the foregrip. As soon as it was out his right hand went to the pistol grip and his finger found the trigger.

Bruder heard the click of a dry fire, then watched Rowe work the pump and dry fire again.

He muttered something to himself inside the mask and pumped the shotgun again before tucking it away to start over.

Bruder stepped in front of him and looked at the safety goggles.

"Any problems? Fog?"

Rowe tapped the hard plastic lens, which was crystal clear.

"Nah. But I'm gonna be sweating like hell in all of this."

Bruder grunted. There wasn't anything to be done about it, so there was no point talking about it.

Kershaw and Gator were at the worktables with the M4 and handguns. Kershaw was working the Glocks and Sig. Gator had the M4 stripped down and spread out along with an open gun cleaning kit and small bottles of solvent and gun oil.

They both wore disposable gloves.

When Bruder stopped next to him Gator said, "You fired this today?"

"It worked fine. Why?"

Gator rubbed at something on the bolt with a rag and squinted at it.

"Somebody else fired it and didn't clean it, before you. Nothing terrible, I just want to make sure you tested it."

"It's fine," Bruder said again.

He'd have some words for Howard the next time he saw him.

Gator started putting the rifle back together.

Kershaw stepped back and snapped his gloves off, the handgun operation a success.

"These are good to go."

"I'll take the Sig," Bruder said.

They left the guns on the table and checked the rest of the gear one last time—the radios, clothes, the bike Avery had found—and it all worked like it had the previous time they checked it.

At ten o'clock Bruder set the alarm on his watch for three in the morning and killed the lights in the warehouse, leaving just the bathroom light on with the door open.

Everyone found their cot except Gator, who crawled into the camper on the back of his truck and closed the door. In the quiet warehouse, Bruder and the rest could hear clicks and thumps coming from inside the truck.

"I bet he has that damn thing boobytrapped," Rowe said.

Nobody disagreed, and they all went to sleep.

CHAPTER 13

WEDNESDAY

Everyone was in place and had been since five a.m.

Bruder and Rowe stood, waiting and sweating and listening to the radio and the sounds of people and traffic moving just a few feet away.

Kershaw was in the gray car watching the front of the Vanguard branch.

Gator was in the back of the van, parked a few spots in front of Kershaw.

Avery was in the park across from the headquarters with the bike and his book, keeping a casual eye on the exit of the underground parking lot.

At 6:34 Kershaw said over the radio, "It's here. One truck."

Bruder flexed his gloved hands and waited some more.

Rowe bounced on the balls of his feet.

After a few long seconds Kershaw said, "One hopper. One bag. Same routine."

Bruder blinked sweat out of his eyes behind the goggles.

Rowe shook his head.

One bag from the armored car wouldn't hold the two point five million plus the usual delivery.

Bruder held up a finger: Wait.

Kershaw said, "Hopper is back out. Truck is gone."

A few seconds later Bruder heard the heavy Diesel engine rumbling beneath the rest of the traffic noise as it passed.

Bruder keyed his mic. "Everybody stay put. Wait for Armstrong."

Rowe's eyes squinted as he grinned inside his respirator mask.

Twenty minutes later Avery's voice came through the earpieces.

"VIP is at work. Vehicle and plate confirmed."

So, Howell and his security team were at Vanguard headquarters.

Bruder figured if the bonus cash was at the branch, the Escalade would have gone straight there or would come back out as soon as Howell had confirmation.

Bruder hit his mic again. "One hour."

***

Nothing happened in the next sixty minutes except more sweating and a phone conversation within earshot of Bruder and Rowe.

A woman had stopped under the scaffolding to berate someone for putting something out on social media, and Rowe's eyes got slowly huge as the venom piled up.

Near the end of the call Kershaw keyed his mic and the woman's voice came through in stereo.

"I think I'm in love," he said.

Avery came on. "Who the hell was that?"

"I'll tell you later. But don't try to steal her from me."

Bruder cut in. Everyone was getting hot and hungry and coming down from what would have been the moment to go.

He said, "Let's wrap it. Coming out on your say-so."

"Copy," Kershaw said.

"Moving," Avery said.

Bruder and Rowe waited some more.

Rowe brought one knee up to his stomach and pulled it with both hands, then did the other. Bruder heard the joints popping and crackling.

A few minutes later Kershaw said, "In five, four, three, two...clear."

Bruder and Rowe stepped out and turned toward the van.

They opened the back doors and got in between Avery's bike and Gator, who sat with his back against the wall. The M4 was next to him under a towel.

Avery was in the driver's seat, breathing hard from the sprint on the bike.

Bruder closed the doors and watched Kershaw pull into traffic and go slow enough for the van to slip out in front of him.

They drove away from the Vanguard branch.

Bruder was almost certain, but not completely, that they weren't driving away from the money.

***

When they got back to the warehouse and started unloading the guns on the folding tables Avery said, "It always feels weird."

Rowe took the bait. "What does?"

"To have relief when something like this happens. I was all ready to go, then nothing happens, and I'm relieved. Disappointed, too, because we don't have the money yet. But mostly relieved."

"Something did happen," Bruder said. "We had a successful test run."

Avery paused with his Glock in one hand and the magazine in the other. "You know what I mean."

He pulled the slide back, ejecting the round in the chamber, then fed the round into the top of the magazine.

"Hell, I'm relieved too," Gator said. "Nobody got shot or arrested or spotted by some civilian with nothing better to do."

The M4 was already unloaded and on the table. With the gun out of his hands, Gator's foot was tapping on the concrete again.

Avery said, "But will I be just as ready tomorrow? It's like a false start at the Olympics. They're off the blocks like a rocket, then have to come back, reset, and do it all again. And you know they're not going to have that same burst a second time. So, did I blow my wad already? Will I go into it tomorrow hoping it gets called off again?"

Bruder was getting irritated.

"It doesn't matter what you hope. It's happening tomorrow whether you're ready or not, so just be ready."

"Of course," Avery said. He had his hands in his jacket pockets now. The jacket was short, some sort of bike messenger thing he'd picked up, and it made his elbows stick out like chicken wings. "Of course, I'll be ready. I'm just talking to get the nervous energy out."

"You have a bike," Bruder said. "Go for a bike ride."

Avery pursed his lips and looked away, considering it.

Rowe started peeling off the damp coveralls. "Put these damn things on for a few hours. You'll sweat it all out, guaranteed."

He hung the coveralls up and headed toward the bathroom for a shower.

Kershaw checked all the weapons again, then looked at his watch.

"Almost nine thirty and nobody's had anything to eat. I'll go grab something."

"I'll drive you," Avery said, apparently deciding against the notion of a bike ride.

They jockeyed vehicles around and got the Impala out and left.

Bruder left Gator alone to tap and shake and bob and went into the office and closed the door.

He tried not to think about the possibility of Howell picking the money up right at that moment, or already riding with it somewhere, the opportunity to snatch it gone forever.

He had all day to not think about it, and he was off to a bad start.

**

Kershaw and Avery came back with a bag full of egg and bacon sandwiches, hash browns in greasy sacks, and a cherry cream cheese coffee cake.

Bruder took a shower while everyone ate, then sifted through the leftovers and got something in his stomach. There was a pile of discarded bread from what Bruder assumed had been sandwiches, the eggs and bacon extracted for Avery. He ate a few of them like toast along with two full sandwiches.

Gator climbed into his camper for a nap while Kershaw and Avery muttered over the gray car's open trunk.

Rowe tried to find something worth listening to on the radio, gave up and said, "I'm going to the movies."

Bruder liked that idea. Something to take everyone's mind off the job.

They knew what they had to do—thinking about it too much would just slow them down when the time came.

He asked Rowe, "What are you going to see?"

"Hell if I know. I'm just gonna go and see what's playing."

"I'll come along."

Kershaw and Avery wanted in as well.

Avery said, "If nothing good is playing I'll just walk around."

They debated on who should check with Gator until Bruder finally walked over to the truck and thumped on the side. He wasn't going near the tailgate.

From inside Gator said, "Huh?"

"You wanna go see a movie?"

"...Yeah, hold on."

After a few minutes he emerged, blinking in the light of the warehouse.

"Now, we can't all go see the same thing," Bruder said.

Rowe said, "Why not?"

"Five grown men all showing up and going to see the same movie together. It'll look weird."

"Nonsense," Avery said. "We're all in town for—what was it—tool and die. We're just killing time between sales calls. Or whatever we do as tool and die men."

"We could be a bachelor party," Gator said.

Bruder didn't want to spend any more time arguing about it.

He said, "At least space it out. I'll get my ticket, then you two, then you two. Or both of you go solo."

Avery shook his head. "Do you have to plan everything?"

"Yes."

***

They watched a movie in Lynbrook, two of them in one theater and the other three seeing something else, then walked around and found a place for an early dinner.

They walked around some more until Rowe and Gator stopped at an ice cream place and Kershaw and Avery went into a shop to look at shoes or something.

Bruder kept walking until he found a spot with no other foot traffic passing close by.

He'd worked to ignore the feeling through the movie and dinner—ever since they'd pulled away from the curb on Pearl Street that morning, actually—but he couldn't ignore it anymore.

He knew it was just his discomfort with how fast the planning had gone and how many questions they'd left unanswered along the way, but if he was going to get any sleep that night, he wanted something concrete to hold onto.

He pulled out the new burner and called James' cell phone.

"Hello?"

"It's me. Anything new?"

"Hold on."

Bruder heard noises from the pub in the background.

They got quieter and James said, "Nope. The last thing I told you is still the last thing I know. And no sign of my guy so far today. He's probably working."

Bruder weighed the risk of holding onto the phone after the call against the risk of new information not getting through.

He said, "If he comes in, call me."

"This number?"

"Yeah."

He hung up and went to collect the others.

Every time he passed a trash can, he had to fight the urge to dump the phone.

***

They got the warehouse ready again with the vehicles staged for the morning, then played cards for a while and went to bed earlier than the night before.

Everyone was worn out from the early wake up, adrenaline rush, then the dragging lull through the rest of the day knowing what was coming on Thursday.

Bruder set his watch alarm again and fell asleep.

CHAPTER 14

THURSDAY

When Bruder pulled the van over on Water Street at 4:45 in the morning they were two blocks away from the Vanguard headquarters on Front and Wall.

Avery hopped out the side door with the bike and rode away, not in a hurry yet.

There was no traffic and Bruder followed Water to Hanover Square, then a left on Pearl, past the Vanguard branch for a couple hundred feet before he pulled over again and parked on the left side of the street, next to the scaffolding.

He got out on the driver's side and Rowe got out of the passenger seat, both of them in the hooded coveralls and respirators and masks.

They didn't say anything to Gator, who was laying down in the back of the van.

Just like the previous morning, the only thing they carried was the fire extinguisher.

Bruder could see some people on the sidewalk, either out very early or very late, none of them close enough to see what was happening.

He and Rowe stepped under the scaffolding and walked to the storefront entrance set back from the sidewalk, which was blocked by the dirty drop cloths hanging from the cross-bars of the scaffolding and had been for twenty-four hours now.

Bruder stepped through the far side of the scaffolding and pushed through the drop cloths.

Rowe followed him, then they both stood there in the small space, looking at each other and waiting to see if anyone hollered or stuck their nose behind the drop cloths.

Nobody did.

Three minutes later Kershaw came through the earpiece: "Parked."

Bruder didn't peer around the drop cloth but knew the gray car was parked two spots behind the van. Kershaw could watch the Vanguard branch in his mirrors and keep an eye on what was happening around Bruder, Rowe, and Gator in front of him.

At 5:15 Avery keyed his mic. "Enjoying nature."

He was back in the park with the bike, reading and watching for Howell.

Everyone settled in and waited for the armored car.

***

At 6:35 Kershaw said, "It's here."

In the rear-view mirror, he watched the hopper get out of the passenger door and enter the Vanguard branch.

He wasn't carrying anything.

Kershaw waited.

The police scanner in the console chattered but didn't say anything that concerned him.

A moment later the hopper came back out and disappeared around the rear of the truck, walking with his hand on the butt of his holstered pistol.

One of the rear doors came into view for a moment as it swung around the back corner of the truck, then Kershaw watched the space between the truck and the Vanguard branch.

Within a few seconds the hopper and another guard rolled a dolly with a large black box attached to it toward the mirrored doors.

The hopper opened the door for the dolly, scanned the sidewalk, and followed the money inside.

Kershaw hit his mic.

"He checked the interior, then came out for the delivery. It's here. Two men inside with it now."

He heard two clicks in response, Bruder acknowledging the message.

Four seconds later Avery came through. His voice sounded a little tight: "VIP is at work early. Just dropped into the garage. One vehicle, same plate."

Bruder responded again with two clicks.

They expected Howell to be early, either here or at the branch, to confirm the delivery. If he'd gone straight to the branch Avery would hustle to Pearl, and if he didn't get there in time Gator would handle Avery's role. Then Avery would have to ride all the way to the warehouse or wherever everyone was holed up, but it looked like that wouldn't be necessary.

Bruder didn't bother to key his mic and tell everyone to be ready.

They already knew, and they already were.

***

At 7:00 on the dot Avery keyed his mic and said, "He's on his way."

Bruder could hear the movement and strain in his voice. He knew Avery was either on the bike or trying to get on it, and now he'd be pedaling like a maniac to get in front of

Howell, circling around to Coentis Slip and coming at the van from the front.

There wasn't any need to track Howell from headquarters to the branch—they knew where he was going.

The radio was silent for almost two minutes while they waited for the Escalade to creep along with the morning traffic, then Kershaw saw it turn left from Hanover Square onto Pearl.

He keyed his mic.

"Visual."

The Escalade bumped onto the curb in front of the Vanguard branch and the rear driver side and front passenger side doors opened.

A thick-necked guy in a suit and sunglasses with brown hair stepped out of the front passenger door and looked around.

Another guy who looked the same except for blond hair got out of the back on the driver's side, scanned the street, and walked around the rear of the vehicle.

He and the first guy exchanged short statements, then the blond opened the rear passenger door.

Another thick-neck got out and stepped away to let a tall man with white hair get out of the back seat.

Kershaw said, "At the spot."

Howell walked through the mirrored doors, held open by one of the security detail, and then the only evidence of his arrival was the illegally parked Escalade, idling halfway into the street.

Kershaw said, "Inside. Three escorts plus driver."

He took his eyes off the mirror long enough to watch Avery skid to a stop next to the driver's side of the van, pull the side doors open and lean in to toss the bike inside.

When he came back out Avery wore a fedora and large Aviator sunglasses and had a bandana tied loosely around his neck, and when he tucked his chin it basically became a mask. With the messenger jacket, he looked like any hipster wandering around for the perfect pour-over coffee.

He glanced at the gray car and puffed his cheeks at Kershaw, then ran across Pearl and stood catching his breath outside the Thai restaurant that had almost killed Bruder.

He pulled out a black chunk of plastic the same size as a phone and bent over it, tucking his chin and ignoring the rest of the world.

Kershaw went back to the mirror and started the gray car.

He flexed his fingers on the steering wheel and waited.

***

At 7:04 the mirrored doors opened and the blond thick-neck came out and looked around.

Traffic had picked up and he watched several vehicles slide around the Escalade and continue down Pearl.

His sunglasses seemed to meet Kershaw's in the rear view and linger for a moment, then he looked away and stepped over to the Escalade and opened the back door on the passenger side.

Howell came out next with the other guard from the back seat, who had a large black duffel bag slung over his shoulder.

The third guard came out last, scanning the whole street, even the windows of the upper floors.

He looked down the sidewalk in Avery's direction but didn't seem to be bothered by anything.

He never looked at Kershaw.

Howell got into the back seat and the guard with the bag took the strap off and hefted the thing onto the floor of the back seat and followed it in.

The blond waited for a break in traffic, then came around the back and got in behind the driver and closed the door.

Kershaw said, "One bag, back seat, two escorts and the VIP with it."

The last guard took one more look around and got into the front passenger seat.

"Rolling," Kershaw said.

The Escalade rocked off the curb and came down the road like a rolling fortress.

***

A silver Lexus was in front of the Escalade with barely enough room for Kershaw to squeeze between.

But the Escalade was picking up speed, closing the gap.

When Avery stepped into the street right behind the Lexus, staring down at his phone, Howell's driver had to tap the brakes to keep from running him down.

Avery never looked over, just moseyed across Pearl while Kershaw pulled into the street and lined up directly in front of the Escalade.

When Avery got under the scaffolding on the other side of the road he turned right, walking toward the van. He ignored the drop cloths when he passed by.

Kershaw rolled forward and touched the gas like he was ramping up to the speed of the traffic ahead.

The Escalade matched him and grew in the rear-view mirror.

Kershaw keyed his mic and said, "Go."

Then he stomped the brake.

The Escalade's massive grille dipped down from the sudden halt and stopped.

Kershaw checked the side mirror and estimated their bumpers were about eighteen inches apart.

Perfect.

***

Bruder and Rowe came out from behind the drop cloths and walked across the sidewalk.

They slapped at their coveralls, kicking dust and dirt loose and making enough of a mess that anyone walking nearby would cover their face and hurry through.

It didn't matter, because no one else was on that part of the sidewalk right then.

The shade under the scaffolding and shadows of the buildings along Pearl kept the morning sun from being too bright, but Bruder still had to squint a little inside his goggles after emerging from the tomb.

The Escalade was right in front of him.

Rowe moved right to swing around behind the vehicle.

Bruder looked that way and checked the car behind the Escalade. It wasn't a police car and the only occupant was a skinny kid trying to fix his tie.

Bruder forgot about it.

When he stepped through the far side of the scaffolding, he was one narrow parking lane away from Howell's vehicle. The tinted windows were so dark he still couldn't see inside, even at that small distance.

Kershaw hit the button when Bruder was halfway across the parking lane.

Compressed air from the portable tank flooded through a solenoid valve into hoses attached to the actuators, which were bolted to the floor of the trunk with the rods pointed toward the back of the car.

The ends of the actuators were attached to the slab of treated lumber, which had replaced the rear bumper of the gray car. It was coated in the gray primer spray paint, which wouldn't last long on the damp wood, but it wouldn't have to.

When the compressed air came through the hoses and forced the actuator rods out, they drove the slab of lumber away from the car and slammed it into the front bumper of the Escalade.

Kershaw had done the math. United States regulations require front airbags to deploy when a vehicle has a sudden deceleration from anything over fourteen miles per hour, or if something strikes the front of a parked vehicle at thirty miles per hour.

Kershaw had engineered the impact of the lumber to be equivalent to a forty mile-per-hour collision, just in case.

The wood slammed into the Escalade's front bumper, crushing it and rocking the huge truck back on its suspension.

Bruder heard the airbags blow and caught a glimpse of something light-colored flash in the sliver of windshield that he could see.

He also heard the doors unlock, which happens when the airbags deploy.

Bruder pulled the rear door open and found carnage inside.

***

The airbags had knocked everybody off their game.

The two guards in the front seat were covering their faces.

Bruder saw blood on the passenger's airbag.

Nobody in the back seat had been wearing a seat belt, and even though the side airbags hadn't deployed and the Escalade hadn't been moving, the two guards flanking Howell were collapsed toward him, either to protect the principle or to get away from the sudden airbags.

Bruder didn't care.

He blasted all three of them in the face with the fire extinguisher, filling the air inside the vehicle with foam and powder.

He let the extinguisher spray for two seconds and cut it off, then he sent a short blast toward the car behind the Escalade, covering the windshield.

The far side door opened and Rowe filled the opening.

He reached down and yanked the duffel bag toward him.

The guard on that side reached down and Rowe hit him

with a short left hook on the point of the chin. The guard sagged.

The guy on Bruder's side swiped at his face to clear the foam and turned toward the door to get out. He was reaching to pull his gun from inside his suit coat.

Bruder hit him with a rabbit punch to the side of the neck, just enough to cut off the blood for a split second. The guard's eyes rolled back.

Bruder checked on Rowe again.

Howell had lunged down without bothering to get the foam off his face and latched onto the duffel like it was a life preserver in a hurricane.

"No!" he yelled. "No!"

He was getting dragged toward Rowe along with the bag.

Bruder hit him under the ribs and Howell let go and whirled on Bruder.

"You morons! That's the Lab's money! The Lab's!"

Bruder stared at him, then looked across the back seat at Rowe, who was frozen in the doorway with the duffel in his hands.

Bruder cuffed Howell under the ear and he flopped over on top of the guard with his mouth hanging open. The fire extinguisher foam flapped as he snored.

Bruder stepped back and slammed the door and sprayed the outside of the Escalade, covering the windows.

"Get back!" he yelled for anyone close enough to hear. "It's gonna blow, get back!"

The driver's door popped open and Bruder closed it with a kick.

He looked ahead and saw Rowe at the van, which had pulled out in front of Kershaw and the gray car.

Bruder sprayed the windshield of the Escalade as he walked past Kershaw, then turned and got into the open side door of the van.

Avery was in the driver's seat and Rowe was already

inside with the duffel.

Gator was crouched at the rear doors with the M4 held low, below the windows.

Bruder closed the side doors and Avery shot forward, followed by Kershaw.

They got to Broad Street and turned right, gone.

***

On Broad Street Bruder and Rowe pulled the goggles and respirators off and shucked the coveralls.

Everything went into the sixth empty suitcase.

They had the quick-dry shorts and t-shirts on underneath, already soaked through with sweat, and when they pulled on the running shoes, they looked like any other jogger knucklehead, if slightly beefier.

Avery turned right on South Williams and Bruder knelt next to the black duffel.

It was made of thick canvas and had a fat zipper with a locking mechanism, but it wasn't engaged.

He unzipped the bag and looked inside.

It looked like two and a half million dollars.

He ran his hand around the inside of the bag for anything that felt like a dye pack, or tracking device, then he and Rowe started pulling out banded stacks of hundred-dollar bills and dropping them into the five suitcases.

They didn't bother to count or divvy up the splits—that would come later.

When the duffel was empty Bruder handed it to Avery, who waited for a good moment and dropped it out the window between two delivery trucks parked along South Williams.

Bruder and Rowe squatted with their backs against opposite sides of the van and braced against the coming turns.

Gator was still by the back doors, out of sight but ready.

The back of the van didn't have any side windows and

Bruder fought the need to get into the passenger seat and look out the window as they came to the five-road intersection with Beaver.

He watched Avery instead, who came to a full stop and looked down toward Pearl.

"All clear," he said, and pulled through the intersection to get onto William.

They kept moving to Wall Street and drove past the secondary hideout, the Holiday Inn Express.

The police scanner didn't say anything interesting until they were almost to the Williamsburg Bridge. The dispatcher told one of the patrol units to check out a bunch of fire extinguisher discharge on Pearl Street, between Hanover Square and Coentis Slip.

Witnesses were calling in about a black Escalade that might have been on fire, but it was gone now.

Rowe raised his eyebrows at Bruder, who nodded.

"Like we figured, he won't go to the cops."

"Yeah, but you heard what he said."

Bruder just looked at the suitcases.

Avery's eyes checked them in the rear-view mirror.

"What did he say?"

Bruder didn't see any reason not to say it out loud.

"He said this is the Lab's money."

Gator turned from his spot below the back windows.

Avery stared at them in the mirror, then had to hit the brakes too hard to avoid tapping the car in front of him.

Bruder kept looking at the luggage, and inside, the money.

Sure, Howell wouldn't go to the police about the robbery.

It was a lot worse than that.

CHAPTER 15

Nobody said anything else until they were inside the warehouse with the overhead door closed behind the van and gray car.

Kershaw looked at the painted wooden bumper, which was crooked now, and the mess inside the trunk where the angle iron was twisted and one of the actuators had popped loose from the bracket at its base.

"It only had to work once," he said, like he was pleased but still had to defend the damage.

They all met at the back of the van and Bruder handed out suitcases of cash.

Avery took his and hesitated, standing there with the luggage dangling from his arm.

He said, "Are we—"

"Later," Bruder said.

Avery lingered for another moment, then walked toward the office in the back corner.

Kershaw noticed it and looked at Bruder. He was the only one who didn't know about the Lab connection.

"Later," Bruder said again.

They each carried a suitcase into the office and left them there and Kershaw locked the door, then they all cleared their guns and left them on the table.

Bruder kept the suitcase with the coveralls and goggles and respirators near the van. He'd spread all of it in separate trash bins when he left.

He listened to the police scanner and didn't hear anything connected to the Escalade, a van, or a gray car. He turned the volume down to a murmur and carried the scanner to the small kitchen area, where everyone else gathered.

Avery was chewing another knife he'd found, leaving dents in the white plastic.

Kershaw glanced at him, then Rowe and Gator, who looked somber.

None of the crew were the type to throw victory cash into the air or roll around on the floor with it, but the mood should have been more upbeat.

Kershaw said, "What happened?"

Everyone looked at Bruder.

"We might have a problem," he said.

***

Avery scoffed around the knife.

"Might? We might have a problem?"

"Easy," Rowe said. "Let the man tell it."

Bruder said, "When we pulled the bag away from Howell, he said it was the Lab's money."

Kershaw blinked a few times. "The Lab's?"

"That's what he said."

"Dude called us morons," Rowe said. "Like how stupid could we be, trying to steal from the Labyrinth?"

"Did you believe him?" Gator said.

Bruder said, "Why would he lie?"

Avery pulled the knife out of his mouth. "Because anyone in their right minds would hear that and turn around and run away. Or, if they were dumb enough to take it anyway, they'd stand around talking about it and decide to give the money back."

"We're not giving it back," Bruder said.

Avery crossed his arms. "Are we going to vote on that?"

"You can do whatever the hell you want with your share. As long as it doesn't come back on any of us."

Everybody thought about that for a moment.

Bruder let them.

There was no way Avery could give his share back to the Lab without uncomfortable questions that would lead to disastrous answers.

So, he wouldn't be giving his share back.

"Well," Avery said, "that's it then. We're fucked."

"No," Kershaw said. "They don't know anything about us. They know Howell had the money, and now it's gone. Howell is the one who's fucked, not us."

Gator's knee was bobbing like a sewing machine.

He said, "But why would he even have the Lab's money?"

Bruder shrugged. "A payoff. Laundering it for them. Who knows? We still don't know if he was lying or not."

"He wasn't lying," Rowe said. "Did you see the look on his face, even behind all that mess? The man was terrified."

"Well…" Kershaw looked at the gray car, then at Bruder and Rowe. "He was being terrorized at the moment."

"Beyond that," Rowe said. "He didn't seem all that shaken up about the airbags or the goons in masks slapping everybody around. He just wanted to keep his hands on that bag."

Avery said, "Whoever in the Lab that money was supposed to be for, whoever was getting it from Howell…they must be pissed. Like, the kind of pissed that comes from humiliation."

He shook his head like it was a shame, then his eyes popped, and he whispered, "Oh, shit. The finger. The guy, the bartender."

"What about him?" Bruder said, but he already knew.

"He can connect us to this. And he knows the guy who works with Howell."

"He got fired," Bruder said.

"What's that got to do with anything? If the bartender finds out this money belongs to the Lab, he won't want to touch his share. He'll find his guy, the accountant or whatever, or Howell, and tell them everything."

"Why?" Bruder said.

Avery leaned toward him. "Because it's the fucking Lab!"

Bruder shook his head. "He's fine."

He didn't want to say James' name again in case Avery had forgotten it.

"You can't know that," Avery said.

And he was right.

"It's my call, either way," Bruder said. "I'll decide if something has to be done with him."

Rowe said, "We don't get a vote on that either, huh?"

Bruder shook his head again.

"Let's do the split," Avery said. "I want to get out of New York as soon as possible."

Bruder said, "We can do the split, but we're staying here overnight. Somebody might still call the cops, or see something from a security feed, and start setting up roadblocks. We don't want to get caught up in that."

"We're off the island," Gator said. "You think they'd run it all the way out here?"

"The Lab will shut down the goddamn tri-state area to get their money back," Avery said. "They'll say it's a terror alert, or a missing kid, or something else, but they'll be looking for us."

Bruder was tired of it.

"So, we're staying here until tomorrow. We'll put the bumper back on the car, sanitize this place, and roll out one by one in the morning."

By the time anyone else stepped foot inside the warehouse there would be enough dust and mouse shit to
cover any remaining trace of the crew.

Gator said, "What about the van?"

"I'll leave it somewhere then get in with Kershaw."

"And never come back to New York again," Avery said.

Bruder shrugged. "That's up to you."

Everyone stood and stared at each other, then Avery said,
"Let's just do the damn split. Maybe that'll cheer me up."

"Maybe," Bruder said.

He didn't care either way.

***

They did the split in the office.

They pulled the banded cash out of the five suitcases and
left the luggage open, one for each man.

$750,000 went into Bruder's suitcase, and the same
amount went into Kershaw's.

$350,000 went into the luggage for Rowe, Avery, and
Gator.

There was plenty of room left for clothes and other items
to hide the cash from a cursory search.

Bruder set the remaining $100,000 aside for James.

He didn't bring up the expenses for the job. With him
and Kershaw each getting $400,000 more than the others,
it might come across as petty.

Nobody pulled any of the hundreds out of the stacks
for walking-around money. Each man had his own way
of laundering the cash, and it would be a shame to go
through the job and the risk just to get busted for spending a C-note with a flagged serial number.

They closed the suitcases and left them in the office,
which Bruder re-locked.

Then they took turns washing the job off with Bruder

going last since he didn't mind the lack of hot water.

He dressed in lightweight outdoor clothes and pulled out his money clip and handed some cash to Kershaw.

"You guys go get some breakfast, on me. You all did outstanding work today."

Avery looked at the others, then Bruder. "You're not coming?"

"I'll stay with the money. And the scanner, just in case."

Rowe gave him a crooked grin. "You don't have a flight out of JFK with five pieces of luggage to check, right?"

"Not a chance," Bruder said. "Bring something back for me though, I'm starving."

They took Gator's crew cab truck, the only vehicle that was strictly legal, and Bruder closed the overhead door as they pulled away.

Then he started to break the warehouse down.

One more night, and it would be empty.

***

They came back a couple hours later with some breakfast sandwiches and a large white box with enough Danish for Bruder and a family of eight.

Kershaw got to work on the gray car with Avery, pulling out the pneumatic components and trying to get the original bumper to look right.

Bruder and Rowe sanitized the van inside and out while Gator wiped the guns down and emptied the magazines and wiped each bullet before putting it back in its box.

When that was done each man collected his own belongings—except the cash—and packed them up.

Rowe, Gator and Avery put their stuff in their vehicles.

Bruder and Kershaw loaded theirs into the gray car.

At the trunk Bruder said, "We'll be the last to leave tomorrow. I saw a few spots when I was driving around, blocks with a lot of broken windows. You follow me, and I'll leave the van with the keys in it. Then we'll take the guns back to Howard. I'll leave James' split with Howard, he can go get it whenever he wants."

"Sounds good," Kershaw said. "Then what?"

"Not sure yet. I haven't been to Miami in a while. How about you?"

"Puerto Rico, I think. But Oregon is nice this time of year too."

"Really?"

Kershaw shrugged and glanced past Bruder at Avery walking over to them, dressed in a linen suit.

He looked back and forth between Bruder and Kershaw a few times, then said, "So are we done talking about the whole Lab thing?"

"What's left to talk about?" Bruder said.

"Uh, the whole Lab thing."

Kershaw smiled. "Did you think nobody was going to come looking for two point five million dollars?"

"Yeah, but I thought it was going to be some Wall Street stiffs. Maybe a private firm that specializes in recovery. Not the goddamn Labyrinth."

Bruder's irritation picked up where it had left off the first time.

"Just don't be stupid with the money. Sit on if for as long as you can, then find a way to sit on it even longer. Do another job, something that keeps you flush for a while."

Avery turned grim. "Oh, shit. You think…the Lab is going to ask around to see who isn't working? Like, who doesn't need to work? Because they hit a big score?"

Bruder shook his head. "Do you have any idea what I'm doing when we're not on the same job? What Kershaw's doing?"

"No, but you two aren't…people talk, man."

"Stupid people talk," Bruder said. "We're not stupid. And we don't work with stupid people. Do we?"

Avery seemed to realize he was talking himself into trouble. "Look, you don't have to worry about me."

He glanced over his shoulder toward Rowe and Gator, who were arguing about whether you had to eat a Danish just because you touched it.

"And you don't have to worry about them," Bruder said.

"Maybe. But what about the people they use? They start cleaning that cash, all it takes is one call. 'Hey, you know that money you're looking for?'"

Bruder said, "So I guess the smart thing would be to kill all of you and burn the money."

Avery stared at him to see if he was serious.

He couldn't tell, so he looked to Kershaw, who shrugged.

"Worry about yourself," Bruder said, and walked away.

***

Bit by bit, they killed the rest of the day.

Rowe and Gator went to a different movie theater and saw a different movie.

Kershaw offered to dump the stuff that needed dumping around town, and Avery offered to drive him, saying he needed some fresh air.

Bruder stayed with the money.

The idea that it was earmarked for the Lab, or had been theirs to begin with, made the take feel a little radioactive.

Like the money was tainted or cursed.

He knew that was nonsense.

Money was money, even if you had to wash some blood off it.

But knowing the Lab could be out there looking, searching, putting the word out, leaning on powerful people who didn't have any choice but to lean on everyone within their power…

Bruder didn't want to be unsettled by it, so he chose to be irritated about the situation trying to make him unsettled instead.

He thought about the plan, the one they already had, and nothing needed to change.

He repeated it to himself: Nothing needs to change.

The scanner was still on and nothing had come up about the Escalade, Howell, the warehouse, roadblocks looking for a van or a gray car or Gator's truck or Avery's Impala... nothing.

But if it was just the Lab looking, and not the cops, it wouldn't necessarily pop up on the scanner.

Bruder folded his cot and carried it into the corner office, then had to shove some things around to make room for it. The office door could still open, barely.

He stretched out on the cot and considered letting every-body leave that night.

Let the nervous energy he'd noticed ever since they got back carry them out of the city and across the country, wherever they wanted to go.

Let them move the cash into their washing machines and start to breathe easier.

It would come as a relief to them, he knew.

But he also knew that's when things went wrong.

When you changed the plan for no reason other than some emotional urge.

The only thing telling them to move out was themselves.

Not the cops closing in, not somebody getting caught and questioned so it was only a matter of time, not some-body getting shot and bleeding all over, so they had to do something.

Just one man blurting something out in a moment of terror, and their own imaginations filling in the rest of the horror story.

Bruder shook his head.

The Labyrinth...

It was better to wait overnight and let anyone on the

hunt—if there really was anyone—assume they were already long gone.

Then slip out of town behind them, or when they gave up and regrouped to try something else.

He'd stick to the plan.

Stay overnight and leave one-by-one in the morning, before dawn.

Thinking about that, Bruder fell asleep.

***

When the warehouse door opened Bruder woke up and lifted the hand holding the .45 to check his watch.

He'd only been asleep for fifty minutes, but it felt longer.

He stood up and looked through the office windows and saw Kershaw and Avery carrying sacks of Chinese food.

He stepped out of the office.

"All set?"

Kershaw said, "Everything is gone. We found some construction Dumpsters for some of it, dropped the rest in various public cans."

"We found one outside a daycare," Avery said with a grin. "Full of diapers and food scraps. Consider that stuff nuked."

They spread the food out on the kitchen table and started eating an early dinner.

Gator and Rowe came in halfway through and joined them.

After a while the only things left were a bunch of fortune cookies and soy sauce packets.

Bruder said, "Let's post a lookout tonight. Anybody snooping around, a patrol car that turns in for a long look at the place—we can sound the alarm and move out. There's a lot across the street from the entrance to this complex, they have some company cars that stay overnight. We'll park there and not stand out too much. Two-hour shifts. Kershaw first, then Rowe, Avery, me, and Gator."

Bruder hoped everyone would be up by the time it was Gator's shift. He wasn't looking forward to knocking on the back of that truck again.

Bruder told Gator, "You're the first one out, leaving from the lookout spot if you're already there. If anyone is camped out and running plates, yours will come back legitimate. Call my burner and let us know. You get ten minutes out, call and give us the all clear."

"What time are we starting?" Gator said.

"Four. We want to be on the right side of rush hour traffic."

"That's coming into the city," Rowe said. "We're heading out."

"What if you see something you don't like and have to turn around?"

Rowe acknowledged the possibility.

Bruder said, "If Gator gets out clean, we'll follow every fifteen minutes. Rowe, then Avery, then me with the van and Kershaw following."

"Why am I last?" Avery said.

Bruder looked at him. "You're not. We are."

"You know what I mean."

The real reason was Bruder wanted to let Avery see there wasn't anything to worry about. When Gator and Rowe both slipped away without incident, he'd calm the hell down and be less of a risk to everyone.

But he didn't want to get into all of that, so he looked at Avery and Rowe and told them, "You two figure it out."

Rowe asked Avery, "Where you driving to?"

"I don't know yet. You?"

"Detroit," Rowe said, like everybody knew it. And they did—Rowe only left Detroit for work. "I got a long drive ahead of me. I'll go first."

"Fifteen minutes is going to make a difference?" Avery said.

Bruder cut in. "Nobody cares. Figure it out later."

Avery asked him, "How long are you going to have that number?"

"Until I'm out of the city. Why?"

"Because if the Lab tracks one of us down, we need to be able to warn the others. If we have time."

Bruder tapped the table a few times with his fingertips.

Maybe he was wrong. Maybe Avery should leave first— even now—to get the stench of his fear away from everybody else.

But Bruder didn't want him out there running around when everyone else was still holed up in the warehouse.

He briefly weighed the option of shooting him, but that left the hassle of getting rid of the body and the Impala. It also might rub Gator and Rowe the wrong way, like disagreeing with Bruder got you a bullet.

It wasn't the disagreement, it was the eroding trust.

Bruder wasn't one-hundred percent certain he could count on Avery anymore.

Not when the Lab was involved, anyway.

Bruder tapped the table again.

Once they were clear of this job, he wouldn't bring Avery into anything else.

He said, "If you need to get in touch with anybody here, use the usual methods."

Avery chewed the end of a chopstick. "Even if it's urgent?"

"Especially if it's urgent. Use the process. You deviate from that just because you're in a hurry, things break down and people pay for it."

Avery shrugged. "Okay. But if the Lab catches you with your pants down because you didn't check your message service, don't blame me."

Bruder had some things to say but kept them to himself.

Avery was one of those people who enjoyed banter.

Bruder, on the other hand, had already decided not to shoot him and didn't want to revisit the pros and cons.

***

They cleaned up and bagged the trash and Kershaw took it out so the warehouse would be ready to vacate in the morning.

They had all been up since three in the morning, gone through a long day, and needed to be up early again on Friday.

Kershaw took the gray car to the lookout spot. It was a small risk, having the car outside, but the model was the closest match to the company cars in the lot and the gray paint would make the car practically invisible once the sun went down.

Rowe and Avery found their cots and Gator climbed into the back of his truck.

Bruder listened to the sounds of whatever Gator did in there to secure his perimeter, then he went into the office and locked the door.

The five suitcases of cash were lined up on the desk, waiting to be carried away into the world, where the money would slowly disappear among its kind, like cards being shuffled into an infinite deck.

***

Bruder was instantly awake when the knob on the office door turned and stopped against the lock mechanism.

He sat up and looked at the door and saw Avery standing outside the glass, giving a small wave.

Was it time for his shift already?

Bruder checked his watch.

He'd only been asleep for an hour.

He frowned at Avery and shook his head and mouthed, What?

Avery pointed down at the knob and made a twisting

motion.

Bruder cursed under his breath, got up and unlocked the office door.

"What?"

Avery said, "Can I talk to you for a minute? Inside—I don't want to wake anybody up."

"Except me," Bruder said. "What is it?"

"It's about today. Can I...?"

He leaned toward the small opening in the doorway.

Bruder stepped back, his irritation growing. Whatever Avery had to say, it wasn't worth the sleep he'd miss.

"Make it fast," he said.

Avery closed the door behind him.

Bruder noticed he was wearing a t-shirt a few sizes too big, which looked strange compared to his usual tailored fit. It made him look like a little kid sleeping in his dad's shirt. Bruder sat on the edge of the desk, scrubbed a hand across his face and waited.

"I just wanted to apologize about today," Avery said. He started pacing in the small space that allowed the door to open.

"Okay," Bruder said. "Good night."

"I wasn't doubting you, or Kershaw. You guys know what you're doing. You're pros. It's just, when the Lab's name came up, I freaked out a little."

He looked over at Bruder with raised eyebrows, like he wanted him to wave it off and say it was no big deal. Bruder just watched him take his two steps and turn around.

Avery said, "The plan is solid. Once we're out of here, we're gone. And you're right, there's no way anyone can find us unless we do something stupid. Even your guy, the bartender. He knows you two, but he doesn't know us. And even if he tells the Lab everything, that just means they're looking for you two. And you two don't get found unless you want to."

Bruder let him babble.

His batteries would run out eventually.

And he looked like a fool every time he spun around, the shirt flapping behind him like a nightie. The material was puckered in a few spots and Bruder realized it wasn't just too big, it was inside out too. The puckering was from screen-printed lettering.

He shook his head.

Avery was a mess, and the mess was costing sleep.

"What?" Avery said. He stopped pacing.

"Nothing."

"Why did you shake your head no? You don't like the idea?"

Bruder frowned. He'd missed something while seething.

"What idea?"

"The serial numbers."

"Tell me again."

Avery started pacing again.

"I know a guy with a way into the Treasury Department. Not like, you know, in with the money, but into their system. Databases. He can check the serial numbers on the cash we stole and let me know if they're flagged."

Bruder glanced over his shoulder at the five suitcases.

"Every one?"

"No, no, just a couple. I figure if one number is flagged, they all must be, right?"

Bruder shrugged. He just knew he didn't want to list the serial numbers on two point five million dollars in hundreds.

He also knew he didn't care that much if they were flagged, but Avery clearly did.

"You trust this database guy?"

"With my life."

"What about my life?"

"Yes. Absolutely."

Bruder looked at the suitcases again.

"It's your money. You can do whatever you want with it. And if it is flagged, letting us know would be good."

Relief fell across Avery's face.

"Great. Thank you."

He stood there, waiting for something.

"Bye," Bruder said.

"Well, I wanted to get the bills out."

"Now?"

"Things are going to be a little crazy in the morning. And I sure as hell don't want to pull into a rest stop and crack open a suitcase full of hundreds, you know?"

Bruder considered him for a moment.

Avery shifted inside the tent of a shirt and tried to smile.

Bruder said, "I don't like the timing. If the bills are clean, and this guy hears something about the job we pulled, he'll put two and two together and get two point five million. Why else would you be asking about flagged hundreds?"

"I'm telling you, this guy is solid. And he owes me."

"For what?"

"Just a thing I did for him."

Bruder wasn't crazy about the whole idea, but if slipping a few bills out would make Avery shut up and go away, probably forever, it was worth it.

And bottom line, he couldn't control what anybody did with their share. If Gator wanted to buy a billboard proclaiming the job they'd pulled on Howell, or the Lab, or whoever the money was supposed to be for, that was his call.

It would get him killed, of course, but it wouldn't mean anything for Bruder's cut of the money.

His methods would keep that safe no matter what.

Bruder stood up and turned to Avery's suitcase, pulling it out so he could lay it on the cot.

He said, "This database guy—he's good with computers?"

Then everything went black.

PART THREE

CHAPTER 16

At ten in the morning Lawrence Howell was in his corner office on the twenty-third floor of what he called the Vanguard Castle—even though that wasn't its name—when his lead administrative assistant buzzed his desk phone.

"Mr. Howell, there's a Mr. McIntyre here to see you?"

She posed it as a question, and Howell felt a moment of panic as he pictured how the last few moments in the plush waiting area outside his office must have gone:

McIntyre walking in like he owned the place and saying he was there to see Howell.

Janice doing her job. "Do you have an appointment?"

McIntyre saying something cruel, or condescending, or just giving her a look, and Janice making the call basically asking Howell if she should let him in or call the police.

"Send him in," Howell said.

Then he stood up and took two steps toward the double doors, thinking he should go out and greet McIntyre instead of having him sent in, but the doors opened, and McIntyre stepped through.

Another man had opened the doors for him, a man in a suit with a mustache and wide shoulders and a shaved head. That man turned and closed the doors behind McIntyre and stood with his back against them, his hands clasped in front of his open suit coat.

He didn't look at Howell, but Howell had the feeling he was being watched.

McIntyre walked past Howell and looked out the floor-to-ceiling windows that showed the East River and beyond that, Brooklyn.

"Are you ready, Lawrence?"

Howell glanced at the man by the doors, then joined McIntyre at the windows. It felt strange to start talking without shaking hands or offering everyone a drink.

"Ready for what?"

McIntyre turned and looked at him with those arid blue eyes of his and broke into a smile.

"For whatever I say next."

Howell wasn't used to this. This was his office, and he was the one who set the pace and tone.

McIntyre was tall and lean and maybe a few years older, with a full head of white hair and a suit that cost as much as a downtown loft's mortgage. His skin looked like he'd spent most of the summer on the golf course or steering a boat.

But Howell golfed too, and he had a boat, and his hair was just fine.

He wanted to start the whole thing over.

He said, "Of course, fire away. But first, would you like a drink?"

He stepped toward the bar along the wall.

McIntyre didn't even glance at the arrangement of bottles and crystal. "Pass. I don't touch the stuff."

"Oh. I see. Maybe some coffee then, or a ginger ale?"

"No, Lawrence. But help yourself."

Howell hesitated. He did want something to drink. His mouth was dry, and he felt better holding something in his hand, but McIntyre was making it seem like a weakness to slake one's thirst.

Howell walked back to the windows empty-handed.

"We're going to bail you out," McIntyre said.

He was looking almost straight down now, frowning at the people and cars moving around on Front Street.

Howell became wary. McIntyre was on the board of a very successful shipping conglomerate, but he was also a part of the other…group.

"Who is 'we'?" Howell said.

McIntyre looked at him. "You know who. We've reviewed the information from your last shareholders meeting, and it's dismal. I would call it inept, but I know that's not the case—you all know better. You just got greedy and careless and thought the bubble would never burst."

McIntyre smiled again.

"Pop."

Howell blinked and wished he had that drink in his hand.

He said, "A bailout will put investors in a panic. We'll spiral out of control."

"Oh, you're already spiraling. Around and around the ol' commode. But you can stop sweating. And please, wipe your brow, man. It's distracting."

Howell pulled a handkerchief from his pocket and swiped it across his face. He was dismayed by how damp it came away.

He didn't know how McIntyre got ahold of the confidential shareholder information, but his assessment was correct.

Things at Vanguard were bad and getting worse.

For decades they had gotten fat on interest rates and investment fees, and now people were defaulting or moving their portfolios and the bottom floors of the ivory tower were getting pulled out one by one.

Whole departments were being cut loose as profits dropped. Why, just tomorrow afternoon, after lunch, the entire senior accounting team would receive notice, along with a box for their things and an escort to show them the door.

Brick by brick, department by department...

Eventually, the top would fall too.

McIntyre said, "We'll inject more than what you need, and we'll do it quietly. No one needs to know beyond the proper officials, and they'll keep their mouths shut. Can your people do the same?"

"Yes, of course. Of course."

McIntyre studied him for a moment with a raised eyebrow.

"I'll try to be optimistic about that."

"Thank you," Howell said, because he didn't know what else to say.

"Well, there is a price to be paid," McIntyre said. "Two point five million."

Howell blinked again. He flashed on selling his boat, or the place on Sanibel, or maybe some of those damn doll-houses...

McIntyre short-circuited the panic chatter.

"The two point five will arrive with the bailout as a bonus for you and your cohorts."

Howell kept a straight face.

McIntyre said, "The moment you have access to that money and I mean the very second—you will withdraw it in cash and deliver it to me. And when I say you, I mean you."

"Me? Howell said.

"Personally," McIntyre said.

"Well, that's fine. That's just fine."

Howell said this while his thoughts churned through risks and exposure and what the money could possibly be for.

It wasn't fine.

Not at all.

This was clearly a laundering process, but where the money originated and where it would go once, he delivered it to McIntyre...Howell was certain he didn't want to know either missing piece.

"Where should I deliver it?"

"I'll let you know when the time comes."

"Oh, of course. And that will be..."

"Next Friday."

Howell found the edge of his desk and sat on the corner. The only items on the desk were a multi-line phone and a stack of papers with figures and charts and projections. He liked to keep the papers there so he could tap the sides and adjust the stack, squaring the edges perfectly. It was a nervous tick, possibly an obsession, and it gave him a few seconds to think when he needed to choose his words carefully.

At that moment he very much wanted to sit and square things up, but he resisted.

"A week from tomorrow?"

"That would be next Friday, yes," McIntyre said.

"That's rather abrupt."

McIntyre turned from the windows with his hands in his pants pockets and surveyed the office but didn't look at Howell.

"This particular transaction has been in the works for some time now. You're just the final box to check, and there wasn't any reason to let you know about it until today. The timeframe won't be an issue."

It wasn't a question, but Howell felt compelled to confirm the statement.

"No. Not at all."

He would need the senior accounting team for this.

Or maybe just one of them.

The fewer people who knew, the better.

"You handle your end," McIntyre said, "and I'll be in touch

about next Friday."

"Very good," Howell said.

His right hand automatically reached out to shake on the agreement.

McIntyre walked past with his hands still in his pockets.

The bald man opened the doors and followed McIntyre out.

He left the doors open.

Janice wandered into the opening, her back to Howell so she could watch the two men leave.

After a moment she turned to Howell with wide eyes.

"Who was that? Are you okay? Mr. Howell?"

Howell looked up from tapping the stack of papers.

"Hm? Yes, I'm fine."

"Who was that?"

"McIntyre."

"Yes, but…who is Mr. McIntyre?"

She said the name like it was a food she'd never heard of.

"He's, ah…I need to see someone from the senior accounting team. Right away."

"Does it matter who?"

"No," Howell said. Then, "Wait. Yes. Get me the single one."

Janice frowned. "Single…?"

"The guy with no wife. What's his name…Fenner."

"David?" Janice said. "Has anything changed with his status?"

"His what? No, no, nothing to do with that. Just get him for me."

"Of course."

Janice closed the doors and went away looking slightly bewildered.

Howell hoped Fenner was the right choice.

He was a hard charger, the work hard, play hard sort. Ambitious, and if Howell had read him right, the sort who can see how the ends justify the means in certain cases.

Fenner would keep his mouth shut, and if need be Howell would throw him some cash or connections.

And if McIntyre and his people at the Labyrinth required more drastic measures, Fenner didn't have a wife or kids who would add to the hassle.

***

Twenty minutes later Janice buzzed and said David Fenner was ready to see him.

"Send him in," Howell said, feeling completely different about the words this time.

He was back in his office, his domain.

Back in control.

He stood by the windows, waiting.

Let Fenner open the damn door himself.

At the last moment Howell realized he was standing exactly where McIntyre had stood, like a dog pissing on the same bush. He made a sour face and took a small step to the side as the door opened.

"Mr. Howell?"

"Fenner. Come in, close that door behind you."

Fenner shut the door and took long strides across the carpet toward Howell's desk. He wore a dark suit and had a tablet computer under his arm and a look of nervous excitement on his face.

"This is a pleasant surprise, sir. How can I help you?"

"Have a seat," Howell said.

Fenner took one of the soft leather chairs in front of Howell's desk and crossed his leg to make a desk for the tablet. Howell noticed his socks had small dollar signs on them.

He'd made the right choice.

"Fenner, I'm going to need you to stay on with us for a few extra days. We might need someone else from the accounting bullpen to assist, but they're not being let go, so that's not a problem."

Fenner looked confused. "Wait, who's being let go?"

Howell shared the confusion for a moment, then looked at the Patek Philippe on his wrist.

Damn, it wasn't even lunch yet.

No one had told the senior accounting team.

Howell said, "It's nothing personal, son. As I'm sure you know, Vanguard is up against some hard decisions. You and your team have seen the numbers. We all need to make some sacrifices to keep the ship going."

Fenner glanced around the corner office with its stocked bar and curved section of carpet with extra low pile so it could be used as a putting green.

"So...I'm in here to get fired?"

"No, that's a separate issue. HR will handle all of that. But as I said, I need you to remain in your position for a few more days, let's say...a week."

"And the rest of my team?"

Howell tried a reassuring smile. "They won't have to worry about the traffic on Monday."

"Well, Mr. Howell, there's a lot of work to be done if the whole team is being fired."

"Let go," Howell corrected.

"Okay, sure. Let go. But I can't handle the transition by myself. We need to get people trained up, we need to get them access to our shared drives and folders, we—"

Howell cut him off. "As I said, HR will handle all of that. I'm sure the people taking over your responsibilities are more than capable of figuring it out. I don't need you for the transition."

Fenner sat back, more confused than ever.

"Then...what?"

Howell said, "We're getting a revenue injection next week."

Fenner brightened. "A bailout?"

"No. Not a bailout. We don't need to be saved. We aren't failing."

"Then why am I being fire—er, let go?"

Howell didn't have an answer for that, so he ignored it.

"It's an injection from investors who see the rebound coming. They are anticipating, not reacting. These are smart, savvy people. And there's a portion of the injection that needs to be transitioned into cash, right away, and available for withdrawal by next Friday."

Fenner frowned. He was an accountant, a numbers guy, and the switch from his doomed employment status to his wheelhouse had him leaning forward, unable to resist.

"That's unusual," he said.

"Nevertheless," Howell said, like that explained it.

Fenner waited, then: "Nevertheless…what?"

"It's what needs to happen."

"Um, okay. What portion of the bail—injection—needs to be withdrawn?"

"Two point five million," Howell said.

Fenner blinked. "In cash?"

"Correct."

"What for?"

"That's a concern for the folks on this floor."

Fenner nodded. The C-Suite. The CEO, COO, and CFO up here on the twenty-third floor.

The people who would typically get a bonus when things were going down the toilet.

He wondered why Shaver, the CFO, wasn't in the room.

"Now this is the sensitive part," Howell said. "This needs to stay between you and me. If our investors catch wind of the injection, they'll see it just as you did, a bailout. And they'll jump ship like rats scurrying for shore. As for the cash portion, I need you to bury that."

"Bury the cash?"

"The trail," Howell said. "I can't have anyone from Treasury asking about where it went."

"Mr. Howell, this sounds dangerous. Illegal, even."

"Don't be naive. Those leeches want nothing more than to find some reason—any reason—to suck more fines out of us. All I'm doing is protecting our assets."

"Well…I know I don't need to be concerned about losing my job over it, because, you know. But this sounds like it could have repercussions beyond my role here. Like, career implications."

"I'll make it worth your time," Howell said.

Now Fenner was very interested.

"How?"

"Use your imagination. Or make a spreadsheet. I'm certain you can figure it out. And if you're worried about legality, bury your involvement too."

Fenner shifted in his seat. "How—"

"Look, son, it's simple. Figure it out. I'm not interested in the minutia. That's why you're here. Figure out how to get it done, do it, and make sure it can't come back on Vanguard."

Fenner seemed resigned to the fact that he wasn't going to get any more comfortable in the chair, or in the room.

"Okay, Mr. Howell."

"Good," Howell said.

Howell knew how to make it happen.

Of course he did.

It would take time, and Janice and others might wonder why he was spending so much time on the computer instead of in meetings and on the phone, but he could do it.

But he needed someone, a buffer, someone to take the fall with McIntyre and the Labyrinth if things went sideways.

Or the Treasury Department, if it came to that.

He told Fenner, "I am your only point of contact on this. I'll tell Janice to put you straight through whenever you call, and here…"

Howell pulled a card from a desk drawer and handed it

to Fenner.

"That's my personal number in case you need anything over the weekend or nights. I'm sure you'll be working both to get this done in time. Don't use that unless you have to, I don't like to be disturbed when I'm not in the office. And I'm sure I don't need to say this, but just in case: don't say anything about this on a phone. Just use the phone so we can set up a face-to-face."

Fenner took the card and stared at it like it might bite him or burst into flames.

He stood up on unsteady legs.

"Oh," Howell said, "and keep quiet about your team losing their jobs. Nothing good will come of letting that news out early."

"Sure, Mr. Howell," Fenner said.

He headed for the door, his steps much smaller than the last time he'd crossed the carpet.

***

Over the next hour Howell sat behind his desk and thought about all the things he'd need to do between the current moment and next Friday.

He tapped the stack of papers and pinched the corners square and thought.

He would need more security.

He had a person—not always the same one—from Platinum Protection who picked him up in the morning and dropped him at home or the FBO or wherever he needed to go at the end of the day.

Years ago, a string of international executive kidnappings had made personal protection details a must for anyone traveling beyond the borders, and the insurance companies had worked with firms like Vanguard to lower premiums so that it was actually cheaper to have protection than it was to pay the rates for kidnapping coverage, sans personal security.

It was also a business expense and could be written off, with the remaining costs foisted upon Vanguard clients via slightly higher fees.

But perhaps the most important aspect was the status it conveyed.

If you weren't important enough to be targeted for kidnapping or harassment or have pig's blood hurled at you a few times, what the hell were you doing with your life?

But he couldn't do more security just for Friday. That could bring too much attention and curiosity around that particular day.

He pressed a button on the desk phone.

"Janice, come in here please."

She came through the doors a moment later with a tablet in hand.

"Are you okay, sir? Mr. Fenner seemed pretty shaken up when he left—I take it you broke the news to him."

"News? Oh, yes. He knows, but he'll be fine. And he'll be staying on for another week to wrap things up."

"Oh?"

She made a note on the tablet.

Howell touched the stack of papers.

"Just some loose ends we can't push onto the subordinate teams. Nothing to worry about, and not why I called you in. I'll need some additional security next week, Monday through, oh, let's say…Friday."

Janice made another note, then raised an eyebrow and swiped and examined the screen.

"Are we making adjustments to the schedule as well? I don't see anything too…dangerous."

Howell almost told her, just to save face. As it stood, he appeared to want more security to get him to and from his home in Chappaqua, thirty-six holes at Winged Foot's West Course, and an endless string of meetings with people who worked in the same building.

"The schedule will be a little fluid," he said. "Nothing to be concerned about, but there will be some people in town who will need to meet at some point. They aren't sure of their schedule yet, hence the uncertainty for us."

"Of course," Janice said.

She knew things weren't looking good for Vanguard, and she knew better than to ask anything too probing about a possible merger, or acquisition partners. Especially right after someone like McIntyre stops by unannounced and gets right in.

She said, "Any changes to this week?"

"No, this week is safe. Thank you, Janice."

She left and closed the door.

Howell touched the corner of the stack and felt the crisp point of each sheet perfectly aligned.

It was satisfying.

He took solace in that, and the fact that all Fenner had to do was exactly what Howell said, and keep his mouth shut, and everything would be over in about a week.

***

Howell called Valerie down at the Sanibel house and told her he wouldn't be coming down for the weekend.

"Well, poop," she said. "Has something happened?"

"Nothing significant, just enough of a hassle to require my presence over the next few days, and I don't want to come down just to turn around and come back up."

"But we're supposed to play tennis with the Traymores Saturday morning. And Clint keeps saying you need to come out on the new boat with him."

Howell knocked the papers out of alignment and started tapping them back into place.

"Clint just wants to ask me about his nephew again."

"Oh, the internship?"

"Yes, the boy from...what was it? Pitt?"

"Penn State, dear."

"Right. They make linebackers, not investment bankers."

"You sound grumpy," Valerie said. "Much too grumpy for Sanibel."

"Yes, well..."

Howell didn't have time for their cute little rule about frowns not being allowed at the Florida house.

"Do you want me to come back up?"

"No, no, that's not necessary. Just say hello to everyone for me, and if Clint asks about the nephew tell him our stable is full."

"I'm not telling him a thing! That's boat talk!"

"Fine, I'll handle it."

"Kisses!"

Howell hung up and nudged the papers around.

Valerie was a fine wife and enthusiastic hostess, and she wasn't too passive-aggressive when it came to the children, who were both grown and lived in California. But the older she got, the more her enthusiasm seemed like kookiness. He could see her in ten years, wearing nightgowns all day long that looked like drapery and forcing small dogs to live in her ridiculous dollhouses.

Mistresses helped, but they came with their own issues, no matter how much you spent on them.

Howell considered calling on his latest, just to clear his head and stop thinking about McIntyre and the Labyrinth and Fenner and the Treasury Department for a few damn minutes.

Give him a pep talk, as he liked to call it.

But no, he needed to stay focused on the pile McIntyre had dropped in his lap.

And there were some positives...maybe.

After all, the Lab was injecting some capital into Vanguard.

And handling the situation well for them could lead to

better things.

That train of thought, of course, led to him fixating on what other caveats might accompany the bailout money, and how worse things could get if he screwed up with the two point five million.

Or if Fenner did.

Howell was wearing the corners of the stack down when Janice buzzed his phone again.

"Mr. Howell, you have a lunch meeting in conference room A starting in ten minutes."

"What about?"

Janice paused. "It's your weekly with Mr. Shaver and Ms. Gordon."

Howell shook his head. The C-Suite and their right hands, eating catered lunches while they tried to figure out how to fix the leaks in Vanguard.

It had been a standing weekly meeting for three full months now, and he wanted to smack himself for drawing a blank.

If Janice was worried about him before...

Howell got up and headed for the door.

He had good news to share with the others about the cash injection, but his focus was on the knot in his gut about the money only he and Fenner knew of.

So far, anyway.

It had to stay that way.

***

Fenner was sweating at his desk inside his half-wall cubicle near the windows, where the senior accounting team bullpen was.

The windows were something to indicate his status, at least, but Vanguard had gone all-in on the open office concept and pretty much everyone on the floor could at least see the windows, if not the view they offered.

Vanguard loved the idea of everyone being accessible to everyone else at all times, but in execution it was a pain in the ass. Sometimes you needed a door to close, something that told everyone to piss off, the senior accounting lead was busy and didn't want to hear about your fantasy football team.

Fenner peered over the top of his half-wall and sure enough, right on cue, there was Rafferty.

Rafferty liked pinstripes and suspenders a lot, and Fenner didn't like Rafferty very much.

He leaned an elbow on Fenner's wall.

"So, what's up?"

"What's up with what?" Fenner said.

"What did old man Howell want?"

"Oh, nothing. Just some stuff about the new portfolio. He wants us to run the projections again."

"Again? Shit, how many times?"

Rafferty frowned.

"And why did Howell tell you? Why not some peon? Or with one of his long-ass emails?"

Fenner shrugged. "He's a hands-on guy."

"Yeah...hey, was anybody else in there with you?"

"No, just me and the boss."

"Rachel was up on twenty-three handing some stuff over to Shaver's goons this morning and some big swinging dick came in for a meeting with Howell. Rachel said Janice was pissed, and Howell's whole staff was all flustered, twitching around like a bunch of pigeons. Cindy told Rachel the guy didn't have a meeting but got right in."

"Cindy..."

Fenner was stalling and trying not to panic, even though he wasn't sure what the panic was about yet.

Rafferty said, "One of Howell's other secretaries. Sorry, my bad: administrative assistants. The one with the bucket ass."

"And the guy was in there right before me?"

"That's what it sounds like. But he wasn't in there with you..."

"No," Fenner confirmed.

Rafferty looked around, about as subtle as a submarine periscope breaking through an ice sheet, then leaned over Fenner. He smelled like coffee and body spray.

"I'm wondering if the guy was a merger situation. Maybe a takeover. Howell didn't say anything about that?"

"Of course not," Fenner said, sweating more now.

"So, our jobs are safe?"

"Well...nobody's really safe anymore."

Rafferty pulled back. "What the hell does that mean?"

"Nothing. It means no job is safe anymore, the way things are. But Howell didn't say anything about a guy or jobs or whatever."

Rafferty squinted at him, either unconvinced or reveling in the conspiracy theories.

"I gotta find out who that guy was."

"Well, good luck. Now go away, I have shit to do."

"We doing the pub tonight?"

"Um, yeah. Wait...maybe. If I can get this stuff done."

"Then get it done."

Rafferty patted the top of the wall and looked around some more as he walked away, like something might be happening in the corners of the room.

Fenner didn't see anyone else coming and pulled up the company calendar on one of his screens.

Howell had two meetings that morning starting at 8:00, both of them routine.

Something about the new marketing strategy, and planning for the shareholder's quarterly.

Then nothing from 9:45 until he'd summoned Fenner around 10:30.

So, the swinging dick, whoever he was, didn't have an

appointment. That part was true.

And now Howell and the rest of the C-Suite had their weekly in conference room A coming up.

Howell, Shaver, and Gordon, plus their sycophants.

Fenner closed the calendar and leaned back in his Aeron chair and chewed the side of his thumbnail.

So, somebody comes to see Howell and gets in without an appointment when he's usually impossible to see unless you book a month in advance, or he summons you.

Then Howell calls him in and basically pulls him into a felony, or at least the conspiracy to commit one.

Then he goes into a weekly meeting with the C-Suite.

So, was it business as usual in that weekly, or was he telling them about the two point five million?

If they all knew about it, it had to be for them, somehow.

Some backdoor bonus for the honchos while the rest of the company got pruned, branch by branch.

With all of it kicked off by a mystery man waltzing into Howell's office and getting everyone spun up.

Fenner chewed his thumb and looked out the window at nothing in particular.

What really got him stewing was the audacity of it.

For Howell to tell him he was fired and ask him to risk his career—whatever that was now—and possibly his freedom in the same breath required a staggering lack of self-aware-ness.

And an impressive amount of balls.

Fenner wanted all of that, someday.

Howell pulled it off because he could.

He didn't care what Fenner or anyone else thought of him.

Because he didn't have to.

He cared about results, and he got them, whatever it took.

Even if it took drafting some schmuck in a cubicle—which should be an office, dammit—to grind for the next week to make sure it got done.

And what did Howell say?

He'd make it worth Fenner's time.

Damn right he would.

"Okay," Fenner muttered to himself.

He started making notes on a legal pad, notes about how he was going to hide two point five million dollars, and make it liquid, and make it accessible for withdrawal within hours of it hitting the Vanguard accounts.

What he was really writing, though he had no way of knowing it, was a suicide note.

***

The end of the day snuck up on Fenner like a snake and sprang out of the bushes when Rafferty slapped the top of his cubicle wall and said, "Pub!"

Fenner blinked at his screens, then peered out the darkening window, and knew he wouldn't get anything else productive done that day.

He'd started the thing for Howell, chipping away at it between emails and meetings and interruptions and his actual day-to-day responsibilities, and the overall progress was depressing.

He still couldn't wrap his head around how to get Howell what he needed, when he needed it, without leaving any footprint and without knowing where it was all coming from in the first place.

He needed more time and more information, but what he really needed right then was a drink.

He shut his computer down and stuffed the legal pad into his leather satchel and followed Rafferty and the others toward the elevators, reminding himself to keep his damn mouth shut about Howell and the money and the whole team getting cut loose tomorrow.

He'd just have one rum and Coke with his burger and fries.

CHAPTER 17

LAST FRIDAY

On Friday morning Fenner almost called in dead.

But he fell out of bed, managed to shower between dry heaves, was pleasantly surprised by the symmetrical knot in his tie on the first shot, then vomited again in the toilet.

He couldn't hold his head up at his desk and had to watch the computer screens past his eyebrows.

Around nine Rafferty walked up with a grin that turned to horror when he saw Fenner's face.

"What the hell happened to you?"

"I'm fine," Fenner said.

"How long did you stay after we left?"

"I don't know. Forever?"

"Damn, dude. So, no martinis at lunch for you, huh?"

Fenner pressed the back of his hand to his mouth.

Rafferty said, "What do you think the meeting is about?"

"What meeting?"

"Today at three. The invite just came through, the whole senior accounting team."

Fenner checked his email and saw the invite.

He shrugged.

But he knew what it was: Everyone was getting fired except him, who got to stay on for one more week and sell his soul and destroy the lining of his stomach.

At least he wouldn't have to suffer Rafferty next week, but that also made him angry.

It was another example of Howell doing whatever the hell he wanted and not giving a shit how it landed on other people.

Ferner wouldn't be a bit surprised if, come next week, Howell blew him off and acted like none of this ever happened.

Because what was Fenner going to do about it?

Maybe it was the leftover tequila in his brain, or the inability to think straight because his screens kept tilting, but he decided right then he wasn't going to let Howell slide on making all of this worth it.

If the old man tried to screw him over, he'd regret it.

And then—maybe because of the alcohol, maybe because of the enormity of the decision—Fenner stood up and pushed past Rafferty and bolted for the bathroom.

***

Friday morning Howell got picked up by a driver from Platinum. He didn't know the driver's name—Paul, maybe—and told him to swing through town to get a cappuccino. He did this a few times a week, partially because he owned stock in the company and considered it to be paying himself, but also because he liked to fly the flag in town, and because he just liked the damn taste of it.

He waited in the Escalade, bumped up on the curb, while Paul (maybe) ran inside to handle the coffee.

He had an early lunch with friends from his cigar club and was on the third hole at Winged Foot when the senior accounting team found out they were all unemployed.

The meeting didn't cross his mind once.

All he could think about was McIntyre and the Labyrinth and what they might be doing at that very moment to get the money they were forcing upon him and Vanguard.

And Fenner and what he was should be doing to make sure it all happened the way it was supposed to.

Howell wasn't too worried about that part.

The steps and details were straightforward enough once you saw them from the proper angle. He had faith that Fenner would come through. He'd prove himself.

He thought about checking in with the man but didn't want to initiate a simple transactional back-and-forth that could easily snowball into a conversation or a perceived invitation for friendlier terms.

He had no interest in babysitting Fenner over the weekend and through next week.

He had a few drinks and a light dinner at the club, then Paul took him home.

As he opened the back door of the Escalade Paul said, "Have a nice evening, Mr. Howell. We'll have a full team for you here on Monday morning."

"Oh, very good," Howell said.

He didn't wish Paul a good evening or a nice weekend or think anything about him while he walked up the steps to the front door and went inside.

The housekeepers and the chef were all gone for the day and the house was silent.

All the windows and doors were shut to keep the summer humidity out, so he couldn't even hear the fountain out back.

"Damn," he said.

He was supposed to be on his way to Florida and hadn't remembered to tell the staff he was going to be around.

He went into the kitchen and looked through the glass of the restaurant-grade refrigerator.

No marinated steaks ready for the grill, no prepared meals that just needed to be warmed up, no bowls of salad.

Nothing ready for him to eat over the next few days.

"Damn," he said again.

He turned on the kitchen TV to have some background noise. It was tuned to CNBC and he half-listened while he got a drink going at the sidebar just around the corner from the kitchen.

He carried the drink upstairs and into the steam shower to wash the golf off, and in the shower, he decided he was tired of thinking about everything so much.

The course was set, things were in motion, and it didn't do any good to fret over it.

After the shower he called his mistress and had her delivered to the house.

***

Howell spent most of the weekend at the golf course, driving himself and choosing a car from the garages that fit his mood in that moment.

Saturday, he took the '67 Shelby Mustang GT500 and tore along the roads like he was trying to muscle them straight.

Sunday felt more serene, plus he'd had a bit too much to drink at the club on Saturday, so he chose the Rolls-Royce Phantom and took pleasure in the glide.

McIntyre and Fenner crept into his thoughts a few times, but never during his backswing, which was a damn good thing.

***

Fenner spent his weekend hunched over his laptop and ignoring texts and calls from people who weren't currently experiencing what could either be the best opportunity or worst catastrophe of their lives.

Late Sunday afternoon he finally cracked it and found a

way to tuck bits and pieces of the two point five million into nooks and crannies without leaving a trail.

When he found the solution, he ran onto his small balcony and whooped like a madman, to which someone unseen yelled, "I'll take some of that, my man!"

Fenner got back to work and began setting things up for the Thursday deposit and Friday withdrawal, and ten minutes into it he saw how he could do the same thing Howell wanted him to do, but move the money so that only he, Fenner, could get to it.

Two point five million.

What could Howell do about it?

Fire him?

Too late, already done.

Call the cops?

He didn't think so. The whole point was to keep Treasury away from the money. If word got out the CEO of Vanguard was hiding bailout cash, things would go from bad to shit-storm, like…immediately.

Fenner paced around his tiny apartment a few times, thinking it through.

He thought about short-term vs. long-term risks and benefits, what the return on two point five million would be if he was smart with it.

Screw Howell and his senior accounting team—Fenner wouldn't need that or any other job. He could move to a beach and teach scuba diving, once he learned how to scuba dive, and survive on fish tacos and cold beer.

That sounded just about right.

He wandered into the bathroom and threw water on his face, and when he looked into the mirror, he forgot all about his grand schemes.

Sure, he could stash the money and leave New York be-hind, but what he couldn't do was spend the rest of his life feeling like he'd felt since that Thursday meeting in Howell's office.

Like he was carrying a bowling ball around inside his chest, and every now and then it would drop down onto his stomach and remind him not to relax.

If he did exactly what Howell asked, it would all be over by Friday.

For the most part, anyway.

There would be some lingering stress about Treasury, of course, but that would fade.

If he stole the money and told Howell to go screw, however...he'd end up resenting every cent of it.

Fenner went back to the laptop and found a flight to Cabo that departed Saturday morning.

His part would be done by then, and it was perfectly normal for someone who just lost a job to finally take that vacation they'd been putting off for years.

Right?

He didn't think it looked suspicious...

No, it was fine.

He booked a seat and instantly felt better.

A week from that moment, he would be on the beach or in a bar, or in a pool with a bar, fantasizing about the ways Howell was going to make all off this worth it for him.

CHAPTER 18

LAST MONDAY

At 5:22 in the morning Howell got picked up by the four-man crew from Platinum.

He opened the front door and saw a man in his late 30s with a thick neck wearing a suit.

Howell told him, "You're two minutes late."

"It won't happen again, Mr. Howell."

Howell walked to the Escalade and stopped at the open back door on the passenger's side. He looked back at the man in the suit.

"Have you driven me before?"

"Yes sir, this will be my twenty-fifth time."

"What's your name again?"

"You can call me Burt, sir."

"Okay Burt, so you know the drill if I want a coffee from town."

"Yes, sir. Are we doing that today?"

Howell said, "I don't know yet. Oh, this is new."

He was looking into the back seat, which usually had two

captain's chairs. This Escalade was different, with a bench seat spanning the width of the vehicle.

At the other end of the bench, another man with a neck that went straight up from his collar to his ears was sitting and looking out his driver's side window, admiring the water feature or scanning for Russian invaders.

"So, I'm in the middle, then," Howell said.

"It's the safest seat," Burt said. "We've tested it with three of us, there's plenty of room."

Howell doubted both of those statements, but he climbed inside and allowed Burt to wedge in next to him.

The driver took off.

Howell said, "Perhaps tomorrow you can bring something more appropriate."

The security team knew "perhaps" meant "you'd better damn do it."

Burt said, "Unfortunately the fleet of Suburbans is devoted elsewhere, but we're working on an additional asset for this purpose."

Each one of those words chafed Howell.

Unfortunately...

Devoted elsewhere...

Working on...

He had things that needed to get done too, and he was getting them done.

Well, Fenner was.

It was just that simple.

Get a job, get it done right.

He said, "This fleet of yours...devoted to whom?"

"I'm afraid I can't discuss ongoing operations," Burt said.

Howell grunted.

It was likely some Saudi foreigner, gobbling up all the Suburbans and the best personnel so he could haul his harem around to the night clubs. Right then, the vehicle that would allow Howell to ride in some semblance of comfort and dignity was probably sitting in a parking garage under the Hotel Elysee, doing absolutely nothing for no one.

Howell knew he was in a foul mood but didn't care to alter it. It was one of the perks of being in charge—everyone else had to adjust, not him.

The driver took them toward the stop sign at Bedford. A left turn would get them heading toward Manhattan, a right would take them into town for the coffee.

Burt showed an acceptable level of recall and situational awareness and asked, "Would you like that coffee, Mr. Howell?"

Howell thought about it while the Escalade coasted to a stop.

The driver and the man in the passenger seat both glanced at the side mirrors.

Howell didn't give a damn if there was anyone waiting behind him.

He was deciding between seeing how quickly this group could get him to the office—say, because something happened with the money from McIntyre—and how they handled his coffee, should he desire it.

It was only Monday.

He could drill them on the office run the rest of the week.

"Coffee," he said, and the Escalade turned right.

No one paid extra attention to the gray car that followed.

***

The Escalade dropped into the parking garage at 6:50, right on time considering the coffee run.

Burt had even gotten the two napkins and stirring stick Howell liked along with the coffee; he enjoyed pinching the stick between his teeth while he reviewed the morning's reports on his tablet.

Howell's mood had improved since the humiliation of the bench seat. He was pleased with himself for testing the most time-consuming routine early in the week. Now he—and more importantly, Burt and his soldiers—knew it could be done in the required amount of time.

His pleasure vanished when the Escalade had to slow down and stop without pulling into his reserved CEO's spot.

They couldn't pull in because another vehicle was already parked there. It was a dark blue Bentley Mulsanne with tinted windows, and Howell didn't recognize it.

The taillights were on and a steady wisp of exhaust drifted from the dual tailpipes.

Burt said, "Stay here, Mr. Howell."

He opened his door and had one foot out when the reverse lights on the Bentley flared and the car crept backwards.

Burt got all the way out and closed the door and stood ready while the Bentley reversed in a tight arc and made room for the Escalade to pull in.

The Platinum man in the front passenger seat also got out and moved with Burt toward the Bentley. Their suit coats were open and both men had their right hands near their hips.

Howell told the driver, "Pull in now."

"Not yet, Mr. Howell. We don't want to get closed in."

Howell gnashed on the stirring stick. The idea of him getting trapped in his own damn parking space was infuriating.

The man sitting on his right must have noticed, or felt him tense up, because he said, "We're handling it, Mr. Howell. This is why you hired us."

And he was exactly right.

The driver's window on the Bentley slid down and Burt spoke with the driver for a moment, then came back to the Escalade with a blank face.

He opened the back door and said, "Mr. Howell, a Mr. McIntyre is in that vehicle and would like a word with you."

Howell forgot about his fury.

He tried to keep his features composed.

"McIntyre, you say? Well, I suppose. Have him step inside for a moment. The rest of you can step out."

To his credit, Burt kept a flat face.

"Yes sir, Mr. Howell. Mr. McIntyre said the invitation was extended to you, and that you should join him in the Bentley. How would you like me to proceed?"

Howell's rage returned.

Oh, that son of a bitch.

That prick.

That white-haired bastard.

For McIntyre to pull this, in Howell's garage beneath Howell's building, on the first day with his new security team...he may as well have unzipped and pissed all over him.

Howell forced a smile onto his face.

"Oh, that's right. Old man McIntyre has that bum hip, boys. I'll make the trip. Otherwise, we'll be here all damn day waiting for him to totter over."

"Yes, Mr. Howell."

Howell got out and flicked his suit coat into place and waited while Burt opened the back door on the driver's side of the Bentley and checked the back seat.

Then Howell got in and Burt closed the door, so it was just McIntyre and Howell in the vehicle, along with McIntyre's driver, the bald man with the mustache.

McIntyre hit him with that smile of his.

"Good morning, Lawrence."

"What do you want?"

"I noticed the additional security. You're not concerned, are you?"

"No, I'm not concerned. I got where I am by being proactive and taking the necessary precautions to counter the necessary risks."

"Where you are," McIntyre echoed, peering out the window. "Your own parking spot and everything. Good for you."

Howell wasn't sure how much more he could take.

McIntyre said, "There's been a change in the process. The money will be deposited Thursday morning, rather than Friday."

Howell received this as good news at first. This would give him—Fenner, really—twenty-four hours to have the two point five million ready for withdrawal.

Then McIntyre said, "And you will deliver the bonus portion to me on that same day."

"Thursday?" Howell said.

"That won't be a problem for you, I'm sure."

Howell's thoughts scurried.

Was McIntyre testing him, to see if he actually knew whether it would be a problem?

Also...would it?

"Of course not," Howell said. "Why the change, though?"

"Not your concern."

Howell pinched the crease in his slacks on one knee.

"Well, do you anticipate any further changes?"

McIntyre spread his hands.

"I anticipate it shall be what it shall be. And I expect us all to adapt accordingly."

Us, Howell thought, meaning me.

And Fenner.

Damn that Fenner, he'd better come through.

"Is that everything?" Howell asked, trying to make it come across like he wasn't waiting to be excused.

"It is."

Howell knocked on the window and Burt was there to open the door for him.

As Howell slid out of the Bentley, McIntyre said, "Lawrence."

Howell stood outside the car and bent over to look in.

"Would you like me to get you a larger vehicle? I imagine it feels like a cattle car, what with all the..." McIntyre glanced at Burt. "...professionals in there."

"It's fine," Howell said, and stalked toward the elevators.

The Bentley rolled away and the Escalade's tires squawked on concrete to get into the parking spot, then the rest of the security team had to run to catch up with Howell and Burt and the other one.

The one from the back seat offered Howell his tablet and what was left of the coffee.

Howell tucked the tablet under an arm and took the coffee, looked at it for a moment, then hurled it against the concrete wall next to the elevators.

There wasn't much liquid left inside, and rather than a satisfying explosion, it merely tapped against the wall and fell to the floor with a hollow-sounding clunk.

One of the men stepped over to pick it up.

"Leave it," Howell said.

The elevator doors opened, and they piled in and all Howell could think about was the look McIntyre would have if he saw the doors closing, like resealing a can of sardines.

***

When Fenner's desk phone rang at 8:35 it made him jump in his chair.

He had been at his desk for a whole five minutes and was already creating more small pockets in which to stuff some of the money that couldn't be traced.

If anyone from accounting wandered over and peeked at his screen, they would ask what the hell he was doing.

Luckily, he was the only one left in the bullpen area—Rafferty and the others were likely out somewhere schlepping resumes—but there were plenty of people left in the department and a few of them had drifted over to see if he was okay, and also, without coming right out with it, why he was at his desk.

He just smiled and spread his hands helplessly.

"I'm the transition team."

"You're kidding," they'd say, and then launch into how unfair that was and how everyone should walk out in solidarity, to make a point, then they'd go back to their desk and drink their free coffee and maybe post something about thoughts and prayers for those who'd been let go while they updated their own resumes.

So, he was keeping an eye out for any more vultures and zipping his mouse around and clacking away at his keyboard when the phone rang and he jumped and cursed and picked up the phone.

"Fenner."

"Mr. Fenner, this is Janice, in Mr. Howell's office. He'd like to see you at your earliest convenience."

"Um, I'm on my way."

"Thank you."

Fenner made sure his computer was locked behind a password, then took three steps away and came back to double-check.

He carried his tablet to the elevators and spent the ride up to the twenty-third floor hoping Howell had something to give him, a taste of what he was going to do to make all off this worth it.

If it is was stock options or some other bullshit, Fenner would tell him to shove it.

Well, he'd request something more tangible.

More immediate.

Since he was within a few days of being unemployed, and all.

The old man loved to golf—what if he presented a membership to Winged Foot?

Could he do that?

Fenner didn't know, and he didn't know if that was valuable to him or not.

The connections would be amazing, but he'd have to live in the locker room because he wouldn't be able to afford the dues and his rent.

No, he wanted cash.

Howell was going to have two point five million of it on Friday.

There was enough to go around, either from that pile or another.

**

Fenner stepped into the lobby outside Howell's office and saw the four large men in suits spread throughout the room, two of them sitting and two standing.

One of the standing men was just inside the lobby doors, while the other was perched outside the doors into Howell's office.

Fenner stopped and said, "Um."

Janice looked up from her screen and smiled.

"Go right in, Mr. Howell is expecting you. These gentlemen may need to search you first."

Fenner clutched his tablet to his ribs and looked at the men, who stared back at him with flat eyes.

The one outside Howell's doors waved him forward.

Fenner stepped over and the man took the tablet away and set it down, then opened Fenner's suit coat and touched the pockets and knelt down and lifted his pantlegs.

"Nice socks," the man said, and Fenner looked down to see he had chosen the ones with tiny Benjamin Franklin faces, the same face from the hundred-dollar bill.

He didn't recall choosing them, and he shook his head in embarrassment.

The man stood up, brushing the inside and outside of Fenner's legs.

He gave the tablet back and opened one of the heavy doors.

"Have a nice meeting."

Fenner went in, the anticipation of what Howell might

have to offer him completely gone.

***

Fenner was struck again by the size of the office and the view, even though half the windows faced the same direction as the ones next to his cubicle.

Howell's windows were floor-to-ceiling and looked down from an additional twelve floors, and the morning sun bouncing off the East River and silhouetting Mr. Howell as he stood with his back to the room seemed more powerful than the one Fenner saw from his chair.

Of course, the other half of the windows looked across Wall Street—maybe that was the biggest factor.

Howell turned and glanced at the door, waiting for it to ease all the way shut.

Then he said, "How are we coming along?"

Fenner walked across the carpet and dropped into the same chair he'd used the previous Thursday.

"I'm making progress. It's going to take some time, but I think I—we'll—be ready."

Howell stood with his hands clasped behind his back, looking down at Fenner.

Fenner could see his jaw muscles working inside his tanned cheeks.

"Please, have a seat," Howell snapped. "Can I get you something? A drink? Perhaps an omelet?"

Fenner realized he'd made a gaffe by presuming to sit. He also noticed Howell was already upset about something.

"No, I'm fine. Thank you, sir."

Howell said, "The timing has changed. The money will be deposited Thursday now, not Friday, and I need to make the withdrawal that same day. Meaning Thursday, first thing in the morning."

Fenner couldn't believe what he was hearing.

Did Howell not listen when he just said it was going to be

tight to make things happen by Friday?

And now he was moving everything up by a day?

"This also means," Howell said, "your last day with us will be Wednesday. So, everything needs to be in place by then."

"You're crazy," Fenner said.

"Excuse me?"

"That's not possible. Not by myself. If you want to make sure there is no trail for the bonus money—"

"What bonus?" Howell said. He released his hands from behind his back and sent them into his pants pockets.

"The, um," Fenner swallowed. "The two point five million."

"I never said anything about that being a bonus. A bonus for whom?"

"I was just speculating, Mr. Howell. I misspoke."

"I see."

Fenner crossed one leg, then the other while Howell stared down at him.

"Son, I'm trying to protect you here. You don't have any idea what—and who—this money is for, and you should do your damn-well best to keep it that way."

"Okay..." Fenner said.

"Do not speculate. Do not assume. Do not attempt to know more than what you've been told. And most important: Do not fuck this up. I can't be any clearer."

Fenner was suddenly embarrassed again by his socks and put his crossed leg down.

"Mr. Howell, I can't get this done by myself before Wednesday night."

Howell moved behind his desk and tapped the stack of papers on it.

"Let's do this: Make sure the money can be withdrawn from the branch on Pearl first thing Thursday morning. The rest of it—whatever is left to make it disappear—can be done afterward."

Howell seemed chuffed with the solution.

Fenner ran the various scenarios. "That would be...more difficult. To erase the footprints instead of preparing the ground to not show footprints, if you know what I mean."

"Yes, I've managed to grasp the concept. So, make a choice. Get it all done before Wednesday night, or make it harder on yourself by dillydallying."

Fenner realized there was no point in discussing it further.

He'd come up to the twenty-third floor anticipating some sort of prize or reward, and instead Howell had kicked him square in the nuts and told him it shouldn't hurt.

"That's all for now," Howell said.

Fenner stood up. He turned toward the doors and remembered who was on the other side.

"Mr. Howell, you say I don't want to know what this money is for. And you have four bodyguards outside your office. Do I need to be worried about my safety?"

"For the love of God, man, yes! Have I been talking to myself this entire time?"

"But..."

"Fenner. Open your damn ears. If you do what I've told you to do, on time, everything will be fine. Worry about doing your job. Everything beyond that is out of your control."

"Right," Fenner said. "Okay."

"Now, I believe you have some work to do."

Fenner tried to think of something to say and came up with nothing, so he just walked out.

He went through the lobby and the sets of eyes watching him, and he glanced back at them, the big men with big necks and small eyes looking at him like he didn't matter.

He left the lobby as angry as he could remember being.

Howell needed him to do this thing for him, this dangerous thing, and the old man could make a call and get four Secret Service-looking goons to keep him safe.

Oh, and what about Fenner?

Fenner could piss off.

He got into the elevator by himself, fantasizing about the day he could hire those same four men and make them sit on their asses all day, waiting for him to decide to go to lunch or the pub or jet skiing or whatever the hell he wanted to do.

The elevator doors closed and Fenner looked at his tablet.

It had a voice memo app, and he hit the Stop button to halt the recording.

The sound file was saved to his sync folder and automatically uploaded to the cloud, where he could access it from anywhere.

Even if someone snapped the tablet in two, the recording was safe.

Fenner hoped Howell was smart enough to do right by him, to make the recording unnecessary.

He hoped.

But so far, it wasn't looking good.

***

Fenner broke away from his desk and went to the pub for lunch.

He knew he wouldn't have time to go again until after Wednesday, and he needed to get out and look at something besides his screens for an hour or so.

James was there, the bartender, and he knew what Fenner wanted before he even sat down.

He also listened and didn't interrupt while Fenner blew out all the steam he'd been holding in, and he even agreed when Fenner said it wasn't fair, that something ought to happen to these people who thought they could do whatever they wanted.

Fenner knew it was part of James' job, to listen and nod and agree, but he still appreciated it.

***

Fenner went back to work after the pub, his head a little

fuzzy but in a good way, and he didn't stop working until two-thirty Thursday morning.

He went back and forth from his apartment to the office, but no matter where he was, he worked.

When he was finally done—the Vanguard branch prepared for the deposit and withdrawal, the armored truck service prepared to make the delivery, the accounts ready for the revenue injection and the accounting system ready to swallow two point five million and make it disappear—when Fenner knew Howell would get everything he wanted, he fell face-first into bed and passed out.

***

Howell spent the week on edge, waiting for McIntyre to show up again or summon him to someplace intended to make him feel small and insignificant, despite his actual status in the community.

But McIntyre didn't show up or call, and Howell made the trip back and forth between Chappaqua and the office with his four-man team on Tuesday and Wednesday without incident.

On Wednesday he stayed up until midnight, nursing a drink on the back patio and waiting for something—anything—from McIntyre to indicate what he was supposed to do with the two point five million once he had it in his possession.

Knowing that bastard, he'd probably order Howell to take it into some strip club and dole it out bill by bill in front of a bunch of manual laborers.

He resisted the urge to check in with Fenner.

Now was not the time to generate a trail of calls or texts, and again, Howell didn't want to open the door to a flood of requests or complaints.

He finally went to bed and woke up to his usual alarm at 4:30 feeling like he hadn't slept at all.

His phone had two text messages.

One was from Fenner, sent at 2:24 in the morning.

It read: "Done."

The other was sent from an unknown number at exactly 4:00 a.m. listing the address for Pier 94 with the note: "Parking lot."

So, not a strip club, but almost as bad.

But at least he knew where the hell he was supposed to go.

He went through his normal morning routine and got picked up at 5:20 on the dot.

When he was in the back of the Escalade, he told Burt, "We have some things to do this morning. We'll go to the Vanguard building first, then I need to visit the Vanguard branch on Pearl to pick up some assets. We'll then take them to this address."

He showed Burt his phone.

Burt nodded. "Very good, Mr. Howell."

If he and his team were surprised, or concerned, or miffed about not being briefed on this sooner, they didn't show it.

Professionals, dammit.

Howell felt good.

This nonsense was almost over, and by eight o'clock or so he would be done with McIntyre and the Lab.

For now, at least.

And who knew, maybe McIntyre would want to have lunch or a round of golf to celebrate and discuss a more sensible, long-term partnership.

Howell skipped the coffee shop and rode into the city, where the end of the world was waiting for him.

**

The pickup at the branch went just fine.

Howell walked in with his armed brigade and everyone at the branch was happy to see him, some of them practically giddy, like they wanted to ask for a photo with the CEO.

Howell basked in it, forgetting for a moment why he was actually there.

Then the branch manager said, "Everything is ready for you, sir."

Howell could tell the manager was curious about the whole production, but she knew better than to ask.

She also knew better than to say anything to anyone outside of the branch.

Burt hefted the currency transfer bag onto his shoulder, and they all walked back out, then Howell waited while Burt shoved the bag onto the floor of the back seat.

Howell wanted it right next to his feet, where he could see it and touch it.

He was minutes away from fulfilling the request—order, really—from McIntyre, and he'd be damned if he'd let anything screw it up now.

He climbed into the back seat vowing to never ride in an Escalade again after the drop was done, even if he was driving the damn thing.

The driver pulled away from the curb and rolled down Pearl and Howell was close to considering the job already done when some hipster wandered into the street and forced the driver to stomp the brakes.

Everyone in the vehicle tilted forward and the three men in the back had to brace themselves against the front seats to keep from sliding off the bench.

"Asshole," the driver said.

He glanced into the rear-view mirror.

"Sorry, Mr. Howell."

"Don't apologize, the man is clearly an asshole."

The men from Platinum laughed, relieved to have a bit of levity in the moment, and Howell piled on with, "He's a fucking asshole."

Burt shook his head and smiled and Howell watched

the hipster cross the road and duck under the scaffolding running along the sidewalk.

The Escalade started rolling again, then braked again, just as suddenly as before.

Howell tilted forward again and said, "'Damn it, man, what—"

The interior of the car exploded, erupting in white powder and white canvas and Howell recoiled away from the front seat, which had disappeared in a blob of white cushions.

He turned toward Burt for help and the door on that side opened. Howell saw a large man in coveralls and a respirator and goggles holding a fire extinguisher, and for a moment he thought it was a firefighter and the Escalade was on fire—but how long ago had the accident happened? and the man pointed the wide black mouth of the hose right at his face and then Howell couldn't see or breathe.

He felt something happen to his right, then the bag at his feet gave a violent yank and Howell forgot all about his face and lungs.

He saw what was left of his future, telling McIntyre the money was gone and he didn't know who had it, and McIntyre making a phone call, then the Lab would systematically dismantle Howell's hard work—possibly even Vanguard— until they got their money back and made their point.

Then they'd leave him to wither away, unable to tell anyone why he was in ruins, or they'd just kill him and be done with it.

So, he scrambled and clawed at the bag until he had both hands wrapped in the thick canvas.

"No!" he yelled. "No!"

His fingertips screamed with agony as the someone dragged the bag toward the door. Howell went with it, using his body as an anchor.

Something slammed into his left side and his arms automatically came in to protect his vital organs, and Howell spun that way, furious now, and bellowed, "You morons! That's the Lab's money! The Lab's!"

The man who had the fire extinguisher stared at him from behind goggles, then he moved his right hand, and the world went dark.

PART FOUR

CHAPTER 19

When Bruder came to he swung his right fist in a wide, clumsy arc and Kershaw and Gator both leapt back to get out of its way.

Bruder's torso followed the fist and he sat up on his cot, looking wildly around like an animal doused with ice water.

"Easy," Kershaw said. "Take it easy."

Bruder blinked and looked around.

They were in the warehouse office.

His head felt like someone had stuffed it with gravel and broken glass and kicked it off a cliff.

Three suitcases stood on the desk.

"Who's gone?" he said, then: "Avery."

He tried to remember what he and Avery had talked about, but his thoughts wouldn't cooperate. They kept peeking out from behind corners and ducking back when he paid attention to them.

"Avery's gone," Kershaw said. "Rowe's dead."

"What?"

Gator stood with his arms crossed, gnawing his lip and bobbing his leg like a jackhammer.

Kershaw lifted a clear plastic trash bag from the desk and showed it to Bruder.

It had a small, ragged hole on one side and matted blood on the other.

"You're lucky you chew in your sleep," he said.

Bruder just squinted at the bag.

Kershaw said, "As far as I can tell, Avery stabbed Rowe, then came in here and knocked you out with that."

He pointed to a foot-long crescent wrench on the floor.

"Then he tied this plastic bag over your head, so you'd suffocate. I guess he didn't want to make too much noise. Then he put all the cash into two suitcases and snuck out past Gator's truck."

"Why'd he spare me?" Gator said.

"No reason to engage you if he didn't have to," Kershaw said. "Plus, you know. Whatever you have rigged up in there."

"Yeah. I wish he'd tried, man. I wish he'd tried."

He went back to gnawing his lip.

Kershaw said, "He left on foot and didn't use the main driveway or any route along the frontage. Otherwise, I would have seen him. And I sure as hell didn't see anybody walking through the dark with two suitcases."

Bruder stood up and tested his feet and legs.

They still worked, for the most part.

"Rowe's dead?"

Kershaw tilted his head toward the warehouse and all three of them went that way.

Rowe was on his cot with his eyes and mouth open. Blood was caked on his chest and pooled in the crook of his throat and puddled around his torso on the cot.

It had dripped through the canvas of the cot onto the concrete below before it got too coagulated.

The thin steel edge of a broken knife blade peeked out of the blood and mess at the base of his throat.

Kershaw touched something with the toe of his shoe, and Bruder looked down and saw the matching handle.

"That's Avery's," Gator said.

Kershaw pointed at a bundle of bloody clothes stuffed next to Rowe's open bag.

"So is that."

Bruder remembered the shirt Avery wore when he came into the office.

Baggy, inside-out.

It had been Rowe's.

Because his real clothes were covered in Rowe's blood.

Rowe, who'd fought like hell to stay alive.

"The bastard," Bruder said.

Gator ran his hands through his hair.

"I never heard a thing, man. I never heard a thing."

"Don't worry about it," Bruder said. "How long has he been gone?"

Kershaw shrugged. "I came back after my two hours and found this, then you with the bag on your head, snoring through that little hole."

Bruder's head was clearing now, and he could remember checking his watch when Avery came in.

He'd been asleep for about an hour at that point, and Kershaw came back an hour later.

"He's got an hour headstart," Bruder said.

"With an hour," Kershaw said, "he could have walked to the next street, found a cab, and gotten on a plane at JFK to just about anywhere in the world. Assuming he didn't get stopped for having all that cash on him. Or the three pistols he took off the table."

Bruder shook his head.

"No. He didn't steal the money to keep it. He's giving it back to the Lab."

Kershaw and Gator both looked at him.

"It's his goddamn job application," Bruder said.

***

Bruder took a fast, scalding shower with thirty seconds of ice at the end that shook more of the gravel and glass out of his head, then he dressed in a clean suit and swallowed twelve hundred milligrams of ibuprofen from the first aid kit in the kitchen.

Kershaw and Gator had wrapped Rowe's body in blankets and were working on the bloodstains.

Bruder said, "You guys can handle the body and the cars. Get this place stripped down. Dump the Charger and Impala at JFK in long-term parking. It doesn't matter how close they are to here anymore."

"Sure," Kershaw said. "We'll figure it out. You need any of the remaining guns?"

Bruder considered. He didn't fantasize about using the M4 or the shotgun on Avery. He just ran through likely scenarios and risks and rewards and decided the guns would be more of a pain in the ass than a benefit.

"No. Dump 'em. Avery knows about Howard, it isn't worth the risk of taking them back."

Kershaw nodded.

"Is there anyone we need to notify about Rowe?"

"Hell if I know," Bruder said. "That's for later. Get the place clean and get moving. Go wherever you were going to go, as long as Avery doesn't know about it. If you told him, go somewhere else."

"You think anybody's coming here?" Gator said.

Bruder shook his head. "Not soon. Avery won't. He's too smart, and too scared. He might tell the Lab about this place, but it won't be tonight. He has to make contact first."

"Howell," Kershaw said.

Bruder said, "Avery knows where he lives. And that he's connected with the Lab, somehow."

Kershaw had a small grin. "Chappaqua's about to get

real lively."

"I'm taking the gray car," Bruder said. "Use the new burn-er number if you have to. Otherwise, I'll be in touch when I have the money back."

Gator said, "Why don't we catch up with you, when we're done here?"

Bruder stopped and turned around with the keys in one hand and the .45 in the other.

"Because this is my mess. I let Avery get the drop on me. And if I have to tangle with the Lab, you don't want any part of it."

Gator looked back and forth between Bruder and Ker-shaw, then said, "Well...why don't we all just walk away now?"

Bruder had considered that too.

"Because Avery hasn't had a chance to say our names to anybody. Not yet. I need to make sure it stays that way."

He dropped the keys in his jacket pocket, which already had two spare magazines for the .45. The other pocket had three.

Kershaw opened the overhead door enough for the gray car to slip underneath and waited by the controls.

Bruder walked to the gray car, did a press check on the .45 and saw the gleam of brass in the chamber. He tucked the gun into his belt and opened the driver's door.

"I hadn't thought about that," Gator said. "If Avery gives our names and faces to the Lab..."

Bruder looked at him over the roof of the car for a mo-ment, then dropped in and got moving.

***

Bruder made the familiar drive out of the city and into the expanding greenery of upstate New York until the idea of a city and skyscrapers seemed ridiculous.

He didn't see Avery hitchhiking with the two suitcases,

which didn't surprise him but was still disappointing. The knock on his head would be worth the look on Avery's face when he peered through the passenger window into the tunnel of the .45.

Bruder wound through White Plains and into New Castle and slipped into Howell's neighborhood just before midnight.

It looked more or less the same as it had at four in the morning on Monday.

Bruder rolled past Howell's driveway and didn't see a fleet of police cars or horde of press camped out to ask him about the robbery.

Through the landscaping he could see the house was lit up, inside and out.

Howell was either having a party, or he was scared, or he was waiting for someone.

Avery.

Or Avery was already in there, spilling it.

He turned the car around and checked the street as he went back toward Howell's driveway.

He didn't see the woman with the visor and dog, which was good—he didn't want to shoot anybody except Avery.

He stopped in the same spot he'd used on Monday to watch Howell and tied a handkerchief around his nose and mouth and put on his sunglasses.

Then he pulled into Howell's driveway and stopped at the closed gate and hit the call button.

***

FRIDAY

A male voice came through the speaker immediately.

"Who are you?"

"A friend of Howell's. We met earlier today. Let me in."

"Remove your mask and glasses."

Bruder didn't look directly into the lens of the video camera mounted above the box.

"When I'm inside."

There was a delay, then: "What's your name?"

"I'm here to see Howell. Were you with him this morning?"

"That was another team."

"Good," Bruder said, "so you don't have a concussion. Open the gate."

Silence from the speaker.

Bruder checked his watch.

He'd give them twenty seconds.

Any longer than that and they were probably calling the police, and he'd be gone.

After seven seconds the gates opened, and he drove through.

He rolled up the smooth, winding driveway toward the house and saw the gates closing behind him.

Bruder grimaced at the idea of being trapped with these fools but took solace in knowing he wasn't trapped with them—it was the other way around.

***

When Bruder swept through the last curve of driveway and finally got a clean look at the front of the house, unobstructed by landscaping, he shook his head.

All that house for two people, plus whoever they hired to take up space for them. And the lights...the place looked like an upside-down chandelier.

It had three levels in the center and sprawled out into one-story wings on both sides. A circular drive wrapped around a water fountain with its own light show, and Bruder turned left at the circle instead of right.

This took him closer to the left wing of the house, the end of which had glass walls and looked to be some sort of sun porch. Nobody was in there that he could see.

He rolled past the huge front doors and the steps leading

up to them, where a large man in a suit stood watching him.

Bruder rolled to the stairs and the man held up a hand, indicating Bruder should stop.

Bruder held up a finger—a polite one—indicating the man should be patient.

He idled past the front stairs toward the wing on the right. The end of the structure had five garage doors, all closed, and beyond those the asphalt curled around the end of the house.

Bruder followed the path and ended up behind the garages, where the back wall had matching doors so whatever was inside could be driven out and around without backing up.

Bruder shut the gray car off and removed the mask and sunglasses. He assumed there were more cameras and his face would be on them, but he was inside now and had a plan for it.

He got out and glanced at the property behind the house, which looked like it should have been behind a castle instead, then he walked back toward the front of the garages while slipping on a pair of the disposable gloves.

He saw two ways to play it with Howell: Assume Avery hadn't made contact yet and claim to be him or do it straight and not try a bluff.

If he bluffed and Howell already knew who Avery was, that would put Bruder at a disadvantage, caught out.

So, he'd just be himself.

That had usually worked out alright.

When Bruder came around the front corner the man in the suit was near the first garage door, moving warily with a gun in his hand.

He pointed the gun at him and said, "Stop. Hands out to your sides, palms up."

Bruder did those things and waited while the man checked him over with one hand, the other still holding the gun pointed more or less at him.

The only thing Bruder had on him was the burner phone. His knife and the .45 and spare magazines were in the car, under the driver's seat. He figured he wouldn't get through the door strapped, and if he really needed a weapon once he was inside there would be plenty to go around.

Like this guy's, for example.

Bruder studied him and didn't see any black eyes or bruised jaw or wounded professional pride.

So, if he wasn't the guy from the gate speaker, he hadn't been in the Escalade either, and was probably one notch better than the morning crew.

And if he was from Platinum, he would want to make up for what had happened on Pearl.

Satisfied, the man stepped back.

"Why didn't you respond to my command?"

"I did," Bruder said, holding his arms out just enough to jog the guy's memory.

"My command to stop the vehicle."

"I don't want the car out here under the stadium lights."

"Why not?"

"Somebody else might be coming here tonight. If he sees that car, he's in the wind."

"Who else is coming?"

"That's between me and your boss."

"He's not my boss. What's with the gloves?"

"My hands are cold."

The guy stared at him for a while, then said, "Let's go."

He let Bruder take the lead toward the front door, and when Bruder glanced back the guy was looking back and forth between Bruder and the driveway, like he expected to see headlights whipping through the trees.

Bruder said, "You with Platinum?"

The guy didn't respond at first.

At the bottom of the front steps he said, "You're lucky

I wasn't there this morning. The Lab would be the least of your worries."

Bruder climbed the steps and broke into a smile that, if the guy in the suit had seen it, would have started a fight.

***

The foyer was grand, Bruder supposed, with lots of marble and columns and rugs and narrow tables along the walls holding stuff nobody was supposed to touch.

One of the tables had a miniature house that looked exactly like this one, and Bruder recalled the wife's obsession with dollhouses. The replica smacked of a conversation starter, with first-time guests commenting on it and the wife pouncing, dragging them into some room dedicated to her pretentious hobby.

Bruder didn't see Howell or the wife, whatever she looked like, so he turned around and waited for the guy in the suit to close the front door and tell him where to go.

"That way."

He pointed toward the back of the house.

Bruder went that way. He crossed a wide hallway that stretched for miles in both directions, then dropped into a cavernous space with plush furniture and a cold fireplace. An open arch on the right showed a restaurant-grade kitchen overlooking the sitting area. Huge windows displayed the back yard with a lit-up fountain and a pool and a rolling yard with landscaping highlighted by low-wattage fixtures.

Another man in a suit stood in the kitchen archway, watching.

"Back left corner," Bruder's tour guide said, then walked over and spoke to the other man, probably about another guest arriving at some point.

Bruder waded through the furniture and found another hallway with more windows along the right wall overlooking a covered patio.

Howell was out there, sitting at the right end of a long stone table with a moat of low flames running down the center of it. He was in a black track suit, smoking a cigar and drinking something golden, staring out at his domain. A large black phone was on the table next to him.

Bruder walked until he found a set of open French doors that led to the patio.

He stepped onto the flagstones and Howell, without turning around, said, "The first damn words out of your damn mouth had better be 'I'm sorry.' The next words had better be, 'Here's your money, Mr. Howell.'"

The table was about twelve feet long and four feet wide with a slate top. The trough down the center was filled with glass pebbles to enhance the flames dancing through them.

Bruder sat at the left end, opposite Howell, so the man would have to move to see him. The tour guide stood just behind Bruder's right shoulder.

Bruder checked the angles and couldn't see the archway into kitchen through the patio windows, which meant the Platinum man in there couldn't see what was happening outside.

Then Bruder sat and waited, and Howell got impatient and finally turned in his chair.

"Well?"

The left side of his jaw was bruised and swollen. Bruder didn't see any reason to point it out yet.

He said, "First, it isn't your money. It's supposed to be the Lab's."

"You're off to a bad start, son."

Bruder ignored him.

"Second, I don't have it."

Howell frowned. "Then what the hell are you doing here?"

"I know who does have it. And I know what he's going to do with it. You're going to help me get it back."

Howell blinked though the cigar smoke and had to turn

all the way around in his chair in order to comprehend what he was hearing.

"So, who has the money?"

"An associate of mine," Bruder said.

A wolfish grin spread across Howell's face.

"One of your crew swiped it. Oh, that's rich."

Bruder said, "The man who has the money was supposed to get a three hundred-thousand-dollar share. That becomes your share, if you help me get it all back."

Howell stared at him.

"Three hundred thousand."

Bruder nodded. "Put it towards the two point five million you owe the Lab."

"Me? I owe them?"

"You're the one who lost their money."

Howell looked past Bruder at the man standing behind him.

"Are you hearing this? I think I'm hearing it, but it makes no sense." To Bruder he said, "You lost the money too, though. One of your men stole it from you. And you claim to know what he's going to do with it."

"That's right."

Howell waited, then: "Well?"

"He's going to give it back to the Lab," Bruder said.

Howell looked surprised, then pleased, then wary as his CEO brain caught up.

"Hold on. He's giving it back to the Lab? Or back to me?"

Bruder said, "He'll use you to get to the Lab. Then cut you out. I assume they already know what happened on Pearl."

Howell's face darkened.

"They do."

"And they're on you to make it right, whatever it takes."

Howell had his tumbler halfway to his mouth and paused to raise it in a mock toast.

"Oh, they are indeed on me, my boy."

"How long did they give you?"

"A whole forty-eight hours."

"Saturday morning."

"I had to cancel another flight to Florida."

Howell emptied the glass and held it out.

The big man behind Bruder walked around the table and took the glass and carried it toward the house.

Howell said, "Would you like one for yourself?"

"What is it?"

"You wouldn't recognize the name."

Bruder shrugged. He was probably right.

"Sure."

Howell struck him as the kind of guy who needed a drink in everyone's hand before he really got down to business.

And he might need to be a bit drunk to agree to Bruder's plan, so Bruder played along.

For now, anyway.

***

The big man in the suit set Howell's refill down in front of him and carried Bruder's drink along the length of the fire table. He thumped the tumbler onto the stone top, sloshing the liquid around and trying to make a point.

Bruder took a sip while Howell watched him, expecting some sort of revelation.

"It's whiskey," Bruder said.

Howell sat back in his chair and studied him like he couldn't figure out what he was made of.

"Who the hell are you people?"

Bruder didn't have time for it.

"The man who has the money is called Avery. When he contacts you, he might use a different name, or no name at all. He's going to want an introduction to someone in the Lab."

"So, he can give the money back."

"Right."

"And then what? Run for his life? He might make it half a step."

Bruder shook his head. "He wants in."

"In," Howell echoed. "In the Labyrinth?"

"Right."

Howell looked amused. "I suppose they need ditch diggers—or their equivalent."

"Who's your contact with the Lab?"

"You don't need to know that."

"I do. Because if Avery finds a way around you or gets what he needs from you and kills you, I need to know who I should talk to next."

"Kills me?" Howell said. "Why on earth would he do that?"

"You asked who the hell we people are. We're the sort of people who don't like loose ends, the kind that can connect us to armed robberies."

"I see. Though I think it's quite clear I can't go to the authorities about any of this."

"You say that now. But if you get squeezed—for fraud or insider trading or whatever the hell you sort of people get up to—you'll give up everything you know."

"I—"

"Save it. And who said anything about authorities, anyway? I'm talking about putting a face and a name together with a crime. For anyone."

"But...I'm looking at your face right now."

"That's right."

Bruder tapped his gloved fingertip on the table.

Howell saw it and blinked a few times and glanced at the big man in the suit, who was in his spot behind Bruder again.

Howell said, "So why shouldn't I treat you like a loose end? Get rid of you right now. And when your man calls, if he does, I take the money and get rid of him too."

"You could try."

Bruder turned and eyed the man behind him, then went back to Howell.

"But I don't think you're cut out for it. It gets messy, fast. And if you kill me, I can't call the man driving down to Sanibel Island right now and tell him not to shoot everyone inside and burn your house down."

"You're bluffing," Howell said, sounding like he was trying to convince himself first.

Bruder just looked at him.

He was bluffing, of course. Killing family members was an amateur's play, something that only led to vendettas and unnecessary attention from the law.

Bruder said, "We put this morning's job together in one week. One week. Think what we can do with no deadline, when we can be patient, and watch, and wait."

He pointed a thumb over his shoulder at the guy in the suit.

At the same time, he reached his other hand toward the glass of whiskey.

"How many of these clowns will we have to run through before we get to you?"

The guy in the suit said, "Mr. Howell, I've heard enough. This asshole—"

When Bruder felt the hand clamp on his right shoulder he picked up the glass of whiskey and used it to scoop up some of the glass pebbles from the fire trough.

He sent everything in the glass over his shoulder into the big man's face, then stood up as the guy was staggering backward.

Bruder punched him in the throat, then kicked him in the groin, then put a left elbow into his right ear as he was falling. The guy collapsed into a lump on the flagstones.

Bruder fished around inside his jacket and came out with a Sig Sauer pistol, then found a hammerless Smith and Wesson Model 638 revolver in an ankle holster. He released the Sig's magazine and worked the slide to eject the round in the chamber, then dumped the revolver's cylinder and left everything spread out on the slate.

He sat down and looked at Howell, who said, "Good lord."

Bruder said, "Avery reaches out to you. You fill me in on the details. I get the money back and give three hundred grand of it to you. We go our separate ways. You pay the Lab back however you can, and lose some face with them, but that's not my problem. And I'm not your problem, anymore. Deal?"

Howell gulped his whiskey and looked down at the man on the patio, who was snoring raggedly.

He looked at Bruder and said, "Deal."

CHAPTER 20

Bruder hooked a thumb over his shoulder at the snoring man.

"How many of them are here? Just this one and the one in the kitchen?"

"Yes, two," Howell said, his voice distant.

"Platinum?"

Howell nodded.

"Why are they here? Did you think we were coming for you?"

"The Lab," Howell said. "I don't know what they're going to do about...what happened this morning."

Bruder grunted. "Who's your contact with them?"

Howell's mouth opened, then he reconsidered what he was about to say.

"What's it matter now?" Bruder said.

"It just does."

Bruder got up and walked the length of the table. Howell shrank back in his chair and started to bring a forearm up to protect his face.

Bruder picked up his phone and hit the button to activate

the screen. It showed the time and a photo of a sunset taken from a boat, but no text or call notifications. It required a passcode or a fingerprint to unlock the screen.

He put the phone back on the table.

"Open it."

Howell fumbled the phone and got it unlocked.

Bruder said, "Turn off the lock feature. I need to be able to get in."

"Well, it's Vanguard's policy that—"

"This isn't Vanguard's phone anymore. It's mine. Open it up."

Howell sputtered some more about that, but he worked through the screens until he found the right one and deactivated the screen lock feature.

"Show me the recent texts and calls," Bruder said.

Howell showed him the calls first, turning the phone and holding it so Bruder could see the screen. He saw a list of names that meant nothing to him so far, and a bunch of missed calls from someone named Fenner.

"Who's Fenner?"

"Eh?"

"The person who's been calling you every hour since noon."

"Oh, that's just work. My assistant."

Bruder looked at Howell's face, then said, "Texts."

Howell hit some buttons and turned the phone again.

Bruder scanned the messages until he saw one from a number instead of a name. The preview of the message looked like an address.

"That one. What is it?"

Howell looked.

"That's from the Lab. It's where I was supposed to deliver the money."

He tapped the message and showed it to Bruder, who checked the address and the note, a simple "Parking lot", and decided none of it mattered anymore. The number would certainly be a one-time use.

"You should delete that."

Howell turned the phone back and deleted the Lab message like it was a ticking time bomb.

Bruder said, "Who's Fenner? And don't bullshit me."

"I'm not bullshitting you."

"There's a message from 2:24 this morning. It says 'Done'. That's just work?"

"Absolutely," Howell said.

"Yeah, the same kind of work I do. That's your team, the grunts moving things around so you could get the Lab's money out."

"Well—"

"Fenner's the team leader? Or was it always just one person?"

Bruder wasn't supposed to know any of this, so his seemingly uncanny powers of deduction were pushing Howell even further off balance.

"Is Fenner a man or a woman?"

Howell resisted for a moment, then must have decided there was no point in it.

"A man. Just one man."

"And he knows everything."

Howell shook his head. "He only knows the money side. Nothing about the Lab."

"And what happens when he catches up to that part?"

"I doubt someone of his...status...is even aware of the Labyrinth. What you're asking is, will he do the same thing your man did? Try to make good with the Lab. Or will he go to the authorities? No. He's been promised a reward for his part in this, and he's a greedy sonofabitch."

"That's why he's calling you every hour. To see what he has coming."

"I assume so."

"Why aren't you picking up?"

Howell's eyelids dropped. "I have slightly more important issues to focus on right now."

Bruder bit his tongue to keep from saying anything about the poor schlub losing his job.

"So, what's the reward?"

"I haven't decided yet," Howell said, like he hadn't given one moment's thought to it.

Bruder carried the phone in a gloved hand toward his end of the table.

Fenner…Bruder wasn't sure what kind of person would kneel down, take the firing, and still stick his neck out like he did for Howell without knowing the payoff.

Like, down to the penny.

An optimist, he figured.

***

Bruder checked the man from Platinum—still snoring—and sat down in his chair

Howell watched him with a sullen look on his face, then said, "How do you know your man will come to me? If he knows the money belongs to the Lab, he could go anywhere in the country and find someone connected to them. Hell, the world, if he knew where to look."

Bruder shook his head. "Because he's too smart for his own good. He's angling for a job, and he can't risk pissing anybody off more than they already are."

Howell frowned, still not getting it.

Bruder didn't want to take the time to explain it to him, but it would probably save a bunch of irritating questions in the long run.

It would also show Howell there was thought behind these actions, not some desperate grasp, which ought to help him relax, which ought to decrease the likelihood that Bruder would have to kill him.

He said, "Avery has to come out of this looking like an asset to them. If he finds some peon in the Lab and works with them to give the money back, that peon will get some of the credit. Maybe all of it. Not good. If he finds somebody higher up than whoever you were giving the money to…"

Bruder waited, and Howell finally looked out at his vast yard, highlighted by sporadic low-wattage fixtures, and said, "McIntyre."

He spoke the name like it was an invasive weed or a snake that only killed sommeliers.

Bruder said, "If Avery gives it to somebody higher up than McIntyre, it makes McIntyre look like a dope. And he'd make sure Avery gets shit on once he's in the Lab, or rejected from the start, or just shot and thrown in a swamp."

"Office politics," Howell said.

"More or less. Just higher stakes."

"Don't be so sure." Howell took a sip from his drink. "Have you considered, even for a moment, the possibility that your man just took the money and left? That he's headed for some beach in Ecuador where he can live on two and a half million dollars for the rest of his life?"

"Sure."

Howell waited. "But?"

"But he's scared to death of the Lab. He'd spend every moment on that beach waiting for a bullet."

"Or for you to show up."

Bruder shook his head. "He thinks I'm dead."

"Well, that's handy. Why does he think that?"

Bruder almost told him it was none of his damn business, but he needed Howell somewhat cooperative, not shut down and pouting. And the best way to make an outsider feel like an insider was to act like you're confiding in them, sharing a secret.

So, he said, "Because he thinks he killed me."

Howell gave a wry, knowing smile and settled deeper

into his chair. "It is hard to hire the right people. What are you going to do if you get your hands on this man of yours? This Avery."

"When."

"Hm?"

"You said 'if' I get my hands on him."

Howell squinted, then said, "Ah. So, what do you plan to do when you find him? Just out of curiosity. I'm not looking for some sort of self-implicating statement. Premeditation and all that."

Bruder just looked at him until Howell got up to refill his drink again.

***

Bruder put Howell's phone and the empty revolver in his pockets, reloaded the Sig Sauer and stuck that into his belt.

He pulled the burner phone out and called Kershaw, watching the hallway through the windows for anyone wandering back.

Kershaw answered. "Yeah."

"How's things?"

"We're making progress."

Whether that meant Rowe's body was gone, or the van was dumped, or the warehouse was empty, or all of it, Bruder didn't know and wasn't about to ask.

Kershaw said, "You're with the man?"

"Yeah. He was supposed to deliver everything to a man named McIntyre at the lot for Pier 94. I think that spot's burned, they won't use it again, but just in case."

"Got it," Kershaw said.

"Our man here used an employee named Fenner to make it all happen. He's no trouble so far, but he's making some noise on our man's phone."

"Noted."

Kershaw wouldn't be writing any of this down, but he'd

remember all of it if he started digging into these men.

He said, "No sign of our missing partner?"

"Not yet," Bruder said.

"You want us up there?"

"I can handle it. If that changes, I'll call back. If you're already gone by then, stay gone."

He killed the call and dropped the phone in his pocket and retraced his steps into the hallway to the massive sitting room.

Howell was busy at a bar to the left of the archway into the kitchen.

The second guy from Platinum, who was slightly leaner than the one still out on the patio, was in the kitchen with a cup of coffee.

He looked at Bruder, then past him, then back down at Bruder, who said, "Yeah."

The man said, "Yeah what?"

"Yeah, your pal is out there taking a nap."

The man looked at Howell, who said, "He's fine. He's fired, but he's fine."

He turned with a full glass and smacked his lips before he took a drink.

Bruder could tell he was getting drunk, or already there, but he'd tagged Howell as the sort of functional alcoholic who could drink all day and instantly sober up when he needed to sign something or take a phone call, then go right back to weaving around the house and making insensitive comments.

Bruder said to the guy in the archway, "What's your name?"

"Why?"

"Because we're going to be here a while, and I don't want to say 'Hey, guy' the whole time."

"Yates."

"Who's the other one?"

"Weddel."

"Good. Okay Yates, Weddel probably already told you somebody I know will be coming here, or calling, and he doesn't need to know I'm here until I let him know. You get me?"

"You're setting up an ambush."

"Let's call it a surprise party," Bruder said.

"Is it someone from the Lab?"

"No."

"When?"

Bruder shrugged. "Sooner rather than later, if he's doing what I think he is."

He sat down on one of the couches and knew he couldn't stay there long—it was so comfortable he'd fall asleep in five minutes.

Yates checked with Howell, who gave an exaggerated nod and a thumbs-up.

Yates asked Bruder, "So what's your name?"

"You can call me guy. You got any more of that coffee, Yates?"

***

Ten minutes later the man from the patio, Weddel, stumbled down the hallway toward the sitting room.

At the end of the hallway, he held onto the corner to keep from spinning across the ceiling.

Bruder watched him until Weddel's eyes locked on him.

"Take it easy," Bruder said. "Have a seat."

Yates walked across the room and reached for his partner, but Weddel shoved him away and staggered toward the furniture with one hand pressed to his head to hold it in place.

Howell watched with a slightly amused expression, like he was socking it all away as a story to tell at the country club.

Weddel dropped into an overstuffed chair and glared

at Bruder.

"I'll take my guns back now."

Yates took a small, embarrassed step away from him.

"Later," Bruder said. "After you've calmed down."

"I'm calm."

"Yeah. Calm like a box of sweaty dynamite. You'll get them before I leave."

"You'll never make it to the door."

Bruder looked at him for a while.

"Maybe sitting is too hard for now. You'd better find another room, someplace dark and quiet, so you can go back to sleep."

"You—"

Weddel had to stop talking so he could vomit down the front of his shirt.

"Ah, hell," Howell said. "The rug! Watch the rug! Get him out of here!"

Yates hauled Weddel to his feet and walked him into the long hallway toward the wing with the garages. Where the help stayed, Bruder assumed.

When they were gone Bruder asked Howell, "How much are you paying Platinum?"

"It doesn't matter. I'm getting my money back."

He glowered over the rim of his glass, then a thought occurred to him and he brightened, turning to Bruder.

"You want a job?"

"No."

"I can make it worth it for you."

"No, you can't."

But with that one question, Bruder knew Howell would work with him to get Avery and, if necessary, McIntyre. He wanted Bruder to like him. The CEO was looking at him like a problem to solve, a puzzle that just needed its pieces turned the right way and nudged into line.

"Don't waste your time," Bruder said.

Yates came back into the kitchen, alone, and washed his hands in the sink.

Bruder stood up and told him, "Show me where the security cameras go."

***

Bruder carried a heavy mug of coffee down the long hallway in the same direction Yates had taken Weddel.

Yates led the way, passing a few closed doors along the way.

"Where'd you stick Weddel?" Bruder said.

Yates pointed at one of the closed doors.

"It's a bathroom. He's on the floor of the shower. He needs medical attention."

"Soon," Bruder said.

They came to an angle in the hallway and Yates opened a door onto a small room with no windows. It looked like it was intended to be for storage, or maybe a laundry room, but it was full of electronic equipment and screens and cables running everywhere. Then Bruder realized, for a house like this, it was probably designed and built to be exactly what it was.

"Mr. Howell calls this the Nexus," Yates said. "Camera feeds, motion sensors, door and window alarms—all of it goes here. You can even adjust the pool temperature and pH."

Bruder searched the four monitors, each one quartered into four camera feeds, until he found the one showing the front gate.

He said, "This is where you were when I drove up?"

Yates pointed at the rolling chair facing the screens.

"Right here. A pressure sensor sets off a chime, then one of us comes in here to see what's going on."

Bruder looked at the rest of the camera feeds. They showed various spots around the house—the front of the garages, the pool, some walking paths that must be out back somewhere—and one showing the back of the garages and Bruder's gray car.

"Where else do the feeds go? Hard drive? Cloud?"

Yates pointed at a shelf holding a row of black boxes that looked like thick books.

"Hard drives. The footage cycles through about every seventy-two hours."

Bruder nodded.

Yates said, "You want to know why I'm being so cooperative?"

Bruder didn't turn from the screens.

"No."

"It's because you crossed the Lab. What's the point in making trouble with you when you're going to be dead in a few days anyway? Maybe a few hours."

Bruder turned and looked at him.

"Why don't you do it for them? Bring in my scalp and make a name for yourself."

Yates held his hands out.

"Look around, man. I sit around in houses like this and drive jackasses like Howell around the city, to restaurants and golf courses. My ambition stops here."

They stared at each other, and Bruder thought about taking Yates' gun, or guns, just in case, and dropping him in the shower with Weddel.

But he could tell the man was speaking the truth.

He wanted no part of whatever Bruder could serve up.

Yates just held the stare with a stupid, tilted grin on his face until a loud chime broke the tension.

***

Bruder looked at the quarter of screen showing the driveway and gate, but no vehicle was there.

"That wasn't the gate chime," Yates said.

Bruder frowned, then pulled Howell's phone out.

The screen showed a new text message from Fenner:

"Are you ducking me or just too busy counting your money?"

Three dots appeared below that message and Bruder waited to see what he was going to send next.

"I can't wait any longer."

"I'm coming to see you."

"30 minutes."

Bruder watched the phone for anything else and tried to figure out if this was good or bad. After a few moments he decided he didn't have enough information yet to make that call.

One thing he did know: This Fenner was going to be a pain in the ass.

***

Bruder told Yates to watch the screens, then found Howell slumped in one of the stuffed chairs with his eyes closed.

"Wake up," Bruder said.

Without opening his eyes Howell said, "I'm awake."

"Fenner is on his way here."

Howell opened his eyes and looked up at Bruder looming over him.

"What?"

"He's thirty minutes out."

"What?" Howell said again.

"He sent these."

Bruder showed the phone to Howell, who frowned at it.

"The damn fool."

"Is he going to be a problem?"

"Give me the phone," Howell said. "I'll send him back home."

"No. It's almost one-thirty in the morning. He's pissed. He's been stewing about this all day and night. You blow him off again, he might get pissed enough to do something stupid. Better to have him here where he can be controlled."

"Controlled. What does that mean?"

"That's up to Fenner," Bruder said.

"But...my home...he doesn't know where I live."

"Neither did I," Bruder said.

Howell frowned some more, then said, "Ah. I know. We had some leadership retreats here, years ago. My wife's idea. I can't say if Fenner was among those people...but I suppose it's possible."

He treated himself to another sip to celebrate the closed case.

Bruder took the glass away from him before he was done.

"Hey!"

"Sober up. You need to figure out what you're giving Fenner, before he gets here. And it better be enough to keep his mouth shut."

Bruder carried the glass to the bar and emptied it in the sink.

"That was three hundred dollars' worth of Scotch!"

"Really? Give the bottle to Fenner. Maybe that'll do it."

Howell tried to push himself out of the chair and lost the fight. He sagged, suddenly pulled down by the weight of the world.

"I don't even know how I'm going to pay McIntyre, let alone Fenner."

"You'll think of something," Bruder said.

Yates appeared in the opening to the hallway.

"A car just drove past, slow. I went outside and could see the headlights going down the road, and it's hard to tell because of the trees, but I think they cut the lights off once they went past."

Howell looked toward the front door with alarm.

"He's here already? You said thirty minutes."

"That's not Fenner," Bruder said. "Avery's here."

CHAPTER 21

Fenner spent half of Thursday drifting in and out of bad sleep woven with fever dreams about Howell and accounting spreadsheets and, for some reason, snakes.

When he finally gave up on anything restful and flung himself out of bed at noon, he immediately started calling and texting Howell.

His part was done, now it was time for payment.

And if whatever Howell served up wasn't good enough, well…Fenner had his notes and recordings, plus a detailed record of where every cent of that two and a half million actually came from, along with the methods he used to cover those holes.

He started drinking at three in the afternoon, hoping that would settle him down.

It did not.

He got steadily more agitated and more drunk and more victimized as the day wore on until he passed out, exhausted from the injustice of it all, and woke up again at eleven o'clock at night.

His apartment was dark, his head hurt, and he had no

idea where he was, but his phone was resting on his chest and when he turned it on to use as a light, he saw there were no missed calls or waiting messages, and it all came flooding back.

He took a furious shower to clear his head, which didn't work, then got into his car and started driving north.

He remembered exactly how to get to Howell's place. The route and the entire estate were seared into his mind from the one time he'd been there for a corporate leadership retreat, which had turned out to be a well-catered tour of Mrs. Howell's dollhouse collection.

But Fenner didn't care. He'd spent the time looking around with gleaming eyes, thinking, "Someday...Someday..."

The mantra had started back up during his midnight drive to Chappaqua, and he muttered the word to himself when he stopped in Elmsford to get gas and a coffee.

While he was waiting for the tank to fill the doubt crept in, short-circuiting his internal pep talk.

Howell was silent because he was planning something big for him and showing up at his house unannounced in the middle of the night would blow it.

Fenner could feel it—he was right there, right on the cusp of tipping over into a dream come true.

All he had to do, maybe, was just wait a little longer.

He couldn't be overeager or come off as unappreciative.

Ungrateful for the opportunity Howell had given him.

Fenner pulled out his phone and went to the one-sided text conversation with Howell.

One more message, just in case, then he'd turn around and go back home and wait.

But as he scrolled through the messages, all of them showing as Delivered, the anger returned.

He'd been waiting his whole damn life for people like Howell to notice him, acknowledge him, appreciate him.

And where had it gotten him?

Shit on, unemployed, exhausted, and pulled into some illegal scheme that so far had no payoff.

He jabbed at his phone:

"Are you ducking me or just too busy counting your money?"

"I can't wait any longer."

"I'm coming to see you."

"30 minutes."

Then he got into the car and threw the phone into the passenger seat and continued north.

***

Fenner's confidence, which had swept back and forth across the spectrum the entire ride, faded the closer he got to the gate.

He turned into the driveway and stared into the lens of the camera, trying to look resolute, but knew he probably looked like a fish on the deck of a yacht.

A man's voice came through the speaker mounted near the driver's window.

"Yes?"

"David Fenner to, uh, to see Mr. Howell."

Fenner waited, unconsciously holding his breath, until the gate slid open.

He waited for the voice to tell him that Mr. Howell was sleeping, or in Florida, or just straight up he ought to consider going to hell, but he was being allowed in.

Holy shit, he thought as he rolled through the gate.

It's actually working.

Then he checked himself, and reset, and gripped the steering wheel.

He was a professional there to conduct business.

To get what he had coming to him.

He was David goddamn Fenner, and he would get his.

He screamed a little when the man with the gun stepped

in front of his car.

***

Fenner's headlights swept across the man and he hit the brakes, then stared over his steering wheel as the man walked toward him and stood outside the driver's window, waiting.

Fenner rolled his window down.

The man smiled and leaned down, putting one hand on top of Fenner's car.

He said, "How are we this evening? Well, morning, I guess."

Fenner frowned at him. He sounded out of breath and was dressed like a ninja—black pants, black jacket with a hood, and even though he wasn't wearing a hat Fenner wouldn't be surprised if he had a black watch cap tucked away somewhere.

"I'm fine. How are you?"

Fenner asked the question on auto-pilot, because that's what you did in society and he didn't know what else to say or do.

"Great," the man said. "You're here to see Mr. Howell?"

"That's right."

"Your name?"

"Uh, David Fenner."

"And your purpose?"

"Well...Mr. Howell knows."

The man's smile wavered.

"And now I want to know."

Fenner scrunched his face up, like he was trying to recall the face and name. "Who are you, again?"

The man looked up toward the house as he said, "Part of the protection detail."

"Yeah, um...You aren't dressed like any of the security guys I've seen with Mr. Howell before."

The man's face came back to Fenner.

"That's the point, buddy. Why are you here? Is it about this morning?"

Fenner froze.

Was this guy a cop? Part of some sting operation or S.W.A.T. assault?

He said, "What happened this morning?"

"Uh-huh. Pop the locks."

The man walked around the front of the car. In the head-lights, Fenner could see he had a blocky pistol in the hand that had been on the roof of the car. The man opened the passenger door and looked down at the thick folder full of printed spreadsheets and Fenner's notepad and tablet on the seat.

"What's all this?"

"Oh, uh, just work."

The man moved the tablet aside and picked the note-book up and flipped through it, then reached in and opened the folder and leafed through the sheets. Then he stared at Fenner for a long moment before closing the folder and dropping the notebook on top of it.

Fenner scooped everything up and put it on the floor of the back seat.

The man got in and shut the door.

"I'll escort you to the front steps and determine if Mr. Howell would like to see you."

"Don't you have a radio or something?"

The man looked at him, his eyes and face completely flat.

"We're being extra careful right now. Drive."

Fenner drove.

***

When Fenner got to the roundabout in front of Howell's mansion the man in the passenger seat told him, "Go left."

Violating every American driving law and habit ingrained

in him, Fenner went left, looping around the water feature and stopping at the bottom of the wide steps leading up to the two massive front doors.

One of the doors opened and a tall, broad man in a suit stepped out.

He called down, "Mr. Fenner?"

"Yes, that's me."

"Who's that with you?"

"Um, I—Isn't he with you?"

The hand yanked Fenner back, away from his open window, and dragged him across the middle console and passenger seat until he found himself standing in the open passenger door. The man was behind him, pressing him against the car, and the gun was digging into the side of his neck.

The man said, "I'm here to see Howell about some business. He'll want to talk to me."

The man on the steps had his jacket open and his hand on the butt of another gun.

He said, "Take it easy, pal. Are you here about this morning?"

"That's right. If he wants it back, he needs to talk to me."

"Hold on. Let me check with him."

The man on the steps kept his eyes on the scene below him while he spoke quietly into a handheld radio.

Fenner blinked and sweated and tried to follow what was happening, but all he could think about was the metal digging into his neck and how, with one twitch of a finger, that metal would explode into him and everything would be gone.

He managed to say, "Be careful. Please be careful."

The man whispered, "I'm not going to shoot you, my friend. You're my safety shield. Just relax and we'll be out of here soon."

Fenner couldn't believe the relief that washed over him. With those few words, he went from victim to partner.

To being in on it.

Whatever it was…

He kept very still and couldn't ignore the gun in his neck, but managed to say, "Howell's getting the money back? From you? You have the money?"

The man paused, then said, "What money are you talking about?"

Fenner was even more confused.

"Are you a cop?"

The man chuckled.

"No."

"You have to tell me if you are," Fenner said.

"No, I don't, that's Hollywood bullshit. But I'm not. Now what money are you talking about?"

Fenner knew this was the tipping point, where he chickened out or went all-in and proved he was a vital part of the whole thing.

He was on the team.

And if this guy had the money, Fenner wanted to be on his team.

"The two point five million."

There was a long pause—enough time for Fenner to think the man was shocked, as though he had no idea about the two point five million; he was here about something else and Fenner had blown it—then a hand patted him on the shoulder.

"That's right, my friend. I'm glad we've had a chance to meet."

Fenner grinned with relief.

But the gun in his neck didn't move.

***

The man at the top of the stairs waved them up.

"You can let the hostage go. Nobody's going to cause trouble."

Fenner said, "Hostage?"

The man behind him said, "Take your gun out with your left hand and drop the mag. Then eject the round in the chamber. Then dismantle the gun and put the parts on the ground."

The man at the top of the stairs did it all with a slightly irritated look on his face.

"Happy now?"

"No. What else you got? Ankle? I don't want to find out about it later."

The man reached down and pulled a smaller pistol out of a holster and held it by the butt with his thumb and forefinger.

"Empty that thing and toss it into the bushes."

He did.

"Now, if we come up there and you pull out some kind of belt buckle peashooter, I'm going to be very disappointed."

"Just come on."

The man kept Fenner between himself and the man at the top of the stairs as they walked around the car and started up.

He said, "Who else is on the job here?"

"Me and one other guy. He's sleeping."

"Sleeping?"

"Yeah, sleeping. We're pulling shifts."

The man behind Fenner said, "After what happened this morning, I thought the old man would have a full battalion here. Snipers on the roof, that kind of thing."

Fenner said, "What happened this morning?"

Both of the men ignored him, which was irking.

The man behind him said, "Howell's awake?"

"He's waiting for you."

"Lead the way, my good man. And, for what it's worth, I'm not the one who hit him."

Fenner turned. "Somebody hit Mr. Howell?"

The man with the gun just grinned at him as they went inside.

CHAPTER 22

Avery kept the Sig Sauer pistol ready and went through the door last, letting the security guard and Fenner go in front of him.

He didn't want anyone between him and the door in the event cops came swarming out or Howell's security team tried something stupid.

He kept Fenner within reach, though. Fenner was soft but would make a good human shield if it came to that.

Avery had one of the warehouse Glocks tucked into the back of his belt. The other was stashed in the car he'd stolen, a three-year-old maroon Jetta that smelled like fast food. He carried the Sig out of spite, knowing Bruder hadn't trusted him with a safety during the job.

Goddamn Bruder.

Good riddance.

When Avery hit him across the back of the head with the wrench it had probably been the scariest moment of his life. He'd fully expected Bruder to take the blow, turn around, and tell him he'd just made a terrible mistake.

But he'd gone down instead, just like any normal human

being would have, and Avery had moved with a purpose putting the bag over his head and wrapping his neck with tape. He'd tried to wrap it tight enough to cut off blood and oxygen, but Bruder's damn neck cords were too taught.

Avery suspected he was having a seizure, or a death spasm, and he thought about stomping Bruder's windpipe but knew he was running out of time and had been lucky with the noise levels so far.

If Bruder started thrashing around, Gator might hear it and poke his head out of that bunker of his, along with a bazooka or flamethrower.

So, Avery had looked down at Bruder, sucking the plastic bag into his open mouth and fogging it up, and knew it wouldn't take long. He moved all off the cash into two suitcases along with his clothes and travel gear and the maps for the job, then slipped out of the office, pausing only to scoop up the three pistols before exiting the warehouse.

From there he'd followed his planned route around the back of the building and through a hole dug under the fence by kids or hobos or woodchucks, then stolen the Jetta from behind a laundromat, which was operating but didn't have any windows along the back of the building.

Then he headed into Manhattan, wanting to get lost in the city as quickly as possible.

He drove around until he found a 24-hour luggage storage facility and stowed the suitcases, then looked at the maps Bruder and Kershaw had used to pinpoint Howell's estate.

After the drive north at two miles under the speed limit and some careful scouting, he'd driven past the house, killed the lights and parked. Then he found what looked like a blind spot in the perimeter and jumped the fence.

He'd been creeping toward the house when sudden headlights poked through the gate, then rolled forward, and Avery saw the perfect way to finish his trip to the front door.

***

Now he walked through the foyer—which was bigger than his last apartment—and across a hallway until he was looking into a sunken living room full of country club furniture.

Howell was there, sitting in one of the chairs and looking at Avery like he wanted to set him on fire.

The security guard moved next to the old man and stood there, unarmed and really only good for taking a bullet intended for Howell. But Avery didn't think this particular guard was the sort to go that far.

Fenner waved at Howell, then turned and glanced at Avery.

He said, "Mr. Howell, do you know this guy?"

Howell gave a wry smile. "I believe we crossed paths this morning. You were the damn hipster, walking across the road."

Avery couldn't help smiling. "It's nice when one's work is appreciated."

Fenner said, "What's all this about this morning? What happened? This man said somebody hit you. And, oh no, I can see it—your face!"

"I'm fine," Howell snapped. "Why are you two together?"

"He just got into my car," Fenner said, pointing toward the front of the house. "Like, right outside."

Howell grunted. "Fenner, we'll talk about why the hell you're here later. Go outside to the patio and wait for me."

Fenner took a step, then stopped. "Actually, I'm here to talk about our agreement. And if something happened this morning, something that affects what we, uh, worked on, I want to know about it."

"No, you don't," Howell said. "Wait outside."

Avery said, "Stay put, Fenner. I like you where I can see you. In fact, let's all have a seat."

He intentionally used the Sig to point Fenner to one of

the chairs near Howell.

Howell frowned at the sight of the gun but didn't protest as Fenner sat down to his right and Avery took a chair directly across from him.

The security guard was at Avery's one o'clock, near Howell's left elbow, and may as well have been a broken lamp for all he was doing.

But Avery didn't like him standing, able to take a step before Avery could stand up.

"You, sit on the floor. Can you cross your legs?"

The guard tried and got about halfway.

"Good enough," Avery said. "You need to work on your hip mobility."

Then he turned to Howell.

"Mr. Howell, I owe you an apology. If I'd known who the money belonged too I never would have interfered."

Fenner looked confused, then alarmed. He opened his mouth to ask Howell something, but Avery cut him off.

"I have all of it. Every dollar. And I'd like to escort it to its proper owners. I'd also like to leave no loose ends dangling behind me."

He glanced at Fenner.

"So, I need two pieces of information from you, Mr. Howell. One: How do I get in touch with the proper owners? And two: Why the hell is this man driving to your home in the middle of the night with a notebook full of details on how to hide two point five million dollars?"

***

Avery watched Howell turn toward Fenner like he was stuck in slow motion.

After a moment of struggle, in which Avery was certain Howell fought to keep from screaming, the old man said, "Notebook? You kept a notebook?"

"Well..." Fenner said.

Avery cut in. "We'll get to that next. Right now, I need to get in touch with the proper owners of the money. I want them to know it's safe."

"Where is it?" Howell said. He was still glaring at Fenner, who had found something fascinating on the floor to hold his gaze.

"Safe," Avery said.

He pulled out a phone and held it toward Howell.

"Call them and give the phone back to me."

Howell finally turned away from Fenner and looked at the phone. He made no move to take it.

"Why should I? Are you going to include me in the return?"

"I don't see any reason to."

Howell nodded. "Well, there you have it. What's in this for me, besides further humiliation?"

"As of this moment you aren't in any physical pain. That could change."

The guard sitting on the floor stiffened.

Avery grinned at him.

"Save it, bubba. You lost the moment you unloaded your guns. Are you getting paid enough to die for this old codger?"

The man didn't say anything, and Howell looked back and forth from the guard to Fenner, completely disgusted by the people he'd surrounded himself with.

Howell curled his lip at Avery. "You people..."

Then he seemed to catch himself, and Avery was too wrapped up in the self-satisfaction of being the best of "you people" to demand Howell elaborate on what that meant.

Howell snatched the phone and said, "They won't answer a number they don't recognize."

"We can use your phone if you like," Avery said.

Howell got even more flustered. "No, it's fine. It's fine."

He stabbed at the buttons and lifted the phone to his ear.

"Speaker," Avery said.

Howell put the call on speaker and the four men sat and listened to it ring until there was a beep.

No outgoing message, just a beep.

Howell said, "This is Mr. Howell. Call me back at this number as soon as possible."

Avery took the phone back and stored the number.

"You think they're awake?"

"They're always awake," Howell said.

And he was right—before Avery could set the phone down it rang.

***

Bruder heard all off the conversation and the ringing phone.

He was down the long hallway to the left, away from the bathroom with Wedell and the security room, standing just inside the cracked door of a room full of dollhouses.

The only light in the room came through a row of windows overlooking the front lawn, but even in the darkness he could feel the hundreds of tiny figurines staring at him from exact replicas of the White House, Windsor Castle, the Biltmore Estate, and a dozen others he didn't recognize.

It felt like they were watching, waiting for him to make his move.

Bruder considered emerging from the room and catching Avery off guard, but it was too unpredictable.

Avery might get a lucky shot off, or Bruder might try to wound him and hit something vital, or this Fenner clown might do something stupid, or Avery might bleed out or pass out before spilling it, grinning at Bruder with blood on his teeth.

So Bruder listened to Avery answer the phone and waited.

***

Avery hit the speaker button.

"Who am I speaking with please?"

There was a pause, then a man said, "Where's Howell?"

"He's here," Avery said, and beckoned Howell to speak.

"I'm here, Mr. McIntyre."

McIntyre said, "Well?"

Avery took over.

"Mr. McIntyre, you're on speaker with Mr. Howell, Mr. Fenner, uh..."

"Yates," the guard said.

"Mr. Yates, and me."

"And who the hell are you?"

"I'm the man with your money."

"Congratulations. You're dead."

Fenner sank back into the chair and covered his face with his hands.

Avery said, "Now now, let's not get off to a bad start here. I had no idea it was yours when we took it, and as soon as I found out, I started working on a way to get it into your hands."

"I'm looking at my hands right now," McIntyre said. "I see no money."

"I'd like to remedy that."

"You can start by telling me where the rest of your crew is. You didn't do this yourself."

Howell shifted in his seat, looking more and more agitated.

Avery said, "Well, two of them are already dead. That's what it took for me to get the money away."

"How many are still breathing?"

"Two," Avery said. "And after I hand your money to you, finding them will be the first of many jobs I do for your organization."

"Is that so?"

"It is," Avery said.

The phone was silent.

Eventually McIntyre said, "How did you find out about

the money?"

"I'm glad you asked. I considered holding that piece of information in reserve as insurance, but I want to extend an offering of good faith. To show you how dedicated I am to our future partnership."

"Go on," McIntyre said.

Howell frowned at Avery and the phone, uncertain where this was leading but curious nonetheless.

Avery said, "But first: time and place. And don't say your office in one hour. It has to be bright, crowded, and I need to be able to drive up to the spot and drive away."

"Rather paranoid coming from a man who wants to work with us."

"I'm showing you I'm not a fool," Avery said. "That I'm careful."

"Mm. You're at Howell's place in Chappaqua?"

"That's right. But the money isn't."

"You know, Mr..."

"Mister is fine for now."

McIntyre chuckled. "You know the money isn't really that important. It's not even that much."

"To some," Avery said. "But I get your point. It's the message."

"Exactly. We will get it back, whether you hand it to us or otherwise."

"I know. That's why I'm going to hand it to you. Personally."

"Indeed. The Yankees have a day game tomorrow, at one o'clock. Is that bright and crowded enough for you?"

"I'm not setting foot inside the stadium. That's a mouse-trap."

"I hadn't finished," McIntyre said. "164th Street, between River and Jerome. There is a park across the street from Yankee Stadium and the parking ramp there. Mullaly Park. Do you know of it?"

"I can find it."

"At noon, there will be an open spot halfway along 164th Street. You will pull in there, you will hand over the money, and you will be on your way."

"And then what?"

"Someone will be in touch at this number. You will not call me again."

Avery chewed his lip.

"If you can make that parking spot happen, you can block the whole street before I get out."

"Obviously," McIntyre said.

"So, it's no good."

"Listen, stickup man. You've proven you can be careful. Ad nauseam. Now it's time to prove you have some balls."

Avery pointed at the phone and looked around the room, the incredulous look on his face saying, Can you believe this guy?

"Okay. We'll do it your way. High noon at Mullaly Park. How will I identify you?"

"I'll be the man waiting for his money."

"Okay, right. But if I see anything I don't like, I—"

"Moving on," McIntyre said. "Your source."

Avery cleared his throat.

"We got the information about the exchange from a bartender, whose name I do not know, but he works at a pub somewhere close to Vanguard's headquarters."

Fenner peeked out from between his fingers, his eyes rolling around like bingo balls in a cage.

"The bartender," Avery continued, "got his information from a drunk accountant who works for Mr. Howell."

Howell flinched and glared at Fenner again, who started making a soft keening sound from somewhere in his throat.

Avery said, "Mr. McIntyre, that accountant is here now— the aforementioned Mr. Fenner—and I believe he brought most if not all of the evidence he amassed with him."

McIntyre's voice turned wary.

"Evidence?"

"A tablet and a notebook and a folder full of spread-sheets," Avery said. "I won't claim to understand any of it, but I'm sure you will when I hand it over along with the money."

Fenner's eyes darted from Avery to Howell and Yates, searching for help.

"And you're sure that's all of it?" McIntyre said.

Avery looked at Fenner, who blurted, "It wasn't...I didn't..."

"I'd say so," Avery said.

"It doesn't matter," McIntyre said. "Whatever Howell's employees do is his problem, not mine."

Avery smiled. "I agree wholeheartedly. But it's also my problem, to a certain extent, being a loose end that could come back to bite me. And I wouldn't want that to jeopardize our partnership in any way."

McIntyre grunted through the phone.

"So, this evidence—that's your show of good faith?"

"That," Avery said, "and this."

He shot Fenner twice in the chest.

***

Bruder didn't blink when the shots came.

He'd been expecting them as soon as Avery started talking about a show of good faith, and the only surprise was that he stopped with two shots.

Bruder figured Avery would clear the whole room, but the shots were timed so closely they had to be focused on a single target.

Fenner.

Bruder shook his head.

This McIntyre guy was right, Fenner was Howell's problem, and Bruder would have left it up to him.

But Avery was out to prove himself, prove he was the man for any job the Lab had for him.

Now Bruder waited to see if Avery—or McIntyre—decided to get rid of all the witnesses.

***

Avery held the gun on Howell and Yates in case they panicked or tried something stupid.

Howell sat frozen like a statue, his mouth hanging open, and stared at Fenner.

Yates' mouth was a thin, compressed line. His eyes darted from Fenner to the gun and back, and Avery knew he was on the verge of fighting for his life.

Fenner was slumped back in his chair looking down at his chest, which made a slightly concave bowl for the blood to pool in.

He watched it well up until it ran over the sides of his ribs.

He tried to block it with his hands, but his arms kept falling away.

Finally, they fell away and he didn't try to lift them again, and then he was dead.

Through the phone McIntyre said, "Who's still on the call?"

Avery said, "Mr. Howell and Mr. Yates. And me, of course. Would you like me to continue the work?"

"I see no need for Howell. He'll stay in line. I don't know Yates and don't care what happens to him."

Avery looked at Yates.

"Are you following along, bubba? You know who you're dealing with?"

Yates nodded.

"You wouldn't think about telling anyone about the meet, would you?"

Yates shook his head.

"No sir."

"You promise?"

"I'm good to go," Yates said.

"Are you?"

Avery lifted the gun and Yates leaned forward, just a fraction, ready to at least die trying.

They stared at each other for a few beats, then Avery grinned at him.

"I think you are. He's straight, Mr. McIntyre."

"I truly don't care. Goodbye."

The call ended.

Avery put the phone in his pocket and stood up.

"Well gentlemen, it's been a productive visit. I'm leaving now. If anyone comes out, or any lights come on, or heaven forbid I hear a siren, we all know what happens."

Howell's mouth opened and closed a few times before he managed to say, "What about this?"

He pointed at Fenner's body.

Avery said, "What about it?"

"What the hell am I supposed to do with it?"

Avery shrugged. "I'm sure Yates has some thoughts."

He backed out of the room and up the steps, crossed the hallway and the foyer, and was gone.

***

Bruder went to the windows and watched Avery sprint across the lawn with the evidence from Fenner's car tucked under his arm.

He could have just taken the whole car, but it was on the wrong side of a closed gate. And if Fenner had someone back home, someone ready to call the cops if Fenner didn't check in, his car would be more of a risk than whatever Avery had out on the street.

Bruder watched him disappear into the landscape, then stayed at the window for three more minutes, just in case.

Then he pulled out his burner phone and called Kershaw.

"You still in town?"

"We are," Kershaw said, answering Bruder's next question about Gator. "What's up?"

"How many vehicles do you still have?"

"Two. The truck and the blue one."

So, they'd already dumped the van and Avery's Impala.

"Keep both, for now. I need some more details from this end. Find a place to wait and I'll call you back."

He hung up and left the room.

***

Bruder stood in the hallway, looking down at the scene in the sitting room.

Yates was handing a glass of water to Howell, who seemed equally disgusted and fascinated by the body of Fenner.

Bruder tossed Howell's phone onto one of the chairs.

"Where's McIntyre?"

Howell kept staring at Fenner so Bruder snapped his fingers.

"Howell. Where's McIntyre?"

Howell turned, in a daze of booze and shock, and frowned at him.

"McIntyre? Why?"

Bruder thought about dragging him outside and tossing him in the pool, but the old man might just drown while he tried to figure out how to float.

"Just tell me where he is."

"You...you can't just go see Mr. McIntyre."

"Why not?"

"Well, because...it...it just isn't done."

Howell leaned forward and turned conspiratorial.

"He's with the Lab, you know."

"You don't say. Where can I find him?"

Bruder could get the man's number from Howell just like

Avery had but he didn't want to go that route if he could help it. Calling or texting from a phone other than Avery's, even from Howell's phone, might spook McIntyre, and if he called Avery's number to see what the hell was going on, it was all blown.

Howell said, "If he finds out I told you..."

"He's not finding out anything, except things have changed. Where is he?"

Howell pulled on his bottom lip, then looked up at Yates, still standing next to him.

"What day is it?"

"Today is Friday, Mr. Howell."

"Yes..."

Howell took a sip from the water and glanced at Fenner's body, then jerked away from it like he'd forgotten it was there.

"Dear lord!"

"Come on, Howell. McIntyre."

"Yes, ah, Friday. Oh..."

"Spill it," Bruder said.

"He has a standing eight o'clock tee time at Winged Foot every Friday morning."

"Winged Foot. That's a golf course?"

Howell looked at Bruder to see if he was joking.

"Yes, it's a golf course. I have no idea if McIntyre will be there today, with all that's going on. But...it wouldn't surprise me."

"You're a member there," Bruder said.

"Of course."

"Do I need you to get in?"

Howell was perplexed.

"You're going to golf?"

Bruder said, "I just need to get into the parking lot. Is there a gate, a checkpoint?"

"Oh, no. You can get to the lot."

He made a point of eyeballing Bruder's overall existence.
"But that's as far as you'll get."

"What does McIntyre look like?"

"A grade-A son of a bitch."

Howell sat back, pleased with his courage to speak such blasphemy.

Bruder stared at him.

Howell said, "Oh, fine. He's tall. Thin. White hair."

"White skin?"

"Sure."

"So he looks like every other person there."

"Well, I don't know about that. We—"

Bruder cut him off before he could launch into a sermon.

"How can I identify him?"

Howell looked at Yates for help again but the guard just shrugged. The exchange seemed to help though, because Howell brightened.

"Oh! He'll have a driver. Not, you know, as in a one or three wood. As in a personal driver and security guard."

"Slightly relevant," Bruder said.

Howell held his hands up near his shoulders, palms out.

"Well, I'm sorry. The man is always with McIntyre, so he just kind of blends in with the scenery."

He glanced at Yates again.

"No offense."

Bruder said, "McIntyre's the only guy there with a driver?"

"Hmm...I think so, at that time of day. Certainly, the only one with an armed guard."

"What's the guard look like?"

"Oh, he's...bald, I think."

"You think?"

"No, I mean yes, he's bald. Shaved head. With a mustache. You know, I've always thought he looks like an English butler."

Bruder dismissed that. He had no idea what Howell's

idea of an English butler looked like, and he didn't bother to conjure up his own image.

He said, "Bald. Mustache. Old?"

Howell shrugged. "Forty...something? They were in a Bentley Mulsanne the last time I saw them, for what it's worth."

"What color?"

"Blue. Dark blue."

Bruder decided that was all he was going to get, and it would have to be enough. He didn't have time for Howell to recall random bits of information that might or might not help and leaning on him wouldn't do any good.

He checked his watch.

It was almost three in the morning and Avery had been gone for five minutes.

"I'm giving Avery another five minutes to get clear, then I'm leaving."

He started down the hallway toward the garages.

Howell blurted, "Your man!"

Bruder stopped and looked at him.

"Call your man. The one driving to Sanibel. Call him off."

Bruder had nearly forgotten the bluff.

He shook his head.

"Not until I have the money. You tip McIntyre, or anybody else, we come crashing down on you."

Howell scoffed. "What do you think the Lab is going to do?"

"Not my problem. All you can do is get them their money and hope for the best. Or pack up and move to Ecuador."

"That wouldn't change anything. And you heard McIntyre. It's the message, not the money. They simply won't allow their property to be stolen."

"It's not up to them. If I were you, I'd start checking these cushions for loose hundreds."

Howell's mouth flapped some more but no words came

out.

Yates pointed at Fenner's body. "What about this?"

Bruder glanced at the corpse.

"I can think of plenty of options."

He walked down the hallway to the security room spent about a minute unplugging one of the hard drives with the camera footage, then got impatient and just tore the rest of them loose.

He carried them under one arm and left the house.

CHAPTER 23

When Kershaw and Gator walked into the 24-hour coffee and donuts place, Bruder was already into his second cup and halfway through the cinnamon roll.

They sat down and put their orders in with the server, a young woman with the left side of her head shaved to the scalp and wearing black leggings under her pink waitress dress. She seemed to relish the irony of her position in life, and she and Gator had an extended exchange that delighted him so much he forgot to start shaking the table with his leg bob.

When she was gone Bruder filled them in on what had happened at Howell's place, and the meet between Avery and McIntyre, and what he wanted to do next.

At the end he said, "And I have the hard drives from Howell's security system in the car."

Kershaw was amused. "What are you going to do with them?"

"Drill them, then run them over, then burn them, then drop them in the East River."

Gator seemed to approve.

"Just give them to me," Kershaw said.

Bruder nodded, glad to be rid of the damn things.

"Listen. You two don't have to be in this. I'm the one who lost the money."

Kershaw sipped his coffee and thought it over.

"The money's a factor. But he killed Rowe. If it had been me in that cot, I'd be the one sinking into the Jersey mud right now. So yeah, the money. But mostly, Avery."

Gator nodded.

"Fair enough," Bruder said.

Then they started working out the details.

***

Just before five in the morning Kershaw drove Gator's truck along the Bronx River Parkway until he found some construction pylons—it didn't take long—and he pulled onto the shoulder with his hazards on.

Three cars went past while he put two of the pylons in the back of Gator's truck, and none of them stopped or slowed or showed any signs of noticing him at all.

He closed the truck and got back up to speed then had to cut over to New Rochelle to find a home improvement store.

He used his laptop to study satellite map views of the area around Yankee Stadium while he waited for the store to open at six, then went inside and bought a hard hat with a neon yellow sun shield for the back, a neon yellow face mask—just a bright yellow sleeve with a reflective strip that he could wear around his neck and pull up over his nose and mouth—a reflective safety vest, an aluminum clipboard with built-in storage, and a can of bright orange spray paint.

He put all of that in the passenger seat and got onto I-95 south into the city.

***

At the same time, Bruder was on his way to the Winged Foot Golf Club, just a twenty-minute drive from the coffee shop.

Gator was behind him in Rowe's Charger.

Bruder called and woke James, the bartender who had been Fenner's confidant.

James mumbled into the phone, "Huh?"

"It's me," Bruder said.

That woke him up.

"Me? Hey! Hey, man, how'd it go?"

"I need your father's number."

James was quiet for a moment.

"My dad?"

"That's right. The number I have for him didn't work."

James said, "Does this have anything to do with the, uh, recent work we did?"

"In a way. Anything else is between me and him. Does he know anything about it?"

"My old man? No, no way. I didn't talk to anybody about it."

"Good."

"And I didn't see anything about it in the news, so... how did it go?"

"It's ongoing. Don't worry about it. What's your father's number?"

"Oh, yeah. Sure."

James gave him the number, then said, "I wonder if my man is going to come in today. And if he's heard anything about what went down."

James was fishing for something, any little detail Bruder would give him.

Bruder wasn't going to give him anything, especially about Fenner being dead.

So, he said, "I guess we'll see. I'll be in touch."

He hung up and kept driving toward Winged Foot.

***

He called the number from James and after a few rings a deep voice that Bruder recognized as Vincenzo Carza's answered.

"Who's this?"

"It's me," Bruder tried.

"Oh, hello Me. Why don't you go fuck yourself, Officer?"

Bruder grinned. "It's the guy you almost blew up in Youngstown."

After a moment Carza burst out laughing.

"Holy mother Mary and Joseph! Now that I know it's you, go fuck yourself twice! How are you, you grumpy bastard?"

"I need a favor."

"Ask it."

Bruder said, "How'd you like to earn five large for standing around looking like an asshole for ten or fifteen minutes?"

Carza said, "Standing around doing what?"

"Standing around."

"What, that's it? That's not worth five large."

"The money's for forgetting all about it as soon as you're done."

"Oh, hey, that goes without saying. What's the money really for? What's my exposure here?"

"Nothing," Bruder said. "You stand there. A guy will come up to you. We'll take it from there and you walk away."

"Do I know this guy?" Carza said.

"No."

"Anybody I know know this guy?"

"No."

Carza thought about it.

"So, all I gotta do for five grand is stand around like an asshole for fifteen minutes?"

"That's what I told you."

Carza laughed. "I might as well. I do it all day for free."

***

The sign for Winged Foot was small and subtle and haughty all at the same time.

The smooth driveway went past an ancient stone gate post and wound through a canopy of mature trees before opening up to two parking lots, one on each side. All of the asphalt was wet from dew or sprinklers, and it made the parking lots look somewhat new.

Bruder could see a low building ahead on the right. The driveway curved away with more buildings farther along on the left, peeking through branches.

According to the map Kershaw found online those would be the pool house and clubhouse, respectively.

He found an angled spot in the lot on the right, facing the road. From there the cars coming in and heading for the lot on the left would have to drive across his windshield, and those coming into his lot would slow and turn in outside the driver's window.

Bruder checked his watch.

It was just past seven. He could hear two-stroke engines somewhere nearby, last-minute trimming or mowing or watering or whatever they did to make the grass look like a carpet.

The gun was under his right thigh, the knife was clipped to his pocket and the phone was in a cupholder in the center console.

He sat back and watched the driveway.

***

Cars started gliding in around 7:30.

The sun was over the trees, making steam rise from the driveway and parking lots, and Bruder could smell wet grass and, every now and then, a whiff of chlorine from the pool.

The cars were all either very large or very small, and

Bruder didn't pay any attention to the colors or makes or models—he didn't know if McIntyre would be in the same car Howell had seen.

He checked the interiors, and so far, they all had one occupant.

There didn't seem to be a pattern to which parking lot they used, but they all clustered toward the spaces closest to the buildings further along the driveway.

Bruder watched as men in shorts and khakis and short-sleeved collared shirts got out and stretched, waved to each other and laughed about golf things.

Some of them glanced at the gray car parked out by itself, but it was bland enough to look like a service or security vehicle—possibly law enforcement—and they promptly ignored it.

At 7:36 a car with tinted windows sizzled down the driveway and turned into the lot across the driveway from Bruder.

He couldn't see through the glass, so Bruder checked the car.

It was a dark blue Bentley Mulsanne.

It coasted along the lot and swung into a spot in the middle, away from the overhanging trees and the cars already parked. The grille was aimed more or less toward the exit.

Bruder picked up the phone and called Gator.

"Yeah."

"Get ready."

He hung up and started the car and drove to the lot's exit, watching the Bentley.

The front door opened and a bald man with a mustache got out and looked around. He wore a dark gray suit, not anything to golf in as far as Bruder could tell.

Then he opened the back door and a tall man with white hair emerged and surveyed the landscape and the cloudless sky like he owned all of it and was responsible for its splendor.

Bruder called Gator again.

"He's here. Lot on the left."

***

Bruder waited at the lot's exit and listened.

After a moment he heard the Charger's engine, then the stereo turned up so loud the music was distorted and un-identifiable. It was just static and rattling and bass thumps and grinding guitars and howling vocals.

Bruder watched McIntyre and his driver and the other golfers walking from their cars toward the clubhouse.

They all stopped what they were doing and looked down the driveway, and when Gator and the Charger emerged from the canopy of trees Bruder watched their confusion turn to outright disapproval.

Gator had his sunglasses on and his arm hanging out the window.

He rumbled past Bruder without looking his way, focused instead on the lot on the left and the men there.

One of the golfers who had been heading for the club-house started waving his arms and shaking his head.

Bruder couldn't hear what he yelled, but it looked like, "Not here! Turn around!"

Gator flashed the peace sign at him and kept going, past the lots and pool house and up toward the clubhouse.

Everyone—including McIntyre and his driver—watched him go. McIntyre was scowling and his driver's face was blank but wary.

Bruder turned left out of the lot, away from Gator's of-fensive parade, then took a quick right into the lot across the driveway.

He looped behind McIntyre's car, parked and popped the trunk.

The racket from the Charger faded for a moment, then started to climb again.

This, Bruder knew, was from Gator banging around the circular drive, in front of the clubhouse and coming back toward the parking lots.

The golfers nearest the clubhouse moved toward the driveway as Gator closed in. Bruder had no idea what they planned to do, but the man who'd waved his arms around stopped to get a golf club from his bag.

Bruder got out of the car and strode around the front toward the Bentley.

McIntyre was still near the back door and the driver was a step ahead and to his left.

They both watched Gator's truck and the posse of golfers about to intercept it.

When Bruder was ten feet away the driver turned and looked at him and reached inside his jacket.

Bruder put an empty hand out and said, "Mr. McIntyre."

McIntyre turned and frowned at Bruder, then at the car, then back at Bruder.

"What?"

Bruder said, "Mr. McIntyre, I apologize for this nuisance. Is that truck bothering you?"

"Yes, of course it is. I've told you people to get a gate and someone manning it, time and time again."

Bruder closed the gap.

"I know sir, let me take care of this. I'll—oh, no."

He looked past them and McIntyre and the driver both turned, but all they saw was the group of golfers pointing Gator and the Charger toward the exit.

Bruder stepped past McIntyre and hit the driver with a left hook just below the left ear. He sagged and fell against the car but didn't go down, and Bruder bounced his head off the edge of the roof and dragged him past McIntyre, who stood there with his mouth hanging open, toward the back of the Bentley.

He dropped him there and reached for McIntyre, who

said, "You son of—"

Bruder hit him in the stomach and McIntyre, who was a few inches taller than Bruder, doubled over. Bruder grabbed the back of his shirt and belt and hauled him to the gray car and bent him over the edge of the trunk, wrapped his wrists in pre-looped zip ties, then did a quick search of his pockets.

He found a phone and a thick money clip.

Bruder pocketed the cash and wanted to toss the phone into the bushes, but it might be the only way for them to get in touch with Avery, so he dropped that into his pocket as well then heaved McIntyre into the trunk.

The man had regained some breath and said, "You have no idea what you're doing."

"Sure," Bruder said.

He tried to get another zip tie around his ankles, but McIntyre kicked at him.

Bruder leaned in and twisted his nose.

"Ahh!"

McIntyre's hands and full attention went to his nose, and while he was blinking and gasping Bruder secured his ankles.

Bruder said, "Did you already set up the parking spot?"

McIntyre blinked through watering blue eyes at Bruder.

"The what?"

"The meet at noon. The cash. Do you have people set up to secure that parking spot on 164th Street?"

"Look here, you Neanderthal. I—"

"When was the last time somebody gave you a smack?"

"I—"

Bruder smacked him, a flat palm against the side of his face. It shocked McIntyre more than it hurt him, but it still hurt him.

Bruder said, "Yes or no."

"No," McIntyre snarled.

"No, you do not have people ready to secure that parking

spot."

"What did I just say, you moron?"

"Why not? Why haven't you set that up yet?"

McIntyre scoffed. "Because I can make it happen in thirty minutes from the time I call."

Satisfied, Bruder closed the trunk on him.

He looked over the top of the Bentley at Gator, who had come to a full stop but kept the engine and stereo going. He was hollering at the golfers through the open passenger window, telling them he couldn't hear what they were saying.

Bruder knelt down behind the Bentley and pulled the driver's forearms together behind his back and zip-tied them together, then did his ankles.

He glanced toward Gator once more, saw he was trying to get the golfers to sing along with him, then dragged the driver around the gray car and dumped him on the floor of the back seat.

He got in and drove around the Bentley and out the lot's entrance, then called Kershaw and gave him the good news.

The sound of Gator's show faded behind him as he got to the end of the driveway and turned left on Fenimore, heading for the next spot.

***

Bruder kept to the speed limit for the five-minute drive along Fenimore and under I-95 into Mamaroneck. There were no ramps to the highway on Fenimore so traffic was light.

He pulled to the curb along the first block in front of a public works garage and waited.

McIntyre thumped and hollered in the trunk but no one was nearby.

Bruder glanced behind the seat at the driver, who was still unconscious. A runner of blood from his left ear had dried on his cheek and neck, but there wan't anything fresh coming out.

Forty seconds later the Charger pulled in behind him.

Bruder got out and met Gator between the two vehicles.

"Anybody chasing after you?"

"Nope," Gator said. "Man, those old farts got riled up."

McIntyre kicked at the inside of the trunk.

Bruder stepped over to it and rapped his knuckles on the lid. He bent down like he was showing something to Gator and said, "Listen up, McIntyre. We're keeping you until the meet is done, then cutting you and your driver loose. Don't make trouble. If it becomes more convenient to just shoot the two of you, we will. Don't push it. Got me?"

From inside the trunk, McIntyre shouted, "I'm going to piss on your ashes!"

"Oh boy," Gator said. "We got us a firecracker."

Bruder stood up.

"I'll call you when we're done. It's up to you what happens to these two."

Gator said, "Ah, we'll drive around for a while and see what's what. They'll behave."

Bruder got into the Charger and drove through Mamaroneck and got onto I-95 south, into the city.

CHAPTER 24

At the same time Bruder was parked at Winged Foot watching the driveway, Kershaw pulled into the 164th street garage next to Yankee Stadium.

This was the risky part.

Kershaw already had the vest and face mask and hard hat with the sun shield on, along with sunglasses, but if Avery was already on-site, watching, and he recognized Gator's truck, it was done.

He'd get spooked and disappear and find another way to get the money to the Lab, and they'd probably never see him again.

They certainly wouldn't see the money again.

Which, to Kershaw, was unacceptable.

It wasn't a retirement score by any means, but he already had some of it earmarked for a trip to Puerto Rico, where he'd lay on the beach and immerse himself in blackjack and the intricacies of retinal scanners and how to defeat them.

In other words, vacation.

He rolled through the parking structure and checked the cars he passed, looking for Avery or any Lab people sent by

McIntyre to claim the parking spot on 164th.

So far, they were all empty.

He pulled into the first spot he found on the ground level and waited, his eyes scanning everything.

Ten minutes later Bruder called.

"There is no one coming to claim the spot. He didn't set it up yet."

"Beautiful," Kershaw said.

He hung up and got out and opened the back of the truck.

He dropped the can of spray paint into one of the large pockets on his safety vest and hauled the pylons out of the back of Gator's truck and put them on his shoulder, then grabbed the clipboard and used whatever limbs he could to close the truck.

He walked out of the parking ramp on Jerome Avenue and turned right onto 164th. The streetlights were still on because of the shade from mature trees, but he kept the sunglasses in place as he kept his head down and trudged onward, just a city worker on a Friday morning doing the next thing on his list.

Dozens of cars were already parked along both sides of the street, but it was a long block and had plenty of options left. Mullaly Park was on the north side, surrounded by a wrought iron fence. The corner closest to Kershaw was a flat patch of grass and had a group of people going through a stretching routine.

He walked until he was about halfway down the block, then crossed the street and dropped the pylons into an empty space along the curb. He dragged them to the outer corners of the spot, leaving extra room so a car could pull in, then pretended to consult the clipboard while he scanned the area from behind his sunglasses.

He didn't expect to see a neon sign pointing down at Avery, but he didn't see any silhouetted heads in the parked cars or men walking away and trying to seem casual about it.

But Avery was good, damn him, and Kershaw truly had no idea if he was around or not.

He pulled out the spray paint and made some X marks and random symbols on the asphalt, places to cut or not to cut, or where to run a new drain, or not to.

He held up the clipboard one more time and scanned over the top of it, didn't see anything of interest, then trudged back to the truck, paid to get out of the ramp, and drove away.

***

When Avery left Howell's estate around 3:30 and got to the stolen Jetta, he sped away as fast as possible until he'd made three turns.

Then he slowed down, remembering it was prime time for cops to bust drunk drivers trying to sneak home from bars and clubs.

He took back roads from Chappaqua all the way down until he had to jump on the Henry Hudson Parkway to take the bridge into Manhattan. Even though it took twice as long, when he parked the car a block away from the luggage storage facility at quarter to six, he knew no one had followed him, and if they had tried to intercept him on the way in, they were out of luck.

He resisted the urge to check the storage locker and the suitcases of money.

Of course, they were safe, and still there, and ready for him to pick up whenever he wanted.

He also thought about a quick trip back to the warehouse near JFK.

If Kershaw or Gator were still in there cleaning up, it ought to be easy to catch them off guard and finish clearing his back trail.

He wasn't too worried about either one of them launching a vendetta campaign—that was all Bruder, and Bruder was dead but the idea of always worrying about crossing paths with those two was irritating, stressful.

It didn't fit with where he was about to be in his life.

Then he realized—hold on—once he was with the Lab, there was a good chance Kershaw and Gator would be too scared to come after him or do anything even if they bumped into each other in the proverbial dark alley.

Now, that lined up perfectly with the new narrative.

Avery wouldn't have dared cross Howell and his security team if he'd known they were affiliated in any way with the Lab, and that's how the rest of society should behave as well.

Avery looked for a restaurant with something proper for a celebratory breakfast on the menu.

Maybe even splurge on some gluten.

He walked and turned corners, knowing he was somewhat in denial, possibly delusional about the circumstances, but he was all in now and there was no point in harboring doubts.

Caution, yes.

Doubt, no.

He turned a corner and found himself looking at Central Park, with the sun kissing the tops of the trees and a glimmer of water showing through the underbrush, and the surprise and joy of the moment nearly overwhelmed him.

He'd done it.

He'd pulled it off.

Now for some waffles, and then a safe place to watch the rendezvous spot until the stroke of noon.

***

"Look at this," Avery said.

"Look. At. This."

It was nine o'clock and he was driving along 164th Street. He rolled past the construction pylons and the fresh orange paint on the asphalt, right there near the entrance to Mullaly Park, just like McIntyre had said.

Avery shook his head and grinned.

He told the dashboard, "That's what I'm talking about! You need a parking spot next to fucking Yankee Stadium on the day of a game, and you damn well get it. Well done, Mr. McIntyre."

He turned right on Jerome Avenue and started to reverse the spiral he'd driven on the way in, looking for anyone who might be looking for him.

So far, he'd seen nothing worth a second glance, except the VIP parking spot.

The two suitcases were in the trunk with the tablet, notebook, and folder he'd taken from Fenner's car, and Avery had the feeling the luggage was glowing back there, harnessing all of his potential. Like a pilot light on a rocket booster.

His plan was to stay mobile, stay moving and watching, until it was time to pull into that cherry spot, look McIntyre in the eye, and finally start to live the life he deserved.

***

Avery was sweating.

It was 11:49 and he was in the parking lot on the northeast corner of River Avenue and 164th Street, looking west across River toward Mullaly Park.

But he couldn't see a damn thing, just glimpses of people in the skate park and a ton of traffic moving on the streets.

The crowd for the Yankee game was swarming in and the loudspeaker from inside the stadium was playing music, interrupted now and then by a man talking about corporate and family packages.

Maybe he'd gone the wrong way with wanting a crowd instead of isolation.

Or at least overcorrected, by agreeing to McIntyre's suggestion to do it here.

There were just too many damn people to watch.

This was good for safety, to a certain extent, because no one would try anything stupid with so many people around.

But if McIntyre and the Lab wanted to do anything other than the agreed-upon handoff, Avery probably wouldn't realize it until it was right on top of him.

He checked his watch again and saw it was 11:56.

Shit.

He'd been sitting there stewing in doubt and the time had flown by.

With the traffic, he wasn't sure could make it the few hundred yards down 164th and get there right at noon.

He pulled to the lot's exit and nosed in between two cars waiting at the light on River.

The car on his left honked and the driver yelled something, but Avery ignored her.

He scanned the sidewalks and the streets and the park and the parking structure, trying to see everything at once and knowing it was futile.

What had McIntyre said?

"Now it's time to prove you have some balls."

Avery nodded.

"Okay, here we go. Here we go."

The light on River turned green and the cars moved forward, some of them turning right, until suddenly the next block of 164th Street was right in front of him, like a runway.

***

He saw the plume of smoke first.

Avery rolled along 164th Street, his eyes boring into the cars parked at both curbs and the people moving on the sidewalks and in Mullaly Park on the other side of the wrought iron fence.

The smoke rose from the sidewalk from somewhere

ahead, and Avery thought it was at or near the reserved spot.

When the front bumper of the Jetta nosed past the first pylon Avery looked over and saw a large man in a suit smoking a cigar, tilting his head back to blow a plume of smoke into the leaves and branches above his head, like a service to those around him. He had gray hair slicked back to show white wings at the temples.

Avery studied him. The suit was tailored and there were flashes of gold from his wrist and fingers. He didn't exactly fit the image Avery had of McIntyre—perhaps a bit too much flash—but Avery's preconceived notion wasn't based on anything other than a voice on the other end of a phone call.

Then the man brought his head down and looked around, and the small smile as he watched people walk by sealed it for Avery.

It was the look of a man who knew his place above those around him, a man who knew he could give and take as he damn well pleased.

The car behind Avery honked with impatience and the man looked over, the smile unfaltering, and Avery pulled into the spot.

***

Avery kept the trunk closed and the engine running when he got out and stood in the crook between the car and the open driver's door.

The Sig Sauer pistol was tucked into his belt near his right kidney. One of the Glocks was in his right jacket pocket, the other was in the left.

He looked over the hood and called, "Mr. McIntyre."

The man nodded.

"Say something," Avery said.

The man frowned but didn't speak. He beckoned Avery over.

"Say something," Avery repeated.

The man just stared at him, and Avery put one foot back in the car.

***

At 11:58 Bruder walked around the corner of Jerome Avenue and 164th Street with a crowd of people and kept pace with them toward the parking spot.

He was on the sidewalk across from Mullally Park so he could have the entire street and park in view just by looking to his left.

He wore a crisp new Yankees hat and a Derek Jeter jersey, white with blue pinstripes, over a t-shirt. His pants and shoes were unchanged—he'd seen enough people wearing a jersey above sweatpants, shorts, khakis, and slacks to decide the pants didn't matter.

A quarter of the way down the block Kershaw's voice came through his earpiece.

"I got him. He's in a maroon Jetta, driving west. He's almost to the spot."

Kershaw was in civilian clothes on the third level of the parking ramp near a set of stairs, far back enough to see the street without highlighting himself for Avery.

Bruder scanned the street from beneath the hat's brim and behind his sunglasses.

"I see it."

"He stopped. He's checking our guy out."

Bruder walked faster, turning his shoulders to cut through the crowd.

"He's pulling in," Kershaw said. "He's out, he's standing in the doorway. He's talking but I have no idea what he's saying."

Bruder thought about it.

"He's heard McIntyre's voice. He's confirming it's him."

"He's gonna spook," Kershaw said. "Move. Go, go."

***

The man looked at his watch and gave Avery a look of waning patience.

Avery wondered if this was some sort of power play, if he had to display the appropriate level of balls before McIntyre would break his silence.

If it really was McIntyre.

With one foot still inside the car Avery pulled his phone out and called the number he'd used to reach McIntyre from Howell's place.

He put it on speaker and let it ring.

He and the man stared at each other, then the man's hand eased inside his jacket and pulled out a cell phone.

It was ringing, and when he answered it the ringing from Avery's phone stopped.

Avery killed the call and offered a victorious grin.

"One can be careful and still have balls, sir."

McIntyre nodded and put his phone away and blew more smoke into the trees.

Avery reached in and popped the trunk, then felt the spot between his shoulder tense.

He turned, still halfway inside the car, and saw a demon crossing the street toward him.

He froze, just for a moment, then reached for the Sig Sauer in his belt.

***

Bruder waited until he was even with the parking spot then cut across the sidewalk and through the cars parked along the curb.

He had to pause there for a break in traffic, and he deliberately kept his eyes off Avery's back.

A person can feel eyes on them, especially eyes like Bruder's, when the intent of the hunter is to do great bodily harm to the prey.

He let two cars go past then got tired of waiting and stepped into the road, forcing a car coming from his left to slow down. The traffic coming from the right had a larger gap, and Avery was right there, one lane of road away, when he turned and looked straight at Bruder.

Avery's face dropped its color and became a gray sheet of pure terror, then his right hand went inside his jacket but Bruder was already there after taking two bounding steps across the lane and slamming into Avery, shoving him against the door frame.

He got his right hand on Avery's right wrist as it crossed his body, going for the gun, and pinned it against his stomach. Bruder pressed in close. His left hand held the .45, hidden between the jacket and the jersey, and Bruder dug it into Avery's ribs as he leaned in, as if to embrace an old friend.

Avery's mouth flapped, then he said, "You."

"Yeah, me. Keep your mouth shut and hold still."

"How—"

"Quiet."

"But you—"

Bruder dug the gun in deeper and Avery shut up.

He slid his hand along Avery's wrist until he felt the butt of the pistol. He took it out and tucked it into his own belt underneath the jersey. A quick check of the jacket pockets told him where the other two Glocks were, but he left them there for the moment.

"Sit down," Bruder said.

Avery melted into the driver's seat and Bruder followed, crouching down and keeping the pressure on the .45 between Avery's ribs.

Avery winced, his face still gray and sweaty.

"It's in the trunk. All of it."

"Shut up."

"I killed you."

"You tried," Bruder said.

He just crouched there, staring at Avery while cars passed a few feet behind him. The Jetta's door was against his left shoulder, so they were somewhat shielded from passing eyes, but just in case, Bruder said, "Who's going to win today?"

Avery looked at him with wild, confused eyes. "What?"

"Who's going to win today?"

"What the hell are you talking about?"

"Nothing. I'm just talking for anybody who happens to look over here, so they'll see two guys talking instead of two guys staring at each other in silence."

"That's..."

Avery glanced over at the man he thought was McIntyre, but no one was there. A faint stain of cigar smoke drifted up into the trees.

Kershaw came through Bruder's earpiece: "At your ten o'clock."

A moment later he was on the sidewalk, knocking on the passenger window and waving like he was happy to see everyone.

Then he went to the trunk and Bruder felt the car shift as things were moved around back there.

Kershaw leaned around the side of the car.

"It's here."

"I told you," Avery said. "It's all there. Just take it. You'll never see me again."

His right hand drifted toward his jacket pocket.

"I know," Bruder said.

Avery's hand darted into the pocket and Bruder leaned all the way into the car and drove the gun up and in, prying the ribs apart, then blew Avery's heart through the back of the seat.

***

The shot was loud inside the car and Bruder glanced at Kershaw, who nodded.

Avery's chest had absorbed most of the sound. With all of the traffic and pedestrian and stadium noise going on, no one took notice of what sounded like the thud of a baseball bat hitting a heavy bag.

Bruder looked back at Avery, their faces about twelve inches apart.

He was already dead.

Bruder took the two Glocks out of Avery's pockets and set them near the brake pedal, then checked him for anything else.

He found Avery's wallet and phone and dropped the wallet next to the guns, then took a moment to pull the battery out of the phone before adding it to the pile.

He reached into his own pocket and did the same to McIntyre's phone.

He wouldn't need either one anymore.

Bruder used the car keys to put the Jetta into accessory mode, rolled up the windows, then threw the keys under the driver's seat.

Kershaw carried one of the suitcases to the door and set it next to Bruder, who used the luggage to block the view of him putting the guns and wallet into a zipped pocket on the front of the suitcase.

Kershaw said, "The stuff he took from Fenner was back there too. I put it in the other case."

Bruder nodded. No reason to leave it behind and cause more trouble or attention.

He put the phones and batteries in his pocket, then leaned the driver's seat back and closed Avery's jacket, covering the entrance wound and the small amount of blood weeping through the stippled hole. The heart wasn't pumping anymore, and gravity would pull any escaping blood out the exit wound and into the seat back.

Bruder hit the power locks and closed the door, then he and Kershaw each hefted a suitcase across 164th Street toward Gator's truck parked on the third level of the ramp.

Along the way, Bruder dropped the phones and batteries into separate trash bins.

No one honked or hollered or paid any attention to them.

CHAPTER 25

They picked up the Charger a few blocks on the other side of Mullaly Park and kept an eye on their mirrors as they crossed the George Washington Bridge into New Jersey.

It took another twenty minutes to get to the park tucked into the armpit of the I-95 Expressway.

The parking lot had two exits and baseball fields on the right and soccer fields on the left, plenty of clear space to see anyone coming at them.

There were, a couple dozen vehicles already in the lot, mostly minivans and SUVs.

Bruder saw Gator and the gray car backed into a spot in the middle row, against a strip of grass and trees with empty spots all around.

Bruder backed into the spot on the other side of the grass and Kershaw parked next to the gray car, creating a triangle with a small private space in the center.

Gator got out and met Bruder and Kershaw on the grassy strip.

He said, "How'd we do?"

"It's done," Bruder said. "Everybody behave?"

"More or less."

Bruder leaned over and looked into the back seat, which was empty. He raised an eyebrow at Gator, who shrugged.

"The driver's a spitter."

Bruder checked around them and didn't see anyone close or looking their way. He popped the trunk and found a pile of arms and legs and eyeballs blinking in the sudden sunshine, trying to glare at him.

McIntyre and the driver both had duct tape wrapped around their mouths.

McIntyre started growling behind his gag, unable to help himself from spewing threats.

Bruder closed the trunk.

***

They took the suitcases into the back of Gator's truck and made the splits.

Bruder and Kershaw exchanged a few looks while they counted, both of them surprised at the tidy minimalism of Gator's living space.

That, and the lack of overt boobytraps.

They used kitchen-sized garbage bags Gator pulled from a small white cabinet for the splits.

Bruder set three hundred thousand aside for Rowe's people, if and when they could be tracked down.

He took another split of the same amount—what would have been Avery's—and put that in a separate bag.

The hundred thousand for James went into another bag, and Bruder took five grand out of his own cut for James' father, Vincenzo, who had done a fine job of standing around like an asshole. That also went into James' bag. Bruder had an address for shipping such things, and he'd add a note about the extra five.

Gator put his share in the same small white cabinet and shook hands with Bruder and Kershaw.

He said, "You think we need to worry about the Lab?"

Bruder shook his head.

"There's nobody left who could connect either of you to any of this."

"What about you?"

"I'll be as careful as I always am. No more, no less. Worrying about it won't change anything."

He and Kershaw carried the suitcases out of the truck with the shares inside and individually wrapped, except for the bag that would have been Avery's.

Bruder kept that in his hand while they put the cases on the back seat of the gray car.

Gator drove away, and after a moment Bruder and Kershaw took the gray car in the opposite direction.

They left the Charger in the lot, wiped clean with the keys in it, for whoever wanted it.

***

About an hour after crossing into Pennsylvania the gray car got off I-80 and pulled into a Park & Ride, a small lot just off the highway with trees and tall weeds coming right up to the asphalt.

The lot was nearly full of cars and trucks but all of the vehicles were empty, the drivers still at work or wherever they'd gone after meeting their ride here.

Bruder found a spot along the perimeter and backed in.

He checked the .45, then he and Kershaw got out and opened the trunk.

The driver seemed to be sleeping, and he stirred when the light and fresh air entered the trunk. Bruder figured he had a mild concussion at the very least.

McIntyre was wide awake and went right back to straining against his duct tape and zip ties, grunting and turning his face dangerously red.

Bruder showed him the .45 tucked into his belt.

"Hold still."

McIntyre bellowed nonsense as Bruder and Kershaw hauled him out and dropped him in the weeds. He rolled and bucked, getting his golf clothes stained with dirt and grass and flecked with burrs.

They dropped the driver next to his boss, and the bald man had to roll toward the woods to keep from getting kicked in the face by McIntyre's thrashing.

Bruder tossed the bag with Avery's share at McIntyre.

"That's from Howell, toward the debt he owes you. Go easy on him, he didn't have a choice."

McIntyre froze, frowning and confused behind his gag, and Bruder and Kershaw left him like that and drove away.

A LOOK AT: THE BOX: A BRUDER HEIST NOVEL

Everybody knows: When you want to steal fourteen million dollars from a group of Romanian thugs, you go to Iowa.

That's exactly what Bruder and his crew are going to do, and they figure the hardest part will be getting into the gang's armored car and grabbing the cash without getting shot.

They're dead wrong.

Because first they have to scout the job and get in tight with a local—somebody expendable who can give them the information they need. But when one of the men gets wrapped in so tight he starts popping loose ends, Bruder has to make a call: Who's more of a threat, the Romanians, or his own crew?

He'll find out when the gang boxes Bruder and the others in, cutting off the few roads out of town and hunting—farm to farm, house to house, room to room.

It's only a matter of time before the Romanians get their shot at vengeance on the crew. But shooting at Bruder hasn't worked out well for anybody...so far.

The Box is the second book in the gritty Bruder Heist Novels. If you like professional hard case criminals with a relentless focus on pulling off the big heist and getting away with it, join the crew and buckle up.

AVAILABLE MAY 2021

ABOUT THE AUTHOR

Jeremy Brown is a novelist working in many genres, including crime thrillers, murder mysteries, and military thrillers. He has worked as a narrative designer and lead writer for a massively popular video game and enjoys kettlebells, stockpiling firewood, and using coffee as a delivery system for cream. He lives in Michigan with his wife, sons, and various animals.

Made in the USA
Monee, IL
20 April 2021